THE
SAPPHIRE
STRATAGEM

Book Three of The Crystal Halls

THOMAS K. CARPENTER

The Sapphire Stratagem
Book Three of The Crystal Halls

Hardcover Version

by Thomas K. Carpenter

Published by Black Moon Books

BLACK·MOON

Cover design by
G&S Cover Designs

Discover other titles by this author on:
www.thomaskcarpenter.com

ISBN-13: 978-1-958498-20-0

THE

SAPPHIRE

STRATAGEM

Foreword
"Or What Came Before"

At the end of book one, *Shadows in Amber*, Kuma Santos refused to kill Pandora during a duel near the Terreno, instead offering her a chance to yield. The unexpected result hurt their standing in their clans.

At the beginning of book two, *The Emerald Eclipse*, Kuma volunteers for a mission in the city with a gang called the Black Crows in hopes of rectifying this loss of honor,. The heist is a test run before Razor clan offers a partnership to the Crows in hopes of improving their position in the Undercity. In return for additional manpower, Razor must train some of their young gang members, including Deacon, who ran the raid.

The Drops clan has discovered that an elixir called Eclipse offers perfect attunement, giving the clan that uses it an advantage as they can match their best stones with their best warriors. Seeing that Razor has allied with the Crows, they worry that they're going to be the first clan wiped out.

Tensions rise between the three sides—Razor, Drops, and Alliance; and we learn that Pandora has been spying for her grandfather, Dominion Thule, and was sent to the Eternal City, the home of the maetrie, for training. But she has growing doubts about her grandfather's mission, and betrays her family to protect her clan. This leads her to ally with Kuma and his friends as they take down a group of Alliance who were carrying a shipment of Eclipse back as payment. The captured elixir is proof that the real enemy is the Alliance and the two sides should work together—but this comes too late when the Black Crows, who were working for Dominion all along, betray Razor and wipe out most of the clan. At the end of the book, the survivors turn to Drops clan, who accept them as long as they pledge their allegiance. While many things are in flux, one thing is certain—the Undercity is at war.

One

The first thing Olek Koval noticed when he entered the room was that the round table had been replaced with a rectangular gray marble slab. The other heads of the alliance clans sat at one end, staring into their cups, not a greeting amongst them. The second thing he noticed was the enormous painting on the wall of an idyllic olden town that reminded him of the Black Forest.

"Whose fucking funeral did I walk into?" asked Olek, chuckling as he tugged on his black leather jacket.

No one spoke or met his gaze. He frowned and started heading towards the empty chairs at the end, but Lionel Diaz, the leader of Demon Dogs, pulled out a chair next to him. The grave expression on the man's face put a hitch in his step. Olek took the offered seat even if he didn't understand.

"What happened to table?" he asked as he leaned back and crossed his legs, wishing he had a cigarette, but the others always complained about the smoke.

"It's been replaced," said Min Li, head of the Blue Daggers. She had a round, pleasant face. Almost kind if you didn't know better, but he'd seen what she did to those that got in her way, which made him confused about how tense she was, as if there was a gun to her head.

Olek drummed his fingers on the marble. "I liked the round one. It like that old story of the knights and their stupid quests."

He studied their body language. They looked like a group of students who'd been caught cheating and were waiting for the principal to deliver the punishment, which didn't make any sense to Olek, since they were the heads of alliance clans, not weak-kneed schoolchildren.

Olek leaned over and asked Lionel in a quieter voice, "What I miss?"

The curly-haired Spaniard frowned, so Olek added, "I was at my daughter's wedding in Prague. I know about Razor clan. I thought everyone would be happy." He frowned and counted the number at the table, wondering who the final three chairs were meant for. "Who missing? Everyone here, right?"

The sound of a door opening, followed by multiple footsteps, had everyone sitting at attention. Olek glanced around wondering if they'd been drugged, or replaced with doppelgangers. The newcomers entered behind him, and as he started to spin around, Lionel tugged on his jacket, keeping him facing forward.

The first figure was familiar. Olek knew Gregor Anderson by reputation as head of the Black Crows, who until recently had been allied with Razor clan. What he didn't understand was why he was in their territory, or taking a spot at the alliance table.

The other two weren't known to Olek, or even human. Their chalky-gray skin and pinched, sour expressions marked them as maetrie, or city elves. He caught a whiff of coal smoke that was covered up by the heavy cologne on Gregor. The first maetrie was broad-shouldered and wearing runed body armor with handguns on each hip. He carried a sheathed sword in his hand rather than having it strapped to his body, which was unusual. The second looked like he'd just come from a corporate board meeting, dressed in an expensive black suit with a striped shirt beneath.

A few seconds after Olek laid eyes upon the maetrie, he felt a wave of euphoria followed by the desire to throw himself at their feet. To combat the aura of the maetrie, Olek pinched his leg using the strength of his topaz, which burst blood vessels and would leave a bruise, but the pain washed away the worst of his subservient feelings.

He understood why his fellow alliance leaders looked like whipped dogs. Money had been flowing into their coffers from an unknown source, and now he saw the reason. What he didn't understand was how this maetrie had already cowed the others, even before he'd arrived.

"Not to be rude," said Olek, leaning on his forearm with a pleasant smile on his lips. He'd always believed that even the harshest words should be delivered with the kindest expressions. "But who the fuck are you?"

The bigger maetrie's hand twitched towards his weapon, but the other one gave a tight shake of the head.

"Olek Koval. I'm sorry we haven't had the pleasure of an introduction since you haven't been in the Undercity as of late. I hope your daughter had a wonderful wedding. I sent along a gift, which I believe she will quite enjoy."

A stone formed in his stomach. Olek's knuckles cracked as he squeezed his hand into a fist.

"I mean no threat," said the maetrie, holding up a hand. "I sent her a jeweled necklace from the Eternal City. A unique piece that she will treasure forever."

"Thank you," said Olek, doubt creeping into his voice, but he didn't unclench his fist.

"My apologies that we didn't have a chance to meet earlier, but I wanted to keep my presence, shall we say, hidden until the proper moment. Events with Razor clan progressed faster than intended due to some unforeseen betrayals, forcing my hand."

His smile might have been considered generous if he were human, but on the gaunt cheeks of the maetrie, it appeared ghoulish.

"My name is Dominion Thule. While you were absent, the alliance clans anointed me their leader, which I gratefully accepted," he said, holding a hand over his heart.

"We didn't have a leader before," said Olek.

"Which is why you failed to dislodge either Razor or Drops from their lofty positions. My guidance, even from afar, did more to improve the prospects of your clans than the muddled response that you'd assembled thus far."

"I didn't vote for you," said Olek.

"I'm sure you would have given the opportunity," said Dominion with a faint smile.

Olek glanced to his fellow clan leaders. "Is this true?"

The few that dared to look up gave him a tight nod before returning to their head bowed positions. Olek wished he hadn't been at his daughter's wedding during this critical time. He'd missed too much and now he was playing from behind and without important information.

"What's the plan?" he asked, meeting Dominion's gaze, which took all of his self-control.

The corner of the maetrie's eyes creased while his mouth stayed a thin line.

"Razor is eliminated, but unfortunately, Drops remains. Our first task is to deal with this final holdout."

Olek gestured wildly. "Shouldn't be too hard between alliance and the Crows. The biggest worry we had before was that whoever acted first would get wiped out by the last."

"I do hope that it's as easy as you say," said Dominion coolly. "But the strength of Razor joined with the Drops. We may have the numbers but their warriors are worth five times ours. Even with my additional support." He nodded to the big armored maetrie at his side. "We cannot make a frontal attack on the Drops."

"You want to have the entire Undercity under your control," said Olek.

"You *are* perceptive," said Dominion with an amused eyebrow raise.

"Why you?" Olek checked back with his fellow alliance leaders. "Why were you elected leader when we never had one before?"

"Because despite your petty stratagems, your scheming and back-stabbing, you humans have barely scratched the surface of what the maetrie carry out every day in the Eternal City. I promise you, Olek Koval, that with me you'll be richer than you ever were before once we have control of the Undercity and, with it, the faez crystal trade."

"And then?"

"That's for me to decide."

Olek nodded, even if he didn't entirely understand.

"But that's not why I called you all here," said Dominion, leaning back in his chair with his hands flat on the marble. He studied each person at the table in turn. When Dominion's gaze settled on Olek, he felt himself wanting to crawl beneath the table.

"I should be discussing our strategy, but recent events from individuals in this room have distracted me. I could be telling you about the trap I've laid for the Drops, one that is currently in motion, but instead I'm forced to discuss the importance of honesty. I know that sounds rich after my little speech about the machinations of the maetrie, but there's scheming to take down your enemies, whoever they might be, and then there's foolish defiance, or petty grabs for insignificant baubles when larger treasures could be enjoyed."

Dominion stared right at Olek, which had him leaning back in his chair as if he couldn't get far enough away. He wanted to reach for the gun in his jacket pocket, but the hulking maetrie at Dominion's side told him he'd never reach it.

"Olek. I understand your arrogance. Maybe even respect it. You don't know me, nor my reputation," said Dominion as if they were discussing how to have their steaks cooked. "But I can tell you that I will not allow it to continue for the sake of this new organization. If you display such wanton petulance on a regular basis then all respect for each other will turn to ash."

The maetrie nodded towards his bodyguard, who pulled a hammer from the back of his black pants and slid it across the marble table. It stopped right before Olek. The tool wasn't the claw hammer of basic home maintenance, but a heavier one used for driving stakes into the ground.

"As a token of your regret and newfound fealty to me, you'll pick up that hammer and use it in one of two ways. You can either turn to Lionel, who has been stealing from me and our organization, and put that hammer through his face using the strength of your topaz, or you can take it and smash the smallest finger on your hand until it is nothing but pulp."

"What?"

The words slipped out of Olek's mouth at the same time Lionel tried to leave his seat, but the maetrie bodyguard pointed the sheathed weapon at the Spaniard's chest.

"You'll decide now or I'll decide for you," said Dominion.

Olek reached for the hammer as Lionel said, "I won't do it again. We always take a little from each other when we're transporting goods. It wasn't much."

He looked to his fellow clan leaders for support. Olek held the hammer in his fist. No one spoke nor moved to stop him. While he knew that Lionel would stab him in the back if given an opportunity, even as their alliance had prospered because they'd set aside their disagreements to focus on the bigger fish in the Undercity, Olek didn't like being used as a tool. The reason he'd fought his way to the top of his clan had been so he never had to take orders from another person.

"I don't—"

What happened next was so fast Olek barely had time to process it before it was too late. Two things happened at once: the first was the hulking maetrie pulled the sword from the sheath in a quick motion, and the second was, while steel was still ringing through the air, Dominion leapt upon the marble table and accepted the blade. Olek barely had the time to flinch as blood splattered across his face. He turned to find Lionel's head sliding from his body, the thump on the carpet like a coconut falling from a tree.

With his legs spread and still wielding the sword, Dominion looked down upon Olek and said, "The choice has been made for you."

Olek glanced briefly to his fellow alliance members before shaking his head and uttering a curse.

"Fuck."

Olek slammed the hammer on his left pinky with the force of his topaz, the impact shattering the bone and turning the flesh to pulp. He grimaced away the pain as Dominion returned to his place at the head of the table, leaving the bloody sword in his fist.

Two

The false breeze pushed past Duro's skin. It was barely enough to upset the fine hairs on his forearms. He held up a flat hand. The others stopped silently, except for one. Duro turned his head, meeting gazes with Xylos, who was right behind him. The younger clan member gave a tight nod, accepting his responsibility for the scuffed foot. The other two, Adrenalynne and Brazio, stayed motionless waiting for his instruction.

Duro found it hard to believe that he was sneaking through the Undercity with a patrol group nearly entirely composed of former Razor members. Yet he had no fear that they would betray him. The wounds of the attack on the Machi were still fresh in their eyes and in the tightness of their jaws. Besides, their honor, once they had given their oaths to Daraja, was lock tight. They would sacrifice themselves for their new clan as quickly as they would have the old.

He flashed hand signals, but in seeing their confusion, he realized that not all of them translated between the clans. Some were unique. Duro mouthed the words, "Others ahead."

After they nodded, Duro continued through the uneven tunnel that had never been widened or made flat since it headed north to the alliance areas. He leapt up, grabbed a handhold on the wall, and shimmied through a tight gap. On the other side, he pulled his blades and waited, even though he knew no one was nearby. But it was one thing to know, and it was another to doubt. The knowledge that a maetrie named Dominion Thule was behind the alliance clans and the Crows' betrayal made Duro more cautious, because the city elves had ways and methods that even he didn't understand. Duro had had few interactions with the city elves in the past, but their reputation and the events that had transpired only four days ago proved that they shouldn't be underestimated. And unlike Daraja, he believed everything Pandora had told them about her relatives. He knew a warrior when he saw one.

Once everyone was through the gap, they climbed at an angle towards the entrance. When he reached the top, Duro duck-walked forward to keep a low profile and peered over the edge at the massive cavern beneath.

Fungus glow along with the waterfall that crashed into the pool on the opposite side gave the space an ethereal feel. When he'd been a young warrior with dreams of glory and little regard for his own safety, he would sneak away from the Pajot and swim in the pool when he grew frustrated with the pace of his progress. The water was ice cold, but there was a carpet of moss that covered the edge of the pool, which made it a great place to lounge after a dip.

He knew the place like the holes in his heart and so he immediately knew that something was wrong. He spotted an object at the center of the cavern on a flat area. It was about the size of a person, wrapped in gauze like a funeral shroud. As Brazio stepped onto the ledge, he nodded towards the object, studying the former warleader of the Razor clan for his reaction.

Brazio frowned at the object then flashed a sign, asking, "Danger?"

The sense that someone was nearby was no longer present. Duro expanded his amber to its maximum range. If someone was in the cavern, they were hiding themselves with sorcerous means. He gave a shrug. To reach the cavern floor would require a fifty-foot climb down a difficult stretch, which made their position extremely defensible. Given the lack of understanding of the Drops' signs, Duro decided it was acceptable to speak out loud.

"I don't think anyone is here now, but they were recently. Maybe even a few minutes ago," said Duro softly.

Xylos leaned on a rocky protrusion, peering into the cavern. "What is that?"

"A body, you dumbass," said Adrenalynne, rolling her eyes.

The woman was the least "Razor" of any that he'd met, with piercings and tattoos and a shaved head. She fit in more easily with the Drops and their practiced disregard of social norms.

Xylos screwed up his face before it smoothed away to understanding.

"Oh."

"Are we going down?" asked Adrenalynne.

Her face was nicked with a few scars, but was otherwise smooth and bore the freshness of youth. Duro couldn't remember when he was like that, even though he knew he had been once.

"Eventually."

"I'll go," said Brazio with a hunger in his gaze.

Duro gestured to the younger waku. "There are entrances to the northwest and to the east by the waterfall. I want you each to cover one."

As the two waku descended the cliff face without ropes, Duro turned to his counterpart. While officially Brazio was a step below him, Duro saw him as his equal. No one else in the Undercity concerned him if it came to a scrap.

"Are you sure?" asked Duro, the question not about the danger, but what he would find beneath the shroud.

"I need to know."

"It's likely a trap," said Duro.

Brazio looked away briefly, the corners of his mouth deepening with wrinkles. Shadows haunted his expression. "Likely."

"I can go. I know it hasn't even been five days," said Duro.

"They gave me new blood," said Brazio with dark circles around his eyes. He looked tired. Duro would have preferred that he hadn't come along, but he hadn't wanted to hurt the man's pride by refusing him.

"That's not what I mean."

Brazio checked over the edge at the two waku who were just reaching the cavern floor. As they hurried across the stone, he asked, "What do you think?"

"Good warriors. Xylos isn't as disciplined, but I would be happy to fight with him at my side."

"What about the Academy? You've had a chance to watch them train," said Duro.

"I have nothing but respect for your warriors, our warriors." Brazio shook his head. "You know what I mean. But we won't survive this if they can't become true warriors in their own right. Even these two, as talented as they are, I could kill without much effort. We're outnumbered and cut off from most of our sources of stones, while the alliance is finding new ones all the time."

"The nervous student, the one your nephew keeps as one of his friends, he has one of them," said Duro.

"Tiger's eye is what they're calling it, though the stone isn't orange, nor is he a warrior. I was surprised when he attuned to an amber," said Brazio.

"You don't think we have enough good warriors," said Duro.

"No," said Brazio. "But we could, if we can push them beyond their limits. The girl Pandora has skills."

"And your nephew and daughter. There are a few others I can see with promise."

"We need more than a few," said Brazio. "Even the ones that finished the Academy need more work."

"What are you suggesting?"

Brazio sighed. "I don't know yet. The stones are still so new. We only learned recently about how adrenaline helps people attune easier. There are other aspects of the faez crystals we surely don't know."

Duro gestured towards his forearm, which had Brazio checking his own. The black lines on his wrist peeked from beneath his sleeve.

"I'll be fine."

"Have you had that before?" asked Duro.

Brazio shook his head. "No. It might be from losing all my blood. Maybe it has something to do with attunement." He checked back to the cavern. "They're in place."

Duro chuckled. "You know the students have been talking about us."

Brazio screwed up his face. "About what?"

"Wondering who would win in a duel."

Brazio nodded. "I've thought about it a time or two. Not seriously. Maybe when this is over."

"When this is over," said Duro, nodding. "If you want to..."

"I do."

As Brazio climbed over the edge, Duro said, "Tonight we should discuss training. I agree that we should do things differently. The other way was too slow."

"Tonight," said Brazio before disappearing below the edge.

As the former Razor moved towards the shrouded body, Duro focused his attention on it. They both agreed it was a trap, but in what way? He had a good idea of who was in the wrappings. It was the reason Brazio had come. Maybe it was simply to enrage Brazio, as he was known for his temper during a fight. To get him to do something stupid. But Duro didn't see that in the man. He'd taken his brother's counsel for years without overstating his hand. He was aggressive in battle, but not reckless. Duro had seen warriors with a death wish. Either they mistakenly thought themselves invincible, or the bloodlust made them foolish. Brazio was neither.

The older warrior—Brazio was at least a decade his senior—approached the shrouded body. His focus was entirely on the object. Duro watched from the ledge, sifting through his senses with the amber. There was something off about the wrappings, or the placement—he wasn't sure. Brazio checked back as if he sensed the same thing. Duro gave him the sign for "Caution, move slow."

Brazio reached the wrapped body. He stared at it as if he'd approached a casket during a funeral. The older warrior put his hand onto the gauze. Even Duro could tell that he'd set the lightest touch. There was no guarantee that it was Niran Santos beneath the wrappings, but why else would they have left the body? On the other hand, there'd been no communication. In the wars of his youth, bodies had been returned after a negotiation, and sent with an honor guard, depending on the station of the deceased. If this truly was Brazio's brother, there should have been a formal handover, probably in the Terreno. Either the alliance's new leader, Dominion Thule, didn't understand their customs, or didn't care. Or it wasn't Niran, but a lesser warrior that had gone unaccounted for.

As Brazio pulled out a blade to cut the shroud from the head, Duro's adrenaline raced into the stratosphere for no obvious reason. It took all his self-control not to tell Brazio to get away. He couldn't figure out what was wrong, only that it was.

When Brazio put a hand on the body to steady it, there was a wobble that even Duro could see. Brazio checked back, then crouched down to look beneath the body. It was only then that Duro knew what was wrong. It wasn't flat. Something had been placed beneath the shroud, likely a bomb that would trigger when the weight was released.

Duro was opening his mouth to shout when the bomb went off. Even from a hundred meters away, he threw himself to the ground as the concussive wave ripped through the cavern. As soon as it passed, Duro scrambled down the cliff and sprinted to the location where the bomb had gone off. Bits of gauze floated in the air. Pieces of the body were splattered against the stalactites. He waved away the younger waku, giving non-verbal instructions to return to their posts.

Brazio was curled into a ball beneath the ledge where the body had been placed. His skin shimmered from dark gray to his normal lightly tanned color. His eyes refocused.

"I don't think the black diamond protects from concussions," said Duro, breathing relief that Brazio had survived.

The older warrior climbed to his feet tentatively. "I'm in your debt for suggesting the black diamond for me. It was a generous offer considering we'd been enemies only a week before."

"There's no time for half-measures," said Duro.

Brazio leaned on the stone platform. "Do you think it was my brother?"

Duro checked around the cavern until he spotted what looked to be the head. Crouched down and using his blade to cut the gauze, Duro revealed a younger man with a pockmarked face beneath the shroud.

"I'm sorry."

"The maetrie have no honor."

"You've dealt with them before?" asked Duro.

"Once. There's one that owns a bar in the seventh ward. He trades in information. After getting what I needed I decided it wasn't worth dealing with him again. He demands a high price," said Brazio.

"Daraja has had minor dealings with a few over the years. She says she'd rather swim naked with sharks wearing a suit of bloody meat than work with them again," said Duro.

"I pity the shark that tries to bite her," said Brazio, chuckling as he put his fingertips to his temple with a grimace. "She could have taken the diamond for herself as a measure of protection."

"The only protection she needs is a working clan."

"She's smart like my brother. She knows the best path forward and doesn't hesitate," said Brazio.

The older warrior pulled back his sleeve. The black lines had multiplied.

"Maybe there are side effects to the black diamond that we're not aware of, or it's just plain cursed, given that everyone who has had it has died," said Brazio, frowning.

"Or you haven't recovered from your near-death and your body is reacting to the new stone."

Brazio pulled the sleeve up. "Either option is not to my liking."

"We should return to the Pajot. You and I have much to discuss in regard to the training of our warriors."

"Maybe too much."

Duro put a hand on Brazio's shoulder. "We'll figure it out, my friend. The circumstances aren't ideal, but I can assure you that there's no one I'd rather have at my side than you."

Brazio held up his arm. "Let's hope I stay there for a long time."

Three

Pandora stood on the Academy training grounds with her friends, Choo-Choo and Navos. The concrete pad where they normally trained was overfull with warriors, both current and former members, along with dozens of Razors. Even though they were technically Drops now, she had a hard time thinking of them like that. She tried not to look at Kuma—she hadn't talked to him since they'd killed the Blue Daggers.

"I'm gonna rip his head off," said Choo-Choo, pacing behind her with sweat beaded up on his bald head as he kept glancing at Kuma, who stood with his friends.

"Emilio," said Navos with worry in his eyes.

"I don't care that he's my brother now. I'm sure he was the reason

Vasy lost her hand, and his fucking uncle is the one that killed Valeria. I hate the Santos family. Every last one of them."

Blotches of red formed on his cheeks and his jaw pulsed. Pandora put a hand on his arm, but he flinched away.

"You can't," said Pandora, then seeing that didn't get past his wall of rage, she added, "You shouldn't. Think about Triana and Vasy. We need Razor to defend the Pajot, and that includes Kuma and Brazio, and every other Razor that swore allegiance to Daraja."

"Fuck," said Choo-Choo, squeezing his eyes shut. "I can't. I can't."

"You have to," she said, then glared at Navos to help.

"Emilio, you know she's right," said Navos, knocking a swoop of dirty blond hair out of his eyes.

"I'll try," said Choo-Choo with bloodshot eyes.

Pandora breathed relief that he'd calmed, for now, though she could see the rage simmering below the surface. She was fixing her uniform when she heard Navos mutter a curse under his breath. She turned to find Kuma approaching, heading right for her and completely ignorant of Choo-Choo's visible animosity.

"Hey," Kuma said, fidgeting with his hands.

She feared what he was going to say. There were so many secrets between them that anything could become a trigger for further problems. Pandora kept her lips clamped shut, silently willing him not to say anything damning.

Kuma hesitated, clearly sensing her apprehension. "I wanted to thank you..."

She furrowed her brow at him.

"For saving my uncle's life. He told me what happened."

"I didn't do that much," she said neutrally.

Kuma tilted his head as if he were only just picking up the undercurrents, but then Choo-Choo stepped around her and jutted his chest forward.

"You're not welcome here."

Kuma's mouth opened and closed like a dying fish. "I...but we're on the same side..."

Choo-Choo spoke low and mean. "Not as far as I'm concerned."

Pandora pulled him back. "Emilio."

"Don't call me that," he said, yanking his shoulder away. "And what's this bullshit about saving his uncle? You know, the one that killed my sister?"

A stone formed in her gut. She'd been told not to reveal what happened around the time of the Crows' betrayal. She'd been telling everyone that she was on message running errands for Duro during that critical time.

"It's an exaggeration," said Pandora as Choo-Choo turned on her. "I was the one that led him to Duro when he came to the gates. He was half-dead."

"You should have finished him off," snarled Choo-Choo. "After everything my family has done for you, welcoming you into our home, you'd betray us like that? Helping the guy who murdered my sister?"

Before Choo-Choo could reach for his weapons, Navos threw his lanky arms around him, hugging him tight from behind. Pandora shot a glare at Kuma, who was already backing away. It wasn't until he'd left that she remembered he'd just lost his father, which sent rage soaring through her.

She turned back to Choo-Choo as heat formed in her chest. "Don't say that. Don't you dare say that. After everything I've given up to protect them. And you."

Choo-Choo looked incredulous. "What have you done? Nothing."

Pandora jawed at the air. She couldn't tell him anything. Not about her mother or grandfather, or that she'd helped bring the two clans together, or that she'd really saved Brazio by killing Irina. Not only would he not understand, but she'd been told to keep her mouth shut about all of it. Only the leadership of the clan knew the truth about her, and they'd promised to keep it a secret because of what she'd done.

"Stay away from me," said Choo-Choo, marching away. Navos gave her a palms-up gesture then followed him.

She slumped against the wall as many eyes bore down on her. Choo-Choo and Navos were her only friends in Drops, and she couldn't go to Kuma without revealing more secrets. The focus on her evaporated when Duro and Brazio appeared in Academy uniforms, followed by the other instructors from both clans that had survived.

"Attention!" called Duro after he leapt upon a smooth rock near the training grounds.

The chaos of the two groups as they tried to form up in lines was fraught with pushing and angry words. Pandora tried to join Choo-Choo and Navos, but they took a spot without room for her. She gravitated to the end of a line, staying in back where no one would be looking at her, hoping that Choo-Choo would come to his senses later.

"Many of you know why you're here. Some do not. I cannot put it any other way. Our enemies outnumber us and have access to resources far beyond our capabilities. The only hope for survival we have as a clan is that we must be better, warrior for warrior, or they will wipe us from the Undercity.

"That means those of you that graduated are being returned to training. No one, including myself, Brazio, and the other instructors, is excused from these activities. Wherever you think you are as a waku or soldado, I want you to improve tenfold. Whatever you thought impossible before, must become commonplace. Your limitations must become your strengths."

Duro paused atop the rock, looking over the sea of faces. Pandora understood the necessity of his words, but she wondered if her fellow clanmates did. They didn't know how brutal her grandfather was, and that the little niceties and points of order between the clans wouldn't be honored like before. They would either survive or die, much as she'd had to during her training in the Eternal City, which if she was being truthful with herself, she'd failed. Only her mother's intervention had stayed his hand. She'd been allowed to leave because they'd needed her in the Undercity. At the time, she'd been desperate to prove herself.

"We will not be doing things as we did them in the past. The physical training will be similar, but we must unlock the stones, find ways of using them that have never been done before. Some of you understand this. But very few. The rest of you will need to learn quickly."

Duro nodded to Brazio, who stepped forward. "Starting with the end of the line, I want everyone to count to five in turn. Remember your number."

The count took a few minutes to wind its way through the lines. When everyone was finished, Brazio continued, "The ones will go with Duro, twos with myself, threes with Instructor Helena, fours with Kai, and fives with Nikolai. These are your groups for now. After we've sufficiently tested you, we'll reorganize by skill, stones, and potential."

Pandora had received the number five. She found Instructor Nikolai by the fountain furthest away from the training building. He was a long-time Drops member with dark hair and a scar through his eye that made it permanently squint. The injury had come from an Undercity critter that had surprised him when he was traveling alone. He was usually in charge of the younger kids, preparing them for the Academy. Despite his fearsome looks, Vasy spoke glowingly about him.

She was one of the first to Instructor Nikolai. The others were a mix of Drops and former Razor, the first group outnumbering the latter by three to one. She half hoped that Kuma would be in her group until she saw Choo-Choo headed her way with his head down, followed by the short-haired girl, Camina, who hadn't trusted her when they took down the Blue Daggers. The last one to join the group was Yara Santos, the daughter of Brazio. She headed straight at Pandora with fists at her side and the burdens of the world on her shoulders.

"You're Pandora, right?" asked Yara with a scowl.

"I am," she said, keeping light on her feet and a wary eye on Yara's fists.

The pain etched into her face ran deep. Yara said nothing as she chewed her words behind clamped lips.

"Thank you." Yara's expression broke. "For saving my father."

She marched away head down before Pandora could respond. She checked to Choo-Choo, who'd heard the exchange but looked away when she met his gaze.

"Fuck," she muttered.

"You're right about that," said Camina, who'd come up from behind, nostrils flaring. There was a brief standoff, but then Instructor Nikolai called them to attention.

"I hope you're warmed up because we're headed to the Deep Basin," said Instructor Nikolai.

He had a deep voice and only a slight Slavic accent. The other groups were heading in other directions. They formed up in two lines. Choo-Choo looked like he was about to take the position next to her when Camina claimed it.

The run started out slow, but then Nikolai increased the pace, which put strain on the others, but Pandora modulated her opal until she was running without effort. Camina glanced to her during the run, screwing up her face.

"Why do you look like you're barely running?" asked Camina between breaths.

The passages to the Deep Basin headed south out of the Pajot. The tunnels had been widened over the years, making stretching their legs easy.

"What stones?"

Camina looked like she wasn't going to answer until she said, "Amber and opal."

"The opal can do more than heal. It can be used to clean the toxins from our muscles as we run, making it easier to go longer, or goose them to move faster. I can show you later."

Camina nodded as sweat dripped from her nose though she still looked suspicious of her motives. The others were laboring, as Nikolai

was increasing the pace until they were almost running full out. After
twenty minutes, they reached their destination, which was a ledge leading down a ramp into a huge cavern. Lights flickered below, leaving the
former Razor members to gawk at the sights.

"What is this place?" asked Camina.

"You'll see," said Pandora, even though it was only her second time
visiting the Deep Basin.

Nikolai led them down the ramp, which gave the students a good
view of the area. The air was moist and warm. As they descended, the
rocky walls became covered in thick moss, or carpets of fungi. Wisps of
plants grew from the nooks and vines clung to the cracks.

The floor of the cavern was thick with plants that grew onto the
path. Rather than hard stone, they walked over chunky dirt speckled with
rocks that hadn't quite finished breaking down. A patch of ghost-eye
illuminated their passage as insects buzzed around them.

"This was one of the first places the Drops tried to grow food.
They gave up after the early years because this cavern was much too
difficult to defend, and creatures tended to find their way into it, but
that early beginning took on a life of its own. Our gardeners sometimes
introduce new plants here to help diversify the ecosystem. Be warned
that creatures big and small make their home here. Some are benign, but
others are quite dangerous."

He took them to a side cavern off the main area. The plants faded away, leaving more rock and walls that went straight up. Nikolai pulled small orbs from a backpack and shook them in turn, which made them glow from within. Then he turned dials on the side and released them into the air. The first few ascended five or ten feet, but later ones went higher, until there was a column of light alongside the rocky wall.

"Today you're going to free climb the Night Wall. It has that name because some of the stone is glassy obsidian, which makes it both beautiful and treacherous. It's a difficult climb, a five point eleven if you want the technical designation."

"Where are the ropes?" asked a first-year student in the back.

Nikolai threw two cloth bags onto the ground. "You'll find no wall spikes, only harnesses and connecting ropes. You won't be climbing alone, but as a group. The goal is for everyone to reach the top together."

The instructor's words were greeted with a mix of disbelief and concern.

"I'm not climbing with a Santos," said Choo-Choo, crossing his arms and glaring at Yara, who stared back ambivalently.

Nikolai spread his arms wide. "Fine. If you do not wish to climb, you can return to the Pajot and train with the kids."

Choo-Choo blinked heavily before hanging his head and returning to the group.

"Good. No other disagreements?" asked the instructor. "You may begin."

They stood around in a circle. There were around thirty of them. No one spoke at first. Pandora moved towards the rope bag at the same time as Yara and Camina. She gave them a welcoming smile, but neither returned it. Choo-Choo showed up a second after the others.

"I'm not letting a couple of Razors fuck this up," he said.

Camina rolled her eyes while Yara gave him a blank-eyed stare that would have made a serial killer proud.

"How do we want to do this?" asked Pandora, crouching by the bags.

Camina dumped the harnesses on the ground and started digging through them while the others stared at the wall, which went up so far it hurt the neck to see the top. The others clumped around them, but gave them space at the same time, signaling the leadership of the group.

"It doesn't look like there are enough harnesses for everyone," said Camina, frowning.

"Okay, some can free climb and some can stay harnessed," said Yara, crossing her arms. "I'm not afraid."

"That wall?" asked Choo-Choo incredulously. "It's over three hundred feet of high difficulty."

"I'm a topaz," said Yara defiantly.

Choo-Choo screwed up his mouth. "I am too, but only, like, last week."

"Then it should be no problem. Big shot Drops can show us how it's done since it's your wall," said Yara.

"Come on, we have to do this together," said Pandora.

Camina shook her head as she opened the rope bag. "It's a fucking snakes' nest. What's going on? Is the instructor trying to kill us?"

"You heard Duro," said Pandora, thinking about when he'd shot her to force her to rapidly attune to the opal. "They're going to make us push our limits. Not giving us all the tools forces us to come up with new solutions."

"Push our limits?" asked Camina, staring at the wall. "They're gonna get us killed."

Four

After the numbers were called, Kuma found himself in Duro's group with few friendly faces except for Xylos. He approached with a slight limp.

"Can't you get that taken care of?" asked Kuma.

"No one can figure out what's wrong," said Xylos, grimacing. "I won't let it stop me."

As the others formed up, Kuma found himself wishing that Pandora was with their group so he could talk to her alone. He knew he'd screwed up somehow when he'd spoken to her before with Choo-Choo. With everything going on, his father's death, and the loss of so many people he loved, his mind wasn't in a good space. He'd hoped to reconnect with Pandora if only to have something good come of the awful situation.

The other three groups had already left, but Duro and Brazio spoke quietly to the side. The last time Kuma had seen Duro Hernandez was in the Pale Sun when the gunman had tried to kill one of them. He was one of the least assuming waku in the Undercity, looking like he would fit in playing pool and drinking a beer after a hard day of construction.

"What's with him?" asked Xylos, looking over Kuma's shoulder.

He turned to find the tall friend of Choo-Choo's staring at them through his blond hair that hung in his face. His lanky frame, tattoos, and gold teeth made him look like a washed-up rock star. When they made eye contact, he approached.

"Navos?" asked Kuma, remembering past interactions.

Navos swallowed. "I'm sorry about what happened earlier with Emilio." He screwed up his face. "Choo-Choo."

"Did my uncle really kill his sister?" asked Kuma.

"In a scrap," said Navos, frowning. "I hope you won't take offense."

Kuma used his amber to read the lanky waku. He was fidgeting like Tick, but Kuma didn't think that was a normal affliction. Navos kept rubbing his heavily tattooed arms.

"We've bigger things to worry about than old grievances. I bear no ill will towards Emilio."

Navos screwed up his face. "I wouldn't use his real name."

"How did he get it? Is it because he's as wide as a train, or runs you over in a fight?"

The tension in Navos' expression broke with laughter, which he stifled behind a cupped hand. It wasn't hard to see Navos had deep feelings for his friend.

"When we were six years old at our first day of training, he brought a toy train to play with and the instructor said, hey Choo-Choo boy, come here, and it stuck." He grimaced. "Please don't tell him I told you that story."

"I won't."

It occurred to Kuma that his reputation from beating Pandora in a duel might lead Navos to believe that if a fight occurred, Choo-Choo would be outclassed. He was trying to protect him.

"I'm a—"

Before Kuma could finish, Duro returned to the group, examining them casually.

"Come with me," he said, heading down the pathway as if he were on a city stroll.

They fell in behind, glancing between themselves curiously. It didn't take long for them to reach their destination, which the Drops members seemed to recognize immediately. The cavern looked like it was a shooting range except the target boards had been pulled from the ground and stacked in a pile. In their place was a long wooden wall that looked like the front of a building but with open windows where some older men and women stood with rifles in their hands.

"From this spot to that wall is one hundred and five meters, or nearly three hundred and fifty feet. The challenge today is for your group to reach the wall without getting shot. Some of the older members of the clan have volunteered to play with us today."

"They're going to shoot us?" asked one of the younger members incredulously.

"Rubber bullets," said Duro. "They hurt like hell and should give you a healthy desire to avoid them. And if you think because they're old they're poor shots, the majority of them are expert marksmen on the range. They have a shooting club every Thursday."

"What's the point of this exercise?" asked Xylos with his hand half raised.

Duro stared at him blankly with the faintest hint of a smile on his lips.

"You have twenty minutes to come up with an idea on how to cross the range. Failure to reach your target will earn the entire group two hundred push-ups."

A collective groan was followed by the group circling around each other.

"Any ideas?" Kuma asked Navos, sensing he was one of the older waku within their group that wasn't a former Razor.

"I, uhm, what kind of stones we got?" asked Navos, clearly unused to being the one in charge.

Everyone talked at once, which made it impossible to pick out the individual stones being shouted out. Navos stared back with a hunched forehead.

"I didn't get that, can we do it again?"

The second time was no better than the first.

"Can I offer a suggestion?" asked Kuma.

"Please," said Navos, relieved.

"Raise your hand if you have an amber," said Kuma.

Nearly the entire group minus a handful raised their hands. He continued with the other stones until they had a count.

"We have lots of amber, and opal is our second but one sapphire, two emeralds, and three topaz. Ideas?" asked Kuma.

"Maybe we can just rush the other end," offered a guy Kuma had heard someone call Einar. "Not pretty, but some of us will get through, right?"

"Not sure if I want to get shot if I don't have to," replied someone in back.

The conversation devolved into various theories, mostly around the odds of making it across that distance with six shooters ready to pick them off.

"Three minutes," called Duro from the side with his arms crossed and a smirk.

"We'd better do something soon," said Kuma.

"What about those old wooden walls where they put the targets? Can we use them as a shield?" asked Navos.

"Great idea," said Kuma. "Can the topaz carry them? The rest of us can stay behind."

They quickly pulled a pair of the walls off the pile. The awkwardness of handling them required two topaz for the first and a topaz and three other waku to carry the second. With half the group behind each wall, they were about to march across the field when Duro stepped forward.

"Now that you have a plan, you have ten seconds from the moment you start to the moment you touch the wall. Anyone not reaching it in that amount of time will have failed."

"Ten seconds? A world-class runner could barely make it across," said Einar.

Duro tilted his head. "You're not world-class runners. You're waku. You should be able to do better. Hurry. If you don't start soon the twenty minutes will be up."

"What do we do?" asked Navos.

"One minute," said Duro.

"Go for it and see what happens?"

"I don't want to do two hundred push-ups," said someone in back.

"We'll never make it behind the shields."

Kuma sighed. "Okay, if you want to go alone, go for it, or if you want to stay behind the shield, that's cool too. But let's go now before we're out of time."

Duro was staring at his watch. Kuma nodded to Navos, who swallowed and called out.

"Go!"

The moment the two walls started forward, a group of the others broke around them, sprinting across the field well ahead. Kuma helped carry his wall forward, but the awkward handholds and unbalanced weight made it difficult. A second later, the shots started. Cries of pain from the waku that had tried to make it without shielding quickly followed. The topaz girl on Kuma's right who was holding the wall flinched and dropped the wall, making it nearly tip forward. She held her arm where one of the sharpshooters had hit the part of her shoulder that had stuck out. More rubber bullets followed and then Duro whistled shrilly by sticking his fingers in his mouth.

"Time's up! Everyone back to the start. Bring your walls or anything you might have dropped and start your push-ups."

The ones who'd been hit by the rubber bullets revealed deep bruises, which were healed with opals, but a lingering yellow stain remained. Kuma finished his two hundred push-ups at the same time as Navos and Xylos, while the others took longer.

"No one reached the halfway mark, and only the runners made it past the quarter. Hopefully you can do better on this attempt. Same rules as before. Twenty minutes to come up with a plan and ten seconds to cross the field."

The impossibleness of the situation left a lot of jaws hanging open and heads shaking. Kuma wasn't optimistic himself, but he wasn't about to give up. He clapped his hands to get their attention.

"Okay, what's the plan this time? Any ideas?"

"We can't run with the walls," said the topaz girl who'd gotten shot. "No way can we make it in ten seconds."

"Free-for-all run?" suggested Einar.

"Not looking forward to getting shot," said someone.

"They can't get us all."

With a lot of shrugged shoulders and harrowed glances down the firing range, the consensus was for no walls. Kuma approached the starting line with the others hoping that he might be able to use his emerald to soar over their firing fields. Given the distance, it was unlikely that he'd make it, but he figured he had a better shot than most. He cycled Heavy in preparation for a Lightness leap.

"Go!" called Navos.

The start announcement was followed by the crack of multiple shots. Kuma had barely jammed his foot into the ground before he was hit in the shoulder, knocking him backwards.

"Fuck."

The rest of his team was picked off before a single person crossed the quarter line. Everyone trudged back to the beginning grimacing and holding the places on their bodies that were shot. What was worse was the old folks in the shooting windows high-fiving each other.

"Be glad that they're only shooting you in the chest," said Duro. "I think you all owe me two hundred push-ups."

The collective groan was followed by everyone falling to the floor on their hands. Kuma massaged the spot where he'd been shot and started on his two hundred next to Xylos.

"It's gonna be a long day."

Five

Pandora clung to the wall, her fingers jammed into a crack. The others were to her left, connected by a webbing of ropes. They'd put the weaker climbers in harnesses to make sure they couldn't fall. Pandora had volunteered to be a free climber because she could halt her descent with the sapphire.

"There's a ledge to your right, Yara," she said.

As a topaz, Yara was a lead climber. She could hold the others even if someone slipped. In a normal climbing situation, they'd be using pitons to anchor themselves to points along the wall, but the challenge hadn't included tools like that.

Yara looked up and to the location she'd indicated. The glow from the floating balls of light cast strange shadows across the rocks as they hovered, moving slightly as if there were a light breeze. The rock smelled wet, even though it felt dry. She would have liked chalk to ensure her fingers could grasp the stone with confidence, but the crack she'd found to maintain her position was better than nothing.

As Yara reached the ledge, the others adjusted below her. There were five free climbers, each of them with either an emerald or sapphire, and the rest were connected by the webbing of lines and harnesses. The number of climbers on the narrow wall made for additional problems that they hadn't anticipated.

Choo-Choo was the other lead climber. His topaz combined with his natural strength had made him an ideal choice. He was to Yara's left, but Pandora couldn't see what the rock looked like to give him instructions.

"Near your left hand there's a crack," Yara called to Choo-Choo. "It's above that little ledge. You should be able to make progress from there."

The bald waku glared in Yara's direction and rather than move in the direction she'd suggested, he reached for a crimp hold that would provide much less anchor strength. He managed to pull himself up, and jammed his foot in a jagged crack.

"Good here. Climb when ready," said Choo-Choo.

As the rest of the group maneuvered below the leads, Pandora moved up a few more lengths, looking for obstacles that would be a problem for the weaker climbers. The entire group was only fifty feet up the wall. She couldn't see the top, only the line of floating glowballs that seemed to go up forever. The light reflected off a shiny piece of wall about ten feet above Yara's line. Obsidian. The slick stone would be impossible to get a grip on. Avoiding it was the only solution.

"Hey Yara, there's some obsidian up here. You're gonna have to move closer to me. Everyone will have to split around it."

"Seriously?" she asked, head tilted back.

"I'm not moving," said Choo-Choo. "I've got a good line here. You'll just have to figure out a way around it."

"Emilio, stop being an asshole," said Pandora. "We've got to get up this wall together. No one can cross the obsidian, not Yara, not the ones below her. Unless you think we can shift left, you'll have to straddle it."

Choo-Choo leaned back with his hands on a jug hold. He frowned as he saw the section of glossy black wall, then gave Yara a nod. As the entire team shifted to the right, which required a lot of shouting and adjustments, Pandora examined the next section, looking for places that would cause them troubles. She was checking back on progress when she spotted a diamond-shaped head sticking from a crack near Choo-Choo. A tiny tongue tasted the air as the snake peered down the wall.

"Choo-Choo," she called. "There's a problem."

"What now, Pan? Can you fucking decide which way we're going because I'm holding a lot of people on this line," he said.

"Yeah, new problem, not a climbing route, but a snake in the crack that's about four feet above your right hand."

Snakes weren't common in the Undercity, but some species had made their home in the Deep Basin due to the rich environment and ample food supply.

"I'm not changing route," yelled Choo-Choo. "Can you slide over and take care of it?"

She was about to tell him no, but then she realized he was right. As a free climber, she had the best shot of removing the obstacle. Pandora worked her way perpendicular, which put her above the rest of the team. If she fell, she would need to push off from the wall so she didn't take down the rest of the group.

When Pandora neared the crack, she found the snake was no longer visible. It'd retreated into its hole.

"Whatever you do, don't knock it on my head," said Choo-Choo, looking up. "I hate snakes."

Pandora sighed, wishing she'd brought her blades, but they hadn't seemed relevant for the climb, so she'd left them at the base.

"The snake went into the hole. Anyone got anything to dislodge it without me getting bit?"

The message went up and down the wall, but no one had anything useful. Pandora maneuvered herself next to the crack with the snake, keeping a wary eye on the hole in case it decided to make a break for it. The variety of reptiles in the Undercity was rather small. She knew of at least two benign snakes, and a third that was poisonous. The one she'd seen hadn't looked like any of the three.

A jug hold gave Pandora a good place to anchor herself for further investigation of the snake hole. She hung by one hand with her foot jammed into a separate crack and leaned towards the shadowy gap, keeping herself ready to flinch backwards. Using her sapphire wasn't an option because she'd have to put herself directly before the hole to Push or Pull.

Pandora tapped on the stone next to the hole in hopes the snake would stick its head out to investigate. She planned on snatching it around the neck and throwing it away from the wall. If it fell on the instructor, then it was his fault for giving them this task.

"Come on, you stupid legless amphibian. Let me see you," said Pandora.

"Not an amphibian. It's a reptile," said Yara, watching from her position below.

"It's still a pain in my ass whatever it is," said Pandora as she kept tapping. Using her sapphire sense, she tried to *feel* where the snake was but the nature of the crack made it hard to see past the hole. Warning that the snake was going to poke its head out came only as a flickering tongue. Pandora had her hand poised by the gap when it stuck its head around the corner at an angle that made grabbing impossible. She froze when she saw its red eyes and the spiny ridge along its back.

"Not a reptile!" she cried as she swung away from the gap.

The creature snapped at the location her hand was a split second before, then let out a horrifying hiss that sounded like it was gargling whiskey.

"It's a damn demon snake, or something like it," she said, holding herself away as the creature kept its flickering tongue pointed at her.

Pandora prepared to hit it with a Push, but she didn't want to knock it onto the others and cause a panic. If she was going to kill it, or dislodge it from the hole, she needed to fling it away.

"I think you all need to move away from the hole."

"We just moved into position and you want us to move away?" asked Choo-Choo.

"Does a demon snake headdress sound more appealing?"

Choo-Choo grumbled but started calling down to the others. Pandora kept her eyes on the creature, readying a pinpoint Push in case it tried to lunge. She heard a second gargled hiss from above her head, drawing her attention upward in time to see a second red-eyed snake peering down at her from a perch about five feet from her head.

In the moment she was distracted, the first snake leapt from the hole, unfolding leathery wings as it hovered in the air. The winged snake snapped at her head, so she Pushed it hard, flinging it away at the same time the second flew down at her. Pandora kicked off from the wall, flinging herself into empty space as the second flying snake followed with fangs bared.

As she pushed away from the cliff, her foot knocked a piece of rock the size of her fist onto Yara's head. She was in the middle of transferring to a new handhold and the impact made her miss the grab. Pandora prepared to halt her fall with a downward Push when the connected webbing of climbers started falling, the cascade starting with Yara's miss, and the chaos of the two flying snakes making others slip in their attempt to get away.

The second snake snapped at her head. Pandora Pushed it away, which only sped her descent. Ignoring the flying reptile, she slammed a Push downward at the last moment, the angle all wrong, sending her catapulting to the side and slamming her shoulder into the hard rock.

With the shock of pain reverberating through her body, Pandora leapt back to her feet in time to see the entire webbing of climbers halt suddenly about thirty feet above the floor. They collapsed towards the center with only a few managing to find holds.

"Ahhh! I can't hold it much longer!"

Choo-Choo had managed to grab the wall. She couldn't imagine how much strain was on his shoulders with twenty people pulling downward. As she ran towards the wall, Pandora kept an eye out for the flying snakes, but she'd lost them in the chaos and gloom.

Instructor Nikolai leapt onto the wall, climbing upward with speed. The other climbers were trying to find holds, but they'd been smashed together and were fighting for the same space, which was making it even harder for Choo-Choo.

Pandora heard the snap of rock breaking before she saw the entire webbing of climbers shift downward. The section Choo-Choo had been holding broke. Standing beneath the descending mass of people, Pandora had two choices: flee or try to stop them.

Ignoring the voice in her head screaming about self-preservation, Pandora put everything she had into a Push upward. The rebounding force knocked her on her rear as twenty people halted momentarily then collapsed upon her. An elbow hit her in the jaw, someone stepped on her stomach. The pile shifted as there were cries of pain. Many people were hurt.

Pandora started suffocating as someone's back was pressed against her face, smashing her head into the angled rock. The urge to Push in all directions and free herself became almost unbearable. The darkness and pressure reminded her of training in the Eternal City, which made her fears worse. She couldn't take it anymore, and Pushed upward, knocking the body from her head. Before they landed, she rolled out of the way, sucking in precious air and hoping no one noticed her panic.

As she climbed to her feet, Pandora saw Camina staring at her with what felt like pity. Pandora turned away under the guise of looking for people to help. Half the group was climbing to their feet while the others looked too injured to move. The opals moved amongst the group, healing the broken bones and other injuries. It could have been much worse. Pandora found Choo-Choo sitting by the wall holding his arms still, his body lying like a rag doll.

"What hurts?"

"Everything," he said, grimacing as he tried not to move

"You saved lives when you caught the wall." Pandora pressed her hands against his shoulders, letting healing energy repair the damage.

"Thank you," he said, testing his shoulders tentatively. He looked up into her face. "I'm still mad at you."

"I wouldn't have it any other way."

After the worst of the wounds were fixed, Instructor Nikolai approached the group.

"Is there anyone else that needs more healing?" When no one answered he continued, "Good. Was a rough fall, but you managed to survive it. There's still plenty of time left in the day for more attempts."

"More attempts?" asked Yara. "People could have died."

"And everyone will die if we cannot stop the Alliance when they attack us," said the instructor.

"They'll be no one left if we die during training," said Yara.

Instructor Nikolai appeared reticent to deliver his message. He opened his mouth twice before finally speaking, gaining momentum with each word.

"My instructions were clear. The training must continue. Remember, you swore an oath to the clan. This is the price of that oath. El Clan Eto Vas. The Clan is All. It would be good for you to remember that."

Red-faced and tight-lipped, Yara nodded, even as she looked ready to erupt.

"Are there any other disagreements?" When no one spoke, he said, "Please return to your training. You've a wall to climb."

Six

The dining area at the Drops Academy was packed with seats bumping into each other since there wasn't room for the entire group. Kuma sat with Camina and Tick near the corner, shoveling greasy rat meat stew into his hungry mouth. Every time he lifted his spoon a spot under his armpit ached from where he'd taken multiple rubber bullets during the course of the day. While the wounds had been healed, his mind was raw from the pain.

"Everything hurts," said Kuma, shaking his head. "I feel like I got trapped in a giant pachinko machine and Tick was at the controls."

Tick mimed flicking the levers while he grinned with glee.

"I'll take getting shot by rubber bullets over actual death," said Camina, hunched over her bowl and using a piece of hard bread to sop up the stew juices. "If I didn't know any better, I'd think they were trying to kill us."

When he and Tick stared at her, Camina gave a rundown of what happened.

"Flying snakes and a three-hundred-foot wall climb?" asked Kuma incredulously.

"We only made it a hundred feet on our best attempt. We never saw the snakes after the first, but the middle section of the wall had too much obsidian and too many of our group were shit at climbing. I have no idea what this mess is trying to prove but it's making me regret coming here."

A few heads shot their direction. Kuma kicked Camina under the table, but she glared back with her jaw pulsing.

"You weren't there. It was a cluster."

Wanting to break the tense mood, he asked Tick, "What did you do?"

"Huh? Our group?" Tick set his spoon into the bowl. "We went to some lake and spent time holding our breath, or diving to the bottom to pick up weights. You're looking at the winner from our group."

Tick wagged his eyebrows.

"You? No offense, but you suck in the water. I swear you could drown in a bathtub," said Kuma.

Tick squeezed one eye closed. "I *did* have some help with my victory. There were some eyeless fish in the lake that might have been harassing the others in my group."

"Tick. It's not a competition. This is serious. Didn't you just hear Camina?"

His friend shrugged. "It felt like a competition. Like the maze run or all the other crap Ol' Fish Lips had us do."

"I wonder what the other two groups did," said Camina, checking over her shoulder.

Tick was about to put his spoon in his mouth, but he left it hovering before his lips.

"Brazio's group scrapped like demons and the other was trying to get through a door without touching it and using only their stones," said Tick.

"Wish I'd been in that one," said Kuma heavily.

"They had to do fifty push-ups for each failure, so I'm not sure about that. Besides, you'll get a chance. Rumor has it that we'll be rotating to a new instructor every day." Tick held his spoon before his mouth. "Maybe we'll get to see Duro and Brazio scrap sometime. Xylos has been taking bets in case that ever happens."

"What the hell are we doing?" asked Kuma.

"Ask your uncle," said Camina.

Kuma frowned. "I would but he's always with Duro. It's not like

I'm the clan leader's son here."

Camina sat up straight, anger smoothing away. "I'm sorry, Kuma. Here we are bitching about training and your father is dead. You've barely had time to grieve and no funeral."

"There'd have to be a body for a funeral," said Kuma with a sigh. "Besides, I'm not the only one that lost someone. Fuck. More than half the people we called family are dead. If I ever get a chance I'm going to pull Deacon's guts out through his nose."

"You'll have to fight your cousin for that honor. She's been pretty vocal about wanting to gut him like a pig, and for once, I can sympathize with her," said Camina.

Tick rose from the table with his empty tray, mouth opening in a yawn.

"I don't know about you two, but I'm exhausted. I'm using my free time for sleep."

"My ass you are, you pervert," said Camina with a smirk, then she rose as well. "I need a shower. I didn't spend all day in a nice cool lake."

"Freezing cold," said Tick. "Did I mention that?"

Left alone, Kuma finished his meal and brought his tray to the front. He was deciding what he planned on doing for the remainder of the evening when Adrenalynne approached him. Her lip was healing from a recent split and her normally bright green hair was returning to its natural dirty blonde color.

"Hey, Little Bear."

"Adrena. You were in the scrapping group?"

She furrowed her brow. "Your uncle ran it. He kicked the crap out of a couple students when he thought they weren't giving it their all. After that, everyone fought like it was for real." She checked over her shoulder. "But that's not why I came to talk to you. I found this note in my pocket. I don't know who put it there."

She handed over a folded piece of paper taped closed. On the outside, it read: For Kuma.

"Thanks."

Adrena gave him side-eye. "Be careful, Little Bear."

Away from prying eyes, Kuma unfolded the note. The interior was blank except for a crudely drawn lantern. The meaning escaped him until he remembered his time with Pandora in the canyon of ghosts. They'd accidentally stepped into a patch of lantern fungi and had barely survived the hallucinations. He headed towards the exit that led past the canyon. He turned on his amber, listening for signs, when he heard his name whispered. Kuma followed the sounds through a side passage that led to the maintenance cavern. Halfway down the path, he heard the clicking of a tongue above him.

Peering over a ledge twenty feet above was the dark-haired Pandora. He checked the passage with his amber before switching to Lightness and scrambling up the side with the ease of a mountain goat.

She stood back from him with her arms crossed, brow furrowed and lips squeezed tight. Her body language had him shuffle to a stop, instead of moving forward to embrace. A world of questions passed across her black eyes, reminding him that she was quarter maetrie—a fact that changed his calculations of their previous interactions. He knew the city fae were duplicitous and cunning, and that their aura could sway thoughts.

"You're the one who summoned me here."

Pandora looked away. "I wanted to...I wanted to talk to you."

"I'm here. Talk."

The words came out harsher than intended. Pandora turned her body slightly.

"I'm sorry about your father."

"I'm gonna kill every last one of the Crows," said Kuma, heat rising.

Pandora offered a crooked smile. "I'll help you."

"Were you ever going to tell me?" he asked suddenly.

"Tell you?" she repeated with wide eyes.

"You were a spy for the alliance all along and a maetrie too. Was I just a tool for you?"

She hung her head. "I'm only a quarter."

"Does it matter?"

Pandora shot back. "It does to me."

"But you were? Using your fae powers on me?"

She screwed up her mouth. "It's more complicated than that. I liked you. Still like you. And I didn't make you like me. I don't have that ability."

"How can I believe you?" he asked at the same time his heart was telling him to throw his arms around her.

"I know it doesn't look good. My past is a mess, but your uncle, Duro, and the rest of the Drops leadership believe me. I nearly died trying to give them the information they wanted."

"I heard."

"Please don't tell anyone," she said.

"I don't break my promises."

Pandora squeezed her eyes shut and rocked on her feet. When she opened them, she looked to the pebble-strewn ground.

"Twenty-three."

"What?"

She shook her head. "Nothing. It's complicated."

"You said that already."

Pandora inhaled deeply as if she were trying to catch her breath. "I never wanted to come here and spy on the clans. I mean, I did at the beginning, but that was my training. It wasn't until later that I realized those were not my choices, but theirs."

"And now?"

"These are mine," she said earnestly. "I turned my back on my mother and grandfather because I don't agree with them. He'll take what's good about the clans and turn them into a pale imitation of the maetrie courts."

"How can I believe you?"

"Kuma. If it weren't for what we did, taking down the Blue Daggers and stopping the alliance from getting involved, none of us would be here right now. Had the alliance hit at the same time as the Crows, he'd have already won."

Kuma hated the way he mistrusted her. "You're right, but I don't know. It's just hard to take. I was raised with honor."

"And I was trained with a clicker and sent into a dark place where horrific creatures feasted on my flesh when I disobeyed," said Pandora.

"Was that in the Eternal City?"

She nodded.

"What's that like?" he asked quietly, trying not to spook her.

Pandora hung her head. "I don't want to talk about that right now. Maybe another time. It's too...raw." She inhaled again with her eyes closed. "I wanted...when you came to talk to me with Choo-Choo there, I was afraid—"

"That I would say something stupid. I did. I'm sorry. My head isn't in a good place lately."

"It's understandable with everything that's happened," she said, the corner of her eyes smoothing to softness. "And please forgive Emilio for how he acts. He's a good person. My friend. My family really. But your uncle killed his sister, and I don't know if he can ever forgive that."

"Is that what you wanted to say?" he asked tightly.

"I also wanted to talk about us."

The word "us" brought a trickle of electricity across his skin. He feared saying something stupid, so he kept his mouth closed.

"I'm still interested, but no one else besides leadership knows about us."

"Camina and Tick know, but they'll keep their mouths shut."

"But Choo-Choo doesn't know and if he finds out, he'll never forgive me. He's the only family I have here. Him and Triana and Vasy. After everything with my mother, I need that. She chose her father rather than me."

The rawness in her expression had Kuma wanting to take a step towards her in hope that they would embrace, but he feared a rebuttal.

"I'm sorry that your family is like that."

"And I wish your father was still alive," she said.

"Me too."

"You should go," she said, screwing up her face. "I'm sorry. It won't look good if we get caught talking to each other. I took a big enough chance just to have this discussion."

The words in his mouth disintegrated to ash. He'd never felt so alone in his life. He briefly reached out with his right hand before collecting it against his chest and turning away. As he dropped to the floor of the cavern with Lightness, he thought he heard her speak his name, but when he looked up, she wasn't there. Kuma headed back to the main areas of the Pajot with a heavy heart.

Seven

Pandora stared across the sparring grounds to her opponent. They stood on the concrete pad in the middle of the Academy grounds with the others members of their group watching from the side. Einar Baros. He was tall, broad shouldered and looked like he could break a two-by-four in half by flexing his muscles. The mustache on his upper lip made him look older despite the fact that he was two years her junior. In the last year, he'd sprouted into a solid figure, and his topaz and emerald made him a formidable opponent, even if the second stone was relatively new. The trick Duro had pulled on her, using pain and adrenaline to increase the chances of attuning, had increased the overall stone level of the clan considerably. Einar gave her a chancer's grin.

"Begin!"

Most of her opponents feared her sapphire. If they were an emerald, they tried to cycle Heavy whenever she Pulled them, or if they were a topaz, they learned how to grab something nearby to hold themselves immobile until she let up. Einar did neither of these even though he had both stones.

He launched himself at her like a missile, using his topaz to power his leap, then as she slammed him with her sapphire Push, he cycled Heavy, landing like a two-ton boulder.

The problem with emeralds she'd found was the moment they switched Heavy, their bodies collapsed under the weight for half a second. It wasn't long. A moment's distraction when they were trying to keep from being pulled to the ground, but it was enough. Pandora launched herself with a Push, bringing her knee up and into his jaw as she soared over his head. She felt the rattle of his teeth when she thrust her hip forward, knocking him out.

Einar fell backwards like a stiff board. His mouth was a bloody mess and his eyes were in the back of his head. Pandora landed facing him even though the fight was over.

She checked back to Brazio, who approached her, stepping over the unconscious Einar as if he were a log. He came up chest to chest.

"Good fight, but do you know where your mistake was?"

"Knocking him out too quickly?" she asked, matching his gaze.

Brazio grabbed her arms lightning quick and pulled them into a defensive position. "You let down your guard before the fight was over. In a real scrap, you won't be fighting one enemy, but multiple. Never let your guard down, even in practice."

He released her wrists and marched away. "Someone wake Einar. Who's next?"

Pandora trudged from the sparring grounds with her chin down. She leaned against the wall as she felt the weight of her fellow group members' gazes upon her. Three fights and three knockouts, all in the first few seconds of the fight.

Choo-Choo and Yara entered the sparring grounds. They bowed and spoke the ritual words before Brazio gave them the signal. The two warriors were evenly matched with topaz and emerald, their blocks and punches coming together as if it were a choreographed dance.

"You haven't lived up to your promise," said Camina, coming up from the side.

"What?"

The short-haired girl had a yellowed bruise across her jaw from an earlier scrap. She was generally out-stoned with only an amber and opal, though she fought well despite her disadvantages.

"You said you'd tell me how I can use my opal to move faster, fight better," she said.

"I did. I will."

"When?" asked Camina aggressively.

Pandora had been looking forward to a cold shower after a morning of training and afternoon of scrapping, but she nodded towards the combatants.

"After we're done."

Camina nodded and leaned against the wall next to Pandora. She sensed there was more to her request than improving her skills, but didn't want to talk with so many others around.

The fight between Yara and Choo-Choo went on for a few minutes, both combatants wearing down the longer it went. Neither was able to hit the other with enough force to knock them out. A well-timed emerald Heavy in addition to the general fortitude of a topaz made it a fight between armored tanks. They weren't black diamonds by any means, but the combination, properly utilized, made for hard targets.

"Stop!"

Brazio walked between the two combatants, who looked confused by the interruption. He looked between them.

"You're both dead. The fight took too long."

Choo-Choo snarled with anger as he gestured at Yara. "We're still scrapping. She never hurt me."

"No, but you didn't take care of her fast enough and the longer you're tied down by one opponent, the more you're vulnerable to a second, or third."

"But we're only fighting one at a time," said Choo-Choo.

Brazio stepped close to Choo-Choo, bumping his chest against him. The former Razor warleader was a few inches taller than Choo-Choo, which put Brazio's chin in his face.

"What did you say?"

Choo-Choo looked like he was going to punch Brazio. He stared back at the instructor with the heat of a thousand burning suns in his gaze.

"Nothing."

"Are you sure?"

The pain in Choo-Choo's eyes was palpable. Everyone around the circle could barely watch.

Brazio turned away, and before he'd gotten two steps away, he said, "At least your sister fought like she wanted to win."

Choo-Choo threw himself at the back of the instructor. The powerful kick was blocked as Brazio spun around, but Choo-Choo didn't let up, coming with furious blows that forced Brazio into a defensive retreat. Even the newest member of the clan could see that Choo-Choo was making Brazio work for his blocks.

When Brazio jammed his foot into the ground to leap away with Lightness, Choo-Choo blocked him. The instructor had to jump backwards onto the wall and before he could pick a direction, Choo-Choo was on him, coming with heavy strikes wearing a mask of revenge.

Brazio flipped over the bald warrior, landing as Choo-Choo reversed with a side kick, which was blocked. But Choo-Choo in his exuberance overextended. The instructor grabbed his ankle and yanked Choo-Choo off his feet, swinging him around before launching him into the brick wall. The impact cracked stone and left Choo-Choo on the ground, glowering.

"*That's* how you scrap," said Brazio, nodding. "Had you come at Yara like that you would have easily bested her. That is the first time today that I've actually believed you were Valeria's brother, not some weak-kneed wayhos with more muscles than sense."

Choo-Choo climbed to his feet to go after the instructor again, but Pandora reached him first, holding him back.

"Get my sister's name out of your mouth," said Choo-Choo, his face breaking with emotion.

Brazio stared back, matching Choo-Choo's intensity. "I grieve for you. Not that you lost your sister, but that you cannot see why she was a warrior, worthy of my respect, while you're still fighting a battle that's long past. We both fought with honor, but only one of us was going to walk away from that scrap. I would hope that you could see that, just the same as I would hope that Yara would see it the same if things had been different. Not that I don't respect the desire for revenge—I plan on visiting my own upon Gregor Anderson for killing my brother—but you can't let it shade you from the truth, or distract you from the task. We need every one of us. Every warrior. I need you to fight like that from now on, but not just when you're angry. We're brothers now, whether you like it or not."

"Fuck you, you're not my brother," said Choo-Choo, knocking away Pandora's arm and marching off the grounds.

Brazio checked back to Yara, who stared after Choo-Choo with a frown. The entire group looked uncomfortable at witnessing the exchange.

"Session over," said Brazio, shaking his head and walking away. The rest of the class glanced amongst themselves before leaving the grounds, heading towards the showers or the cafeteria.

"He killed Choo-Choo's sister?" asked Camina when no one else was around.

"Years ago. She was supposed to be the best warrior of her generation but it wasn't enough. The whole family grieves her loss as if it'd happened yesterday," said Pandora.

"Is that why he hates Kuma?"

Pandora shrugged. "Maybe he knows he could never beat Brazio."

"But why not hate Yara?"

Pandora turned to Camina as she furrowed her brow. "I'm sure he does, but it's not the same as Kuma. It's just women at home. Maybe he instinctively wants to protect her like he does his mother and sister, like he couldn't for Valeria." She gestured to the empty grounds. "Want to work on your opal?"

Camina glanced around, frowning. "Here?"

"Afraid to be seen with me?"

Camina pulled a small black box from her pocket and set it on the brick wall after pressing a button.

"I want help with my opal, but I also wanted to talk to you," said Camina, crossing her arms.

"And?"

"Stop fucking with Kuma's head. I've known him my entire life and he has it bad for you. Given everything with Choo-Choo, it'd probably be a bad idea for you two to be together."

Pandora widened her eyes. "I already told him as much."

"You did?" she asked incredulously.

"What we had was great. Nothing like the thrill of forbidden sex, but now's not a good time and we have more important things to worry about, like survival," said Pandora.

Camina squinted suspiciously. "You're not just telling me this so I stop bothering you."

"I talked to him two days ago privately and told him that it's over."

Camina reached for the black box. Her hand hovered over it. "Don't fuck things up." Then she pressed the button.

"You still want training with the opal?"

"You think I'm out here for fun? I'm an amber and an opal. The two least useful stones for scrapping. If I don't find a way to create an advantage, I'm gonna be bug food after the first scrap."

"Good, because the opal is more of a scrapping stone than you think."

Pandora went on to explain the things Duro had taught her. The two of them worked together for the next few hours. Camina was a quick learner and made progress in a short amount of time, and while Pandora was focused on training, there was a part of her that kept going back to what she'd said to Kuma, and how she told him that they couldn't see each other anymore. It was the furthest thing from what she really wanted.

Eight

The runed Kevlar jacket fit tightly around Deacon's chest as he pulled it on, the Velcro making loud noises in his ears as he adjusted the straps. He retied his boots, making sure no lace was loose or could come undone and trip him up during the journey. The other raiders were putting on their gear, laughing and joking about a few days before when Syn knocked the tooth out of the mouthy owner of the Devil's Lipstick in Big Dave's Town.

"What a fuckin' rube," said Laird as he leaned on his knees with a cigarette dangling from his lower lip. "The aww...aww—fuck, the nerve of that bitch to think she could talk to you like that."

"Audacity," said Deacon as he checked his rifle to make sure the safety was on and he had the right ammo clips in his black shoulder bag.

"Whatever, Deacon," said Laird as he took his cigarette and stabbed it in his direction. "The point is that they don't know what's good for 'em. New boss in town and if they got a problem with how we run things, they need to shut the hell up."

The others laughed, except for the greasy-haired kid with fresh blue dagger tattoos on his forearms. He was sitting quietly, his knees bouncing, glancing about. Deacon moved next to the kid.

"Hey, Jax. Nervous?" he asked quietly.

A few of his fellow Crows glanced over, so he frowned back, letting them know it wasn't the time for games. Jax kept his knees bouncing furiously as he licked his lips. He swallowed before nodding intensely.

"Nerves are normal, man. I nearly pissed myself the first time we knocked off a shop. Lucky I didn't shoot the old man when he barked back at me, but once you've had your first, it gets easier."

"Really?" asked Jax.

The kid had pimples on his forehead and barely looked the part of the waku, with freshly tattooed arms and a dusting of a mustache.

"How'd you get that stone anyway? You don't look like the other Blue Daggers I've met."

"Joined up a couple months ago. Mostly been fetching tea and beer for the uppers, but when it came time to try a new stone they'd found, I volunteered. Sometimes dudes go crazy and run off, or they shoot them, but sometimes you get a new stone."

"Right. You figured it was a faster way to respect in the clan. I get that, I get that. I stabbed a guy for the same reason when I was fourteen. No one gave me lip after that," said Deacon.

"Really?"

"Cold, hard truth, man.

"Ruby, huh?" asked Deacon, pulling the kid's hair back so he could see the stone on his ear. "Not very red. More like watered-down blood."

"It is when you flash a light through it." Jax blew out a breath. "When are we...?"

"Soon. Real soon." Deacon put a hand on Jax's shoulder, gave it a comforting squeeze along with a wink. "Don't worry, Jax. You do your thing with the ruby and we'll take care of the rest. Once we get there, it'll be like shooting fish in a barrel. Or a lake in this case. You don't have to kill anyone, unless you want to."

The corners of Jax's eyes creased. The kid wanted to prove himself. "I'd like a gun. I know how to shoot."

Deacon grabbed a pistol hanging in its holster on the wall next to the other automatics. He checked the weapon to make sure it was on safety, and handed it over to Jax, who strapped it on with the confidence of someone who'd handled a gun before.

He left Jax to finish putting on the belt, entering the second room, where the others had collected. They stood around in their black Kevlar gear watching Laird. He was holding his automatic weapon at his hip, acting like he was spraying bullets in an arc. His helmet and headset were hanging off the back of his head, about to fall off.

"Stop fucking around, Laird. Get your damn headset on straight. Once we're moving, we have to be quick and silent," barked Deacon.

"I'm just messin' around, keepin' everyone light for the show, you know?"

Deacon got into Laird's face. "I don't *know*. What I know is this mission better go perfect, or I'm taking it out of your ass."

"What the fuck happened to you?" asked Laird as he straightened his helmet and adjusted the headset. "You act like those stuck-up Razors now. Their honor didn't do shit to keep us from mowing them down like kids."

Deacon grabbed Laird by the Kevlar jacket and lifted him into the air.

"It's not their honor I care about, but their discipline. Brazio still lives, and if we're stupid or unlucky, we'll have to scrap with him. But if we don't fuck things up, we'll be in and out and no one will be the wiser. Need I remind you that the new boss doesn't take kindly to mistakes."

"Sorry, Deacon," said Laird from above him.

"I don't want sorry, I want you to take this seriously."

He slammed Laird onto the ground hard enough to make his teeth clack together.

"Grab your gear, everyone, and drain those pots."

The entire team of thirteen Crows and one Blue Dagger pulled elixirs from their pockets, popped the lids, and threw them back. The cool liquid went down with a spicy aftertaste that made Deacon belch. As they headed towards the western exit of the Machi, the effects of the elixir took hold. His eyes felt puffy as if he'd had numbing drops put into them. By the time they passed the guarded gate and entered the darkness, his eyes were picking up the outlines of the walls and stalactites.

"Everyone's vision good?" he asked in the headset, receiving nods. "Laird, you got point. Don't get lost."

The team traveled through the caverns in a western direction, holding their weapons. Deacon kept watch to make sure they were keeping good muzzle control, not swinging them around like a dick in a whorehouse. A few had swords sticking from their backs, but only a handful of Crows were decent hand-to-hand fighters, unlike their enemies, who grew up with a blade in their fist. The blades were more show than real steel. Best for the rubes in Big Dave's Town. The Drops wouldn't be intimidated.

At first they took the main routes that were under Crow control, passing guard stations, but after fifteen minutes, they headed south, taking a more circuitous route to the Drops territory. It was a route that he'd scouted a few days before when Titus had come to him with the plan.

The big maetrie bothered Deacon like no one had before. He was used to being around killers and thieves. It was the way of his world. But the city elves were different. Some said the maetrie had no remorse for their actions, but Deacon didn't see it that way. To him, they were like surgeons. They cut right through the flesh, and bone if necessary, to get at the problem, whatever it was. The maetrie were surgical in their actions. The speed with which the new boss, Dominion Thule, took over the alliance was proof of that. He'd barely had to kill anyone, which was a mark of his ruthless efficiency. Skinning one mouthy clan leader alive while the others watched was enough to keep them from opening their mouths too wide.

The new boss was generous too. He'd promised that those who performed well and without mistakes would receive the best new stones. Deacon had his eye on a black diamond. The clan only had a few at the moment, but having one would give him a measure of protection, especially since he knew former Razors, like Brazio or Kuma, would love to have their revenge. And despite Deacon's position as one of the top waku in the alliance, he knew he was no match for Brazio, and probably two steps behind Kuma.

A part of Deacon regretted the betrayal, not because he held any special loyalty towards the Razor clan, but because he knew how much they'd made him a better person—more disciplined and focused. Not the fuckup with the wise mouth that had gotten him beat within an inch

of his life in the past. The kind of changes that would make him successful in the new regime. Once they eliminated the Drops and had control of the entire Undercity and the faez crystal trade, Deacon planned
on using his newfound attention to detail to climb the ranks. He wanted
to be a top lieutenant for Dominion Thule.

As they neared the Drops territory, the team moved at a slower pace.
Laird could be a mouthy idiot, but his amber was the best amongst the
Crows. If they were spotted before they reached the target, they'd have
to retreat back to the Machi.

The cavern they entered had a light greenish glow. The variety of
fungi in the Undercity was extensive. Deacon toggled his headset to let
them know to halt. He jogged to the front, taking position next to Laird,
giving him a nod of approval for leading the team to their destination.

"Two minutes. Check your gear, get a drink, eat a snack, but make
sure you're fucking ready when we head out. We'll be moving fast and
light."

They were currently southeast of the Pajot. The journey had taken
them two hours, and now that the task was near, his adrenaline spiked
briefly before settling to a nice calm. Deacon approached Jax, who was
wide-eyed and tapping on his own chest.

"You ready? This next part is all you."

"I've been practicing," said Jax as he nodded rapidly.

The comment was less reassuring than the kid probably intended, but Deacon gave him a smile as if nothing was wrong.

He caught Laird staring at him with burning hatred. The moment he turned his head, his former friend looked away. Deacon wasn't surprised. The gangs were a ladder. You stepped on others to climb upward, knowing the whole time that the ones below you wanted to pull you down and the ones ahead would put a boot into your forehead if they could.

Deacon grabbed a piece of rock the size of his fist, concentrated on his topaz, and *squeezed*. The sharp edges of the rock bit into his flesh, but he continued until it cracked and shattered into pieces. He dusted the remnants on his pant leg.

"Whoa, Deac," said Syn, knocking the hair out of her eyes. "That was tight."

"Been practicing. Good to warm up before a scrap," he said.

Syn gave him a crooked smile. He wouldn't be surprised if they hooked up later on. The adrenaline of a scrap could only be tempered by a bout of amber-fueled sex.

"Everyone good?" he asked the others. "Form up like we prac-ticed."

Syn stood next to him and Jax took the position behind them both. The others clustered around them, more front and back, but staying within range of the ruby waku.

"We start, or you start?" he asked Jax over his shoulder.

"You."

Deacon nodded to Syn. She focused inward on her emerald as he did the same with his topaz.

"You're up, Jax."

A tingling sensation formed across Deacon's skin as if he were caught in a low-level electrical field. It felt like warm water had risen up around them. A lightness invaded his bones, and he checked with Syn, who smiled back, clearly feeling the strength of his topaz.

"Start slow at first, then we can pick up speed. We have about a quarter mile until we near the first Drops guard station. We want to be full speed by the time we reach it."

They started walking, then gradually moved into a run. The ruby felt like a wave pushing them gently forward. Deacon could tell when Syn cycled Light and Heavy. The latter was brief, but with his topaz, the entire group moved with speed. By the time they reached the edge of the Drops territory, the group of fourteen moved faster than any normal human. He felt like they were on an invisible train together, speeding forward. As they neared the first guard station, Deacon called for safeties off.

Nine

The bottom of the lake was peaceful, even as it was brutally cold. The heavy weight sat in his lap, keeping him anchored to the slick stone. The lake was new. Maybe only fifteen years old, so the bottom wasn't muddy or filled with strange creatures like other watery areas of the Undercity. Except for the eyeless pale fish that Tick had played with using his tiger's eye, he was alone.

He thought about his father, wishing he could have had one last discussion with him before he died by the Crows' treachery. It wasn't that he didn't know that Niran loved him, but he wanted to know if he thought he was worthy enough.

As the ache in his lungs grew and the desire to open his mouth became unbearable, he let the weight slip between his legs to settle on the lake floor and pushed off. The moment before he broke through the surface, he wondered if that was why Pandora had broken it off with him. He was no longer the clan leader's son. He was just a waku. Hierarchy and status meant something in the maetrie society. He didn't know much about them, but he knew that.

Instructor Kai stood by the edge of the water with a stopwatch in her hand when he surfaced. She frowned.

"Two minutes and eighteen seconds. Average, Little Bear. Your friend Tick had a better time."

"What? Tick?"

"Nearly twice yours," said the instructor. "Seventh place for today."

Kuma waded out of the water to join the others as he tried to imagine how Tick could have beaten him. Beaten anyone for that matter. He was always near last during their games. *Maybe Tick is getting better? Or I'm getting worse?*

The chill from being submerged made him shiver. Kuma stepped away from the others and did push-ups to warm up. After sixty repetitions, his muscles weren't stiff. Afterwards, he joined Xylos, who was sitting on the stone with his arms around his knees.

"What's wrong?"

Kuma frowned as he took a spot by the older waku. "I know I think I'm screwing up, but does everyone else think so too?"

Xylos raised an eyebrow. "You're usually top of the class, or one of the tops."

"Not feeling it today, I guess."

"Don't let any of the instructors hear you say that. Especially not your uncle. He'd whip you silly," said Xylos.

"I know, and I'd deserve it."

Xylos put a hand on Kuma's shoulder. "Grieve your father, but don't let it affect your training. We need everyone at the top of their game."

Instructor Kai clapped her hands. She stood further down the edge of the lake. "Everyone, with me. We're headed to the other end for diving."

The lake was shallow at one end and deep at the other. When he looked at the water he tried not to imagine the tentacled creature that had pulled Camina and Tick into the depths. He'd thought he'd lost them. He knew there wasn't anything like that in this lake, but his mind wouldn't let go.

"There are twenty-two of you. I put an equal number of weights along the slope. The deeper you go, the heavier the weight. Go as deep as you can, but you must bring back one and only one weight. The best three dives will earn extra free time, the rest of you will get fifty push-ups and sit-ups for every place below those top three."

"That's nine hundred sit-ups and push-ups for last place," said Nato.

"Don't be last." Instructor Kai surveyed the group. "Xylos, you're first."

Xylos stood up and stripped off his shirt, revealing lean muscles. He cracked his knuckles and stretched his arms, giving the rest of them a wink.

"Me and my opal are taking first place," he said as he waded into the water. He inhaled and exhaled slowly, shaking his limbs and taking on a slackened expression. After a minute of preparation, Xylos walked into the deeper section, disappearing below the surface.

Kuma watched from the edge of the lake with his arms wrapped around his knees. He kept expecting Xylos to reappear. The longer it took, the more he worried, but Instructor Kai didn't seem bothered.

"Should we—"

As the words passed his lips, the surface exploded. Xylos appeared with a metal weight clutched within his arms. He strained to carry it out of the lake, dropping it on the side with a splash near Instructor Kai's feet.

"Took you long enough," said the instructor with a smirk.

"Hard time getting it back up. I tried for one of the deeper ones, but it was too heavy," he said as he breathed heavily. "But this should be good enough for one of the top places."

"We'll see. You pick the next diver."

Xylos grinned in Kuma's direction. "Little Bear's next."

Since the instructor was watching, he tried not to make a face, but his expression must have betrayed him because Kai said, "None of this seventh-place bullshit, Kuma. I expect better."

After removing his shirt, Kuma waded into the water, shivering as the cold penetrated his skin. He started breathing exercises that would maximize his oxygen for the dive. Inhale slowly, exhale through the mouth, relax the body—it made him a little dizzy.

Every stone had its advantages and disadvantages in the water. Xylos, using his opal on himself, could maximize his oxygen intake and stay below for much longer. Kuma's emerald would make the diving part easier, but give him no reprieve for the ascent. Rather than swim down the slope like the others would have to do, Kuma stroked into the middle where the deepest part of the lake was located and after cycling Light as long as he could hold it, he switched to Heavy and plunged beneath the surface. As he dropped down through the darkness, he had a moment of panic that he'd gone too far, too fast, and he wouldn't be able to get back up.

He reached out with his amber, using the faint lights above the surface to pick out the details of his surroundings. He passed a few of the pale eyeless fish, which darted away from his sudden appearance. Kuma could pick out the increasingly larger weights along the slope that led steadily downward, but he wasn't interested in those—he wanted the one at the bottom to ensure first place.

The pressure on his lungs and ears made him want to veer to the slope and pick an easier weight. He was already concerned that he wouldn't be able to carry one out. His stones wouldn't provide any benefit, but he continued downward. The water was icy cold. He expected to see ice crystals floating. Almost no light made it to his depth. He figured he had to be close to two hundred feet below the surface and still he hadn't seen the bottom.

When his heels hit the thin layer of mud, swirling it around him, he let go of his Heavy and searched for the weights. He'd gotten turned around during the descent and had to use his amber to find the largest one at the bottom. The size of the weight had him wondering if he was crazy. It had to be a hundred pounds. At least there was a handle he could grab.

While it'd only taken him fifteen seconds to descend to the bottom, swimming back to the surface with a hundred extra pounds was going to be extremely difficult, especially since he needed both hands for the ascent. Kuma grabbed the handle and lifted, pushing off from the bottom and kicking his feet furiously. The time it had taken him to get to the bottom had been longer than he'd wanted, but climbing from the depths was going to take a long time. The weight Xylos had grabbed was at least forty pounds lighter and fifty feet up.

He was aware that if he had to drop the weight and swim back without it, he'd be in last place. A part of him wondered if he was overextending so he'd be forced to fail. His whole life had been spent in the shadow of his father and now with him no longer alive and the clan destroyed, what reason did he have to push himself to be the best? He knew his thoughts were useless self-pity, but he couldn't help it. Despite the danger to his new clan and the good chance that they could all be dead in a few short months, Kuma wanted to wallow in his pain and forget everything he'd been working for all his life.

Around halfway back to the surface, Kuma was certain he was going to die. His lungs felt like fire and he wanted to open his mouth to breathe more than anything. Kicking furiously to swim to the surface had used up his oxygen fast and now he was starting to black out. He kept going, switching hands holding the weight to give his other arm a break. Progress reminded him of a video of a jellyfish pulsing upward in the murky depths of the ocean.

When he reached the final fifty feet, he knew he could make it. Then he heard echoing thumps, confusing him. Most of the lights that had been dispersed around the training area were no longer working, or had been turned off. Something was wrong. Or was he hallucinating? Kuma thought he should drop the weight and swim to the surface to see what had happened, but if he was mistaken then he'd be giving up his first-place dive for nothing.

More thumps—a staccato pulse—had him certain that something was wrong. Kuma released the weight, letting it descend through the darkness below as he switched to Lightness, swimming upward until he

broke the surface as gently as he could. It took all his self-control not to

heave with breath, as his lungs shouted for air.

As soon as the water dripped from his eyes, he saw the carnage. At

least a dozen bodies were strewn along the shore, blood running into the

water. Gunfire echoed from other caverns, flashing muzzle blasts reflect-

ing through the exits.

"No," he whispered.

Kuma swam to the shore, keeping his movements slow and his body

low in the water in case someone returned. He crawled next to Nato,

who stared upward with blank, open eyes. Kuma didn't see the instruc-

tor's body since she wore a black uniform, but the rest were hard to tell

as most were on their sides or fronts. He hoped Xylos got away.

He looked around for his blades, but the strewn bodies made it hard

for him to recognize where he'd been sitting before he went into the

water. Kuma reached into Nato's uniform, but couldn't find his weapons.

With no one moving in range of his amber, Kuma stood up so he could

find something with which to defend himself. He spied the glint of a

blade in a fallen hand when he heard the click of a handgun.

"Don't move or I'll blow your brains out your eyes," said a quivering

voice.

Kuma turned slowly with his hands out to show he didn't have a

weapon. A pimple-faced kid clutched a handgun, shaking slightly. He must have been sitting quietly, which was why Kuma thought he was

another body, not an enemy. There was twenty-five feet between them.

Too far for him to cross without getting shot. The flash of gunfire

echoed from other caverns, making the kid twitch.

"You're my captive," said the kid with a grin. "I got 'em here with

my ruby and now they'll see how useful I am when they return."

"Your ruby?" asked Kuma.

"Shut up, I didn't say you could speak," said the kid, shaking the

weapon for emphasis.

Kuma spied the glint of a stone in the kid's ear. He'd never heard of

a ruby, nor had any idea what it might do, but clearly it was important for

the mission. When more gunfire distracted him, Kuma took a single step

forward, freezing when the kid looked back. He couldn't have been more

than fifteen.

"I said, don't move."

Kuma spied one of the fallen moving near the kid's feet. He

couldn't tell who it was, but they were reaching out towards his leg with a

free hand. When the fingers wrapped around his ankle, the kid jumped,

firing wildly as Kuma leapt with Lightness. He landed with a kick to the

kid's head, knocking him onto his rear. The gun splashed into the lake.

Kuma was about to put a foot through the kid's forehead when he

heard someone returning. Spinning behind the ruby waku, Kuma pulled

him upright and held the kid before him as a shield to find Deacon across the lake with an automatic weapon in his hands.

"I hoped I'd find you here," said Deacon.

The Crow wore body armor and looked the part of a mercenary. But it wasn't just that. There was something different about his former classmate. He still wore the cocky attitude, but it'd been tempered with discipline.

"I should have known it would be you, fucking wayhos," said Kuma with barely constrained rage.

"I'm sorry it had to be this way," said Deacon. "I respected your clan, even if your father never saw what was coming."

"I knew you were a traitor from the first time I met you. We should have never let you into the Machi," said Kuma.

"You're right. You shouldn't have, but it's too late now. You should know as well as I that there's no room for mistakes. Your father made too many in the end, though he did manage to evade being questioned."

It was the first time Kuma had proof that his father was dead. Numbness rose up from the depths.

"It doesn't matter, Kuma. My new boss, Dominion Thule, you've probably already heard about him. I'm glad I'm on this end, and not yours. Every rumor I ever heard about the maetrie is true. He'll own the Undercity and the faez crystal trade in no time, and after that, who knows? He doesn't seem like the type to have small ambitions."

Kuma searched for the nearest weapon, but he only saw the glint of a few blades amongst the fallen. That wouldn't help against Deacon and his automatic weapon.

"Give up, Kuma. It's too late. I'd offer amnesty and a chance to swear allegiance but we know you could never do that. Far too much honor, not enough self-preservation."

Deacon started walking around the lake. There was seventy feet between them. Not far enough considering the weapon.

As Kuma checked around him, he realized the pimple-faced kid's ruby stone was in his right ear. Deacon wasn't shooting because he didn't want to hit their new waku, which gave him a narrow opportunity for escape. Kuma bit down on the kid's earlobe, ripping through the thick flesh as he screamed at the top of his lungs. When the bloody hunk came free into his mouth, he pushed him away and leapt backwards with Lightness, staying low as not to provide a tempting target.

Gunfire chased Kuma across the cave. He circled the lake as Deacon pursued, using cycled Light and Heavy to zigzag. Then when he reached the narrow end of the lake, Kuma leapt. It was fifty feet, further than he'd ever traveled before, but it was his only chance to get away as Deacon was coming up from behind fast with his topaz.

The landing was made with Heavy as he'd been cycling between them too quickly. He hit hard, the piece of earlobe with the ruby slipping down his throat upon impact, making him choke, but once he recovered, he sprinted towards an exit as bullets sprayed across the wall.

When he slipped around the corner, Deacon screamed with rage.

Kuma kept running. While he was new to the Drops clan, he'd made sure to memorize the maps around the Pajot for situations like this. He headed south, knowing he could circle back around to the main settlement from a safer passage. He hoped there was something left to return to.

Ten

Pandora heard the news after their seventh attempt at crossing the field. They were just discussing how to lighten the shields they'd crafted when a runner appeared and gave Duro the awful report. The entire class raced back to the main area with the instructor, who headed into the tunnels towards the training lake once he heard the details.

When she found Choo-Choo, he looked close to tears, marching in a circle with his fists at his side, bald head glistening with sweat. The number of dead varied wildly as they heard reports from others. The entire Pajot was on full alert, expecting attacks from other directions. She overheard someone say that Instructor Kai's entire class had been wiped out in the ambush, which left Choo-Choo barely able to stand.

"I'm sure he survived," she told him. "He's a sapphire. They don't go down that easy."

Choo-Choo swallowed. He couldn't speak as he held onto her arm, squeezing so hard it would leave a heavy bruise. While she stayed with him, her thoughts trended to Kuma. He was in Navos' group. Even though she'd told him that they could no longer be together, her heart still had feelings for him.

When a limping and bloody Xylos appeared, Choo-Choo ran straight to him. The former Razor looked stunned. Pandora couldn't tell whose blood was all over him.

"Is Navos alive? Anyone?" asked Choo-Choo.

Xylos checked over his shoulder and then examined the blade in his fist that was covered in dried blood.

"I saw him get away from the lake. Pulled himself to safety, but after that, I don't know. There were Crows everywhere."

As they spoke, the lanky blond waku emerged from the tunnel. He ran straight for Choo-Choo. The pair embraced, squeezing tight and cupping the back of each other's heads.

"Anyone else? Who else did you see go down?" she asked vaguely, even though she only had one person in mind.

Xylos watched Choo-Choo and Navos for a moment before returning his attention to her. He blinked as he tried to access the memories.

"I'd just gotten done with my dive. Kuma was in the water when the shooting started. Everyone else minus a few of us were slaughtered on the shore."

Pandora bit the inside of her cheek, trying not to imagine that Kuma had been caught when he surfaced, even as she chastised herself that it wasn't him alone she should be thinking about. The loss of more than half of a class was tragic and would have a major impact on the defense of the Pajot and their long-term survival.

"Was it the Crows or the Alliance?" she asked.

"It was the fucking Crows and that traitor Deacon," said Xylos.

She'd heard the story of the Crows' attack on Razor to know the name Deacon. As if summoned by his name, Yara appeared and went straight to Xylos.

"Is it true? Was it Deacon?"

He nodded, and Yara started to move away, but Xylos grabbed her arm.

"He's already gone by now. Duro and Brazio went after them, but they're probably halfway back to the Machi by now. I had to hide while they were searching for us. It's been over an hour since the attack."

Yara yanked her arm away, but froze when Kuma appeared. He stumbled into the cavern and dropped to one knee. Flecks of dried blood surrounded his mouth.

"Did you kill him? Please say you ripped his throat out," said Yara.

Kuma lifted his chin. His eyes were hazy as if he'd been poisoned and he appeared hesitant to speak.

"He had the drop on me. It was enough to get away," said Kuma.

His gaze flickered to Pandora, which brought a warmth to her gut, then he turned back to his cousin.

"I'm sorry, Yara. If I'd had a chance, I would have taken it, but I'd just surfaced after my dive."

She squeezed her lips white, nodding absently.

"One thing's for sure," said Xylos, "never break Yara's heart."

"Fuck you, Xylos."

Yara strode towards the Academy with her arms crossed. Each step was a stamp of anger.

"Not sure why she took that out on me." Xylos glanced around. "I'm going to check and see who else made it back."

"Glad you made it out," Navos said to Kuma once it was only the four of them. Choo-Choo elbowed his friend, but Navos shook his head. "Emilio. We need everyone."

Kuma was still on one knee. He closed his eyes momentarily. "I came out of the water to find everyone dead."

Navos started to ask a question, but Choo-Choo marched away, which prompted him to follow. He gave them lifted shoulders before he disappeared with Choo-Choo.

"You okay?"

Kuma nodded. "Attunement vertigo."

"Attunement?"

He rocked on his one knee. "There was a young waku with a new stone. A ruby. When Deacon appeared, I grabbed the kid as a shield, then before I left I bit his earlobe with the stone off but accidentally swallowed it when I was escaping."

"Oh no." She paused. "A ruby?"

"That's what he called it. No idea what it does, but given he wasn't geared like the others, I'm assuming it was what helped get them into the area."

"Do you need help?"

"I need to lie down," he said.

She was about to offer to take him when Navos appeared. "Hey Pan, they need you near the HQ. More wounded came in. The guards got pretty shot up when the Crows left."

Pandora hesitated, but Kuma waved her off. "Go. They need you."

She ran with Navos back to the front, wondering if cutting herself off from Kuma was a good idea. On the other hand, her desires seemed petty in comparison to the fate of annihilation that the entire clan was facing.

Eleven

After dropping off the majority of his team at the Machi, Deacon took the stone-less Jax and a small group northwest to the Alliance HQ. The fight at the lake had been six hours ago and Deacon really wanted a long shower and a beer, but he had to report back on the success of his mission. He wished there were tunnels that led in that direction, but Razor had always been careful not to dig them in areas they couldn't control.

"I'm going to be in trouble for losing the ruby, aren't I?" asked Jax for the fifth time during their travels.

"I'm sure you'll be fine. Punishment for sure, but if you can attune to one, you can probably attune to others," he told the kid.

Jax smiled, but it never reached his eyes, which looked one step from full-blown panic. As they traveled through the caverns, climbing over rocky sections or crossing ravines by way of rickety rope bridges, Deacon longed for the days of the past riding in tricked-out cars with amped stereos and a cooler of beer in back. It'd been months since he'd seen the sun. Once the business with the Drops was finished, he hoped to take a break in the city, visit some of his old haunts, maybe an ex-girlfriend or two.

The first guard post came about an hour after they left the Machi. When they stepped out, Deacon was surprised to see two Eights with a Voyna when he was expecting Demon Dogs. He gave the password and they let him through.

Deacon spotted the communication lines being run through the tunnels. It'd surprised him the first time he'd come this way that they didn't have better connections between the clans, but they'd kept their separate spaces and traditions. Cooperation came only in response to the threat of Razor and Drops.

He was surprised by the condition of the main cavern when they entered. From Gregor's description, he was expecting a smoky mess with the residents living in hovels and burning trash or other junk as cooking fires. Not a trace of smoke remained, and the hovels had been cleared out, replaced with actual buildings much like the Terreno. Clan members climbed over the newer constructions with hammers. Deacon spotted a lot of fresh faces.

"When did all this happen?" he asked Jax.

"Started about two or three months ago. I was brought in when we were tearing down the old buildings."

"Where were you before?"

"Lived in a place in the twelfth ward with, like, nine others. We slept on the floor, drank a lot, and went out on smash runs when green got tight," said Jax.

Deacon nodded absently. He knew the life. He'd been in a similar situation when he was younger. The trick of getting out was finding the right crew to run with and not screwing it up.

"This used to be Demon Dogs home," said Jax.

"I know, kid."

He hadn't been at the meeting, but Gregor had told him in exquisite detail about how Dominion had sliced the head off Lionel Diaz, the head of the Demon Dogs, and had taken control of his clan, using them as his private security team. There'd been a few disagreements, but after a few more heads had been removed, no one else complained. The Demon Dogs had been the largest clan in the alliance and their home territory had typically been the place the clans met.

When he spotted a new-looking bar called the Eleventh Gonka, he let his team grab a drink while he took Jax into the main area.

"What kind of name is that?" he asked Jax.

The kid lifted his shoulders. "Something from the Eternal City."

"No shit."

He didn't bother pressing Jax, since he seemed to be rather clueless. At his age, Deacon had made it a point to know everything and everyone, because not knowing was a recipe for getting killed when you pissed off the wrong person.

The sound of falling water increased as they headed to the back of the cavern. When they came around the corner, he saw two things. The first was the waterfall that crashed over the right side into a deep pool that wasn't visible from this area. The pool led to a swift stream that washed away to the east through narrow and dangerous canyons called Canter's Folly.

The second was that next to the waterfall was a long ledge on the high cliff that was about a hundred and eighty feet above the ground. It led to the main building that Demon Dogs, and now the alliance, called its home. To his surprise, an open cage elevator had been installed to take them up to the main area. Deacon had to give up his weapons at the guard station. As the cage rose, he saw the purpose of the openness. If someone tried to come up this way, they'd be easy to gun down without walls to protect them.

When they exited the cage onto the ledge, another group of guards greeted them, checking them for weapons and verifying their identities. The last time he'd been here, they'd barely checked him once he'd passed the main guard station out front. The attention to detail didn't surprise him, and it was one more reminder that he'd better keep to the path he'd set himself on, and not revert to old Deacon habits.

To the left, he could hear the rumble of generators. The facilities that powered the space had been expanded in that direction. To enter the main building, they went into a set of double doors that led to a room with another set made of stainless steel and etched with runes. Deacon sensed they were being observed through a one-way window with his amber, and after a long wait, the inner doors opened.

Passing through, he got a good look at the thick interior barrier, which looked like it'd been repurposed from a bank vault. It had to be enchanted steel at least a foot thick. They were led through hallways that looked more like corporate offices, until they were left in a side room with a leather couch and a small refrigerator.

Deacon was disappointed to find bottled water rather than beer, but he handed one to Jax and took a seat. The pimple-faced kid paced opposite while he sipped his water.

"You're getting on my nerves," he told him after a few minutes of pacing.

"Sorry."

Jax crouched in the corner rather than sit on the couch with him, which was the first smart thing he'd seen Jax do in a while. The kid was only starting to see the impact of his decisions, but it might be too late.

He could have clued the kid in on his probable fate, but like cows being herded for the slaughter, no reason to get him worked up.

The door opened, revealing a squat waku with tattoos covering his entire body including his bald head. Deacon recognized him as a Yami no Kishi, or Knights of Darkness.

"Come with me," he said to Jax.

The kid looked to Deacon. "You'll be fine, kid. Go with him and answer their questions truthfully."

When the door closed, Deacon shook his head. He hoped it was quick for the kid's sake. He'd done good in getting them to the lake with minimum interference, but losing the ruby had been a dumb move. Better if he'd gotten shot and then healed later.

Without Jax's unresolved energy clogging up the room, Deacon curled into the corner and fell asleep. He awoke to the door opening and reached for his weapon that wasn't there. It took a moment of disoriented waking to remember where he was and why he didn't have his gun.

The Demon Dog who'd come to get him wore runed Kevlar and had a sword on his hip. Deacon wondered if he could take it from him if necessary. He was led to a room he recognized from Gregor's explanation and checked the carpet for signs of Lionel's blood.

"Sit here. He'll be with you in a moment."

The "he" didn't require a question. While Titus had given him the mission, he knew it'd come from his boss.

An enormous painting on the wall depicting a thick forest with a strange town along the river immediately drew his notice. Deacon stared at it briefly, but the details gave him the creeps. It felt like a cursed object that he would get dragged into if he stared too long, so he spent his time flexing his hands and picking at his fingernails while avoiding even a glance at the painting.

When the door opened, Deacon rose to his feet. The figure that entered wore a black suit and purple tie. Deacon resisted the urge to throw himself at his feet. The aura of the maetrie was like a geas on his mind. He managed a stiff bow, remaining in the bent position.

"Your time in Razor served you well," said Dominion Thule. "You may take a seat."

The tension in his entire body loosened slightly at the command. Deacon found himself wanting to please the head of the alliance with every bone in his body. Dominion studied him, while Deacon tried not to make eye contact in case it was an insult.

"The raid was mostly a success I hear," said Dominion as he took the spot at the end of the table.

Deacon couldn't shake the feeling that he was in a cage getting sized up for how easily his skin could be peeled off.

"We killed many Drops, but lost the ruby. I shouldn't have left Jax alone at the lake. I thought there was no one alive, but one of them had been in the water when we hit them."

"You don't have to worry about Jax any longer," said Dominion dryly.

The announcement brought shuddering relief to Deacon even as he knew that Jax was no longer alive.

"Gregor speaks highly of you. He says that the raid on the Machi wouldn't have been possible without you on the inside."

Deacon bent his neck, staring at the gray marble. He started to talk about his role, but the training from Instructor Kazuki overrode his mouth. "The raid was a success because the Crows worked together. I felt lucky to have contributed."

Dominion chuckled lightly, which was like hearing a dead man laugh. His gray skin and gaunt cheeks made him ghoulish, but there was no doubt he was alive.

"That's good. The time in Razor was instructive for you."

"My only regret from the raid was that it ended my time of study," said Deacon.

"I'm pleased to hear that from you," said Dominion.

The compliment brought a wave of euphoria, but knowing its false-ness, Deacon buried it. Distracted by his feelings, he didn't notice the door opening until a figure stepped through it.

If Dominion was a serial killer, the kind that watched his victims for months before systematically taking them apart, limb by limb, then the maetrie who stepped into view was a quick blade to the heart. Black hair swooped over his eyes as one shoulder dipped lower than the other. A sword hung on his hip. Everything about the maetrie was both casual and deadly. The smirk alone could have cut a throat, and his black eyes reflected a thousand thousand deaths.

"You already know Titus, but this is one of my other...friends." Dominion smiled like a corpse as he turned his shoulders. "Kavano is a fixer. There are no problems he cannot solve. This is Deacon, and he's one of the more promising waku in my retinue."

Kavano inclined his head ever so slightly, barely the width of a single hair. The presence of the fixer had Deacon's heart racing, which brought a curl to the corner of Kavano's lips. Like a true predator, he sensed fear, and never in his life had Deacon felt so completely outmatched.

"Deacon wishes to continue his studies," said Dominion with faint amusement. "Since Razor no longer exists and I wouldn't trust the clans in my service to train a dog, I'm sending him to the Eternal City."

Deacon's heart seized up at the thought. He'd always wanted to travel to another realm, but not the home of the maetrie. Tales of the Eternal City made the voyeuristic splatter-punk movies of his youth seem childish.

"Since you have to make a trip back, I would like you to take him. You know the place."

Kavano let his eyelids drift half closed in response.

"What about my team?" asked Deacon when it was clear that he would be leaving right away.

"They'll be informed of your temporary absence." Dominion reached into an inner pocket and produced a small box. "You can attune to this when you're settled."

Deacon's heart was bouncing around in his chest. He took the box and slipped it into a side pouch, desperately wanting to know which one he'd been given. If it was a black diamond it would make this trip to the Eternal City worth it. He rose and followed Kavano from the room while Dominion stared at the strange painting on the wall with a grim longing.

Kavano led them through hallways and eventually through a runed door that glowed upon their approach. In the room beyond was a wall of slick obsidian that looked hacked out of the earth. The edges were sharp and the glossy surface acted like a fun-house mirror.

"We're leaving now?"

"Unless you'd like to tell him that you can't go yet," said Kavano.

"I guess I didn't realize... How far is the trip?"

"Not long, but very far," said Kavano with a barely restrained grin. "Are you afraid?"

"No," lied Deacon right away.

"You should be."

Deacon swallowed away his fears and reminded himself that his younger version would have been thrilled by the chance to train in the Eternal City, even as the idea of it frightened him. In a kill or be killed world, the better warrior would always prevail. This was a chance to catch up and surpass Kuma and the rest of the Drops clan. Of course, they might all be gone by the time he was done with his training. He couldn't imagine that his journey would be brief.

"How long have you worked for him?" asked Deacon.

Kavano scowled. "I do not work for him except by contract. He wishes me to solve a vexing problem. Nothing more."

Deacon knew that Titus Cabone was on long-term retainer in addition to promises of a cut of the faez crystal trade for his leading role, but there was something familiar about the mercenary. His needs and actions were almost human and worked in ways that made sense to Deacon. Kavano left him with a sense his motivations were entirely unique.

"Put your hand on the obsidian. Once we travel over, you must do everything I tell you."

To Deacon's surprise, the glossy black stone was warm, almost alive. Kavano shook the sleeve away from his wrist, exposing a pale white band with brightly colored stones imbedded. At second glance, Deacon realized it was bone. Kavano breathed black smoke over the jewels, which woke with a faint glow, and then he placed his hand next to Deacon's on the obsidian. Before he could ask a question, a punch of vertigo hit him in the gut and the room faded from view.

Twelve

Pandora woke from her slumber in the middle of the night when a note slid beneath the door of her Academy room. She hurried to the hallway to find no one in view, and her sapphire radar revealed nothing more. She collected the note and sat on the bed. It was chunky parchment, the kind people wrote calligraphy on. Unfolding the paper revealed a brief note written in a swirling cursive.

Come to the Deep Basin. Tell no one. — Duro

The secrecy bothered her, but it looked like his handwriting. She remembered it from the war room in the HQ near the maps. But that didn't mean someone hadn't forged it. She slipped into her training uniform, grabbed her travel pack, and snacked on a food bar made of dried crickets, peanuts, and cranberries on the way out of the Academy grounds.

She took the back way out of the Pajot and immediately ran into Navos, who was coming the other way. They both froze and then she said, "You got a note."

He nodded, knocking the bleach blond hair out of his eyes.

"Any idea what's at the basin?"

Pandora lifted a shoulder. "Guess we'll find out."

Shortly after they entered the tunnels, a voice called from behind.

"You got a note too?" asked Camina when she ran up. "Ideas?"

"None, but we should know soon," said Pandora.

The slope leading into Deep Basin had the scuffs of recent passage. The air grew warmer and wetter as they descended. When a swarm of buzzing insects formed a cloud around Camina, she spun around, searching.

"Tick? Where are you so I can rip your ears off?"

Laughter from behind a thick clump of leafy ferns revealed the smallish waku. He waved his hand and the insects dissipated into the air. When he joined them, Camina flicked his ear, which made him flinch.

"It was worth it."

"You're such a child, Tick."

"In all ways except the one that counts," he said, gesturing towards his crotch, which earned him a second flick.

When they arrived at the Night Wall, they found nine others including three of the instructors—Duro, Brazio, and Nikolai—and other students from their groups. She spotted Kuma right away, and Choo-Choo standing on the opposite side, followed by Yara, Einar, Xylos, and Adrenalynne.

"Hey," said Tick, grinning and strutting forward. "Only the best waku are here." No one laughed.

The three instructors were chatting amongst themselves and staring at the enormous cliff wall. There were no lights except for a small lantern set in the middle of the group. Duro approached the group, taking on a stern persona.

"The raid on the lake a few days ago has necessitated a change in our preparations. We'd hoped to continue with the larger group for training reasons, but losing those thirteen put a big hit on our defenses, which were already stretched thin. Guarding the training sites in addition to our regular locations was too much. I take full responsibility for the loss of our clanmates," said Duro grimly.

The announcement erased any smiles. Even Tick hung his head in reverence.

"From this moment forward, training will only consist of this group. There will be times that not all of us can be present, especially Brazio and myself, but every moment you do spend on the tasks we've given you will be of utmost importance. Questions?"

"What will we be training for?" asked Navos.

Duro pursed his lips and glanced briefly at Brazio, who had a sly grin.

"For the time being, that doesn't matter. What does matter is that this training and everything related to it is a secret from the rest of the clan. Daraja and the other instructors know, but beyond that, no one else can know what we're doing. That includes your former classmates, your families, your grandmothers"—Duro smiled at Tick—"and even your pet cave cricket. In time, we'll give you more information, but until we're happy with progress of your activities, be satisfied with giving us your all." He placed his hands behind his back. "The good news is that you won't be weighed down by your lesser peers. The bad news is we won't be coddling you anymore."

"Coddling? That's coddling?" asked Tick, bringing laughter from the group, even the instructors.

Duro nodded to the diminutive waku, then added a playful wink. "You'll find the parameters of your challenges much tighter. For instance, the wall climb, which no group even reached the halfway mark on, will be in complete darkness and must be achieved without making noise." He nodded to Brazio, who held up a black box. "See that box? It will detect even the smallest sound."

"Shall we give them an example?" asked Brazio, receiving a nod. He put a finger over his lips and then switched the box on, after which he crouched down and picked up a pebble with exaggerated motions, tossing it into the air. When it landed, the box blared an ear-rattling alarm that made everyone flinch away. Pandora put her hands over her ears until he clicked it off.

"Eventually you'll need to be able to climb it in less than thirty minutes. That means the entire group of you, but for now, let's concentrate on completing it together without noise, light, and in one piece."

"And no flying snakes," said Tick, grinning at the group, only because he'd used his stone to move them to another location in the Deep Basin.

"You'll be in good hands with Instructor Nikolai. Brazio and I have some other tasks to attend to, but don't worry about surprise raids— we've tripled our guard around the area."

The two warleaders left them next to the cliff. Nikolai approached with two backpacks, dropping them on the ground.

"This time you have complete access to gear and if you want something else, let me know."

"A rope hanging from the top of the cliff?" asked Navos, revealing a gold tooth when he spoke.

"The lantern will stay on until you start climbing and then I'll turn on the noise box. If the alarm goes off, you have to start over."

The nine of them formed a circle. Choo-Choo took the opposite side from Kuma, but he hadn't said anything, which was progress. The raid by the Crows was probably too fresh in his mind.

"Ideas?" asked Adrenalynne.

Her closely shorn head was a mixed patchwork of purple and crimson, and her eyes glowed faintly.

Einar stroked his bushy mustache and said, "We got four topaz including myself. We should be the anchors in front."

No one disagreed. Kuma spoke up. "Weakest climbers in the middle with the sapphires, Pandora and Navos, to help in case of problems?"

"I'll take lead climb," said Choo-Choo, cracking his knuckles.

Kuma hesitated, then spoke reluctantly. "It should probably be Einar and Yara since they have both emerald and topaz. If things go sideways, they can hold a lot of weight."

"I'm the better climber," said Choo-Choo aggressively. "And I know you're just looking out for your cuz."

"I'm just trying to find the best mix for the climb," said Kuma exasperatedly.

Yara said, "You can have my spot, Choo-Choo."

The offer was a complete surprise. Once they'd determined roles, they slipped into their gear, which included hooking lines between each other in a loose webbing. Pandora took the right position, which would allow her to support Choo-Choo, who would be above her.

The group approached the wall. When Choo-Choo put his hand on the stone, Instructor Nikolai switched the lantern off.

"Noise detector is on…now."

Pandora stood two steps to Choo-Choo's right. There was enough luminous fungi in the cavern behind them to see the cliff as a glistening wall. He pulled himself onto the vertical surface at the same time as Einar on the opposite side, moving at the speed of a patient spider. Pandora found a jug hold and pulled to a spot near Choo-Choo. The others made their way onto the wall. Pandora looked for the crack she was—

The black box blared the ear-splitting alarm.

"What the hell?" asked Einar.

"Everyone back down," said Instructor Nikolai.

"Are you sure that thing isn't too sensitive?" asked Tick.

Nikolai crouched down and switched the box off. "It's the parameters Brazio gave me."

"Augh," said Tick.

"Who made the noise?" asked Yara.

No one spoke for a long time until Navos said, "I thought I heard a shoe scrape, like when you jam it into a crack."

Silence returned.

"No one?" asked Yara. "Come on, we can't get better if no one will fess up."

"Let's just try again," said Kuma.

Pandora heard Choo-Choo mutter under his breath, "It was probably you."

No one acknowledged the comment, even as they'd all probably heard it.

The second attempt lasted as long as the first when Xylos knocked a pebble from the wall. The third ended when Tick sneezed, offering an apology immediately after. There were four more failures, and in each one, the entire team never made it on the wall.

"Shall we try again?" asked Choo-Choo reluctantly.

"No," said Pandora. "We need to make adjustments. Too many foot scrapes are causing the alarm. Those climbing shoes are great for gripping, but they're loud. We need to take them off."

"Barefoot?"

"It's not like we all haven't climbed without shoes," said Kuma. "I'm sure you all were just like us as kids, climbing over everything, getting in trouble for being too high on the wall."

"My momma whipped me silly," said Navos.

A few sighs later, the entire group was removing their footwear. With a pile of shoes near the sound detector, the group managed to make it completely onto the wall. Pandora climbed to the bottom-right of Choo-Choo, relishing the cold stone on her callused feet. They made it forty feet above the ground before Adrenalynne knocked a rock from a ledge, which set off the alarm.

"My fault," she said right away.

When they returned to the bottom, Choo-Choo said, "Can we just send someone up to knock away all the loose material first before our real attempt?"

Kuma rubbed the back of his neck. "As much as I'd love to agree, that probably won't help us on the real wall we're eventually going to have to climb."

Everyone contemplated his words. Pandora had already thought about the implications of the trials, but without the specifics there was no point in speculating.

"I was wondering if we were going to be climbing the Spire," said Tick.

"The Spire? Why the hell would you think that, you little tunnel rat?" asked Camina.

"All the obsidian is like a glass window."

"What the hell would we do in the Spire anyway? That's all Hall business," said Camina.

"Dunno. Maybe steal some crazy cool artifact that will help us defeat the alliance."

"Come on," said Adrenalynne. "Let's try again. Maybe we'll make it further this time."

Pandora was as optimistic, but to no avail. They only made it back to that height two other times; the rest of their attempts were foiled at lower levels. After ten hours of climbing, Instructor Nikolai called it, and they returned to the Academy grounds to find their belongings had been moved to a separate building that typically housed the instructors. Duro greeted them inside, where bunk beds had been set up in a space that was barely big enough for the ten of them.

"Why'd we get moved?" asked Choo-Choo, clearly frustrated.

"You need to get better at working as a team," said Duro with an eyebrow raised. "The best way to do that is to be in constant contact with each other."

"But—"

"Is there something wrong, Choo-Choo?"

The broad-shouldered waku shook his bald head. "Nothing, Shadowmaster."

"Get some rest tonight," said Duro to the group. "Tomorrow you'll be working on crossing the firing field."

A collective groan brought a chuckle from Duro. "If you don't like getting shot, then do a better job."

After he left, they had to sort out their bunk assignments. Choo-Choo and Navos took one, Xylos and Adrenalynne were another, followed by Camina and Tick, then Yara and Einar took the one in the corner. Pandora stared across the room at Kuma when they both realized they were the only ones left. He lifted his shoulders and approached with a sly grin.

"Top or bottom?"

"Do you get up in the middle of the night to use the bathroom?"

"Sometimes."

She threw her bag onto the top bed. "Then you're on the bottom. I don't want to hear you climbing down all night."

Kuma looked like he wanted to say something smart, but then he checked to the others before grabbing his duffle bag and placing his gear in the footlocker at the end of their bunk bed.

Pandora was used to sleeping alone or with only one other person, so having nine others making noises, snoring, or breathing loudly left her wide awake until the middle of the night when exhaustion finally set in.

Thirteen

The team had only started diving in the lake when Duro appeared and pulled Instructor Nikolai to the side for a discussion. Kuma was sitting on the slope, waiting for his turn, trying not to notice the bullet casings left between the rocks near where he was sitting. He kept checking the far side of the lake, expecting to see Deacon and his Crow buddies burst into the cavern with automatic weapons flashing. He'd never been close with Nato since he was a year older, but it was another one of his childhood cohort that was no longer alive. Nato. Botan. Carlos. Jando. Omar. There were many others that had died when the Crows had raided the Machi, but it hurt too much even thinking about the ones he knew well, let alone his father.

"Kuma. Pandora. I need to see you," said Duro from the edge of the lake.

Kuma approached the warleader, catching a side-eye from Pandora when she joined them.

"How's that new stone?" asked Duro. "Figure anything out?"

Kuma blushed with embarrassment, letting his chin drift towards his chest.

"I'm sorry, warleader, between the trials and everything else, I've not spent much time trying to figure out what it does. Mostly I'm just happy I'm not dizzy anymore."

Duro let his mouth shift to the side. "There were no clues from when you took it from the kid?"

"He said something about getting them there with his ruby, but I've never been able to make any sense of it."

Duro nodded and looked away. "The guards said the entire group of Crows ran through the cavern at high speed like they were all enchanted or had topaz stones, but we know some of them were stoneless."

"The ruby made them run fast?"

"Maybe," said Duro. "But I assume you would have determined that already."

Pandora was listening quietly, glancing between them. "Why am I here, sir?"

"Because we're taking a trip. Head back to the Academy and dress like you're a lighter. Something nice, we'll be going to a fancy restaurant. Meet me at the Lazona exit."

Many heads lifted at the description of their destination, followed by furrowed brows.

"But...I haven't gone yet," said Kuma, nodding towards the lake.

"Don't worry. This isn't a pleasure trip. You're not getting out of anything," said Duro loud enough for the others to hear. "Now hurry up, we have reservations."

"Sir, I don't have any nice clothes."

Duro looked him over with a tilted head. "I'll have something for you, but both of you shower. You stink."

Kuma burst into a run with Pandora right beside him. When he looked her direction, she offered a shrug.

"No idea."

"I heard you went on trips with Duro."

Pandora chuckled. "I think we both know the one I went on. I'd hardly call myself his regular companion, but he always has a reason."

After the run, Kuma was covered in a sheen of sweat. The showers were in the same room, but separated by curtains. He heard Pandora enter the shower two up from him. He briefly imagined her soaping up and washing her hair.

"Concentrate, Kuma," he muttered to himself.

When he returned to their group quarters, a dark suit hung on the bunk. The pants were a little loose around his waist, but he cinched the belt to make them fit. The shirt and jacket snugged tightly to his muscled frame.

"Not bad," said Pandora, entering the room, wearing a tight black dress with extra buckles and zippers. He couldn't help but imagine her with a whip in hand.

"That dress suits you," he said.

She unzipped a pocket on her hip, revealing a slim blade. "Never go anywhere without a weapon."

They met Duro at the indicated exit. He was wearing a royal blue silk suit with a black tie. His hair was slicked back and he wore a hint of eyeliner, looking like he was ready to stroll down the catwalk at a Paris fashion show.

"You brought your weapons?" he asked.

Kuma opened up his jacket revealing twin blades while Pandora produced hers from locations he was certain couldn't fit them. She raised an eyebrow.

"I told you a girl doesn't go anywhere without her weapons."

The tunnels led them towards the Lazona. Kuma had a thousand questions, but traveling through unguarded caverns wasn't the time for making unwanted noise.

When they entered the Lazona, Kuma whistled softly when he realized he couldn't see the ceiling. The space was a cylinder with businesses crowded around the walls at an ever-increasing height. Some of the neon signs were dull, but a few like the Lime Duck buzzed with electricity.

"Seems different," said Pandora, frowning.

"About a quarter of them left once Razor was taken over. They've moved to the Terreno or Big Dave's or out of the Undercity entirely." Duro gestured towards a tunnel on the opposite side. "Come on. We're not going up that way."

Kuma followed, craning his neck and trying to take in the space. The Terreno always felt a little like Vegas to him—not that he'd ever been—while Big Dave's was like an obscure corner of some strange otherworldly realm. The Lazona felt like he was in some post-apocalyptic town beneath the earth.

The opposite tunnel brought them to a construction area. Welding tanks and earth moving equipment sat lifeless along the wall. A single floodlight illuminated the area, buzzing and crackling.

"The workers stopped the project, said we couldn't protect them anymore," said Duro.

He led them through the construction zone to a metal door which he unlocked with a key. Steel stairs traveled up through the darkness.

"Ready to climb?"

"Seriously?" asked Kuma.

"Afraid of a few stairs?" asked Duro, laughing.

Kuma patted the suit. "I just got cleaned up. I'll be a sweaty mess by the time we reach the top."

Duro winked and started climbing. The stairs circled the area that had been dug out for the elevator that would never be put in, or at least not by the Drops anytime soon. Kuma followed, the ponderous steps ringing in the narrow space. He wasn't paying attention and nearly ran into Pandora's backside about six floors above the ground. Duro opened a door with the same key, leading them across a bridge to a round cage that looked barely big enough to hold three people.

"Construction workers used this to get down here. It's slow and rattles so hard you'll want earplugs, but it's better than walking."

Kuma packed inside next to Pandora and Duro. His shoulders pressed against the other two, so he turned sideways. The elevator lurched into motion, heading upward at a dreary pace. Within seconds, the rattling started, forcing Kuma to clamp his teeth to keep them from clacking together. Diesel fumes chased them upward, giving Kuma a minor headache. The elevator had no interior lights except for a few buttons, so they passed upward through the earth in near darkness. Kuma eventually closed his eyes and tried to forget the passage of time.

As the elevator took him up, Kuma thought about his father and the final hours of Razor clan. If he hadn't gotten distracted with trying to be a hero, he might have been at the Machi when things went down and his father wouldn't have died. Kuma stole a glance at Pandora, who had her head down and her fingers jammed in her ears. She was mumbling, but he couldn't hear, nor did he want to use his amber to find out. Her plan had been a good one, but he shouldn't have been sneaking around the Undercity defying his father's edict to stay in the Machi.

And now that Niran was dead, Kuma had done nothing to avenge him. The weight of that responsibility hung on his shoulders. He tried to tell himself that his uncle Brazio hadn't gone after Gregor either, but logic did nothing to remove the ache in his chest.

When the elevator lurched to a stop, Kuma stumbled out of the door once he'd gotten it wrenched open. He bent over and inhaled deeply.

Duro clapped him on the shoulder and said, "Come on. The walk will clear your head."

After two more sets of locked doors, Kuma stepped into a warehouse stacked with crates and shipping pallets. The concrete floor was smooth and completely clean except for a few old pieces of plastic that had probably been wrapped around a pallet. Their shoes echoed.

When they stepped outside, Kuma squinted against the bright light and stayed in the safety of the doorway. Outside, the warehouse was surrounded by dilapidated buildings. Tufts of grass stuck through the cracked streets, but beyond them, the Spire rose into the sky, twice as high as the nearest skyscrapers. He held up his arm to block the sunlight.

"You gonna be okay?" asked Duro.

Kuma nodded, but found it was easier to walk near the building than closer to the street. At the corner of the block, a black SUV waited for them. Duro climbed in back.

"Hey fam," said a dark-haired guy in the driver's seat.

"Thanks for getting us on short notice, Dane," said Duro.

"What else am I here for then?" he said, chuckling as he pulled onto the street. "You all look hella sharp." There wasn't traffic until they passed closer to the ring road, after leaving the twelfth ward and entering the eleventh.

The interior of the SUV was comforting to Kuma, unlike the streets outside. He hated that he felt weak in the open air. He'd spent his whole life underground, so coming to the surface was like being in a foreign realm.

"Gonna be okay?" whispered Pandora, leaning over.

"Huh?"

She nodded towards his hand, which was squeezing the inner handle hard enough to make his veins stick out.

"Oh, right."

Kuma pulled it to his chest, massaging the muscles. Duro looked out the window. He couldn't decide if it was the open skies or the fact that the last time he left his home, it'd been wiped out. He worried that when they returned to the Pajot, there'd be nothing but smoking ruins.

"Okay, we're almost there. We're going to be meeting with someone who might be able to help Kuma figure out the ruby and a few other things. It took me a bit to set this up. Be warned, from the stories I've heard, he can be rather odd. Take no offense to whatever he says."

"Who is he?" asked Kuma as the vehicle stopped outside a fancy restaurant. A thick brass sign read: Other Realms. A valet in a red jacket approached.

Duro shot them a grin. "Ivan Charmer. He's the guy that discovered faez crystals."

Kuma shared a look of incredulity with Pandora as they followed the warleader out of the SUV. The gap between the SUV and the entrance was mercifully short. A valet opened the door and Kuma followed them inside. A woman in a red dress took their names, nodding enthusiastically and motioning for them to follow.

"Close your mouth, or have you never been in a restaurant in the city?" whispered Pandora.

"Niran took me a few times, but it's been years. Before the invasion and the faez crystals."

He kept his mouth closed but he couldn't help but stare at the people dressed in their finest, eating in a big room together. It was much different than the Terreno or Big Dave's. The fanciest place he visited was the Onyx and that felt like owning fake jewelry. They were led to a back room behind a set of fancy wooden double doors with painted glass at the center. Two bodyguards with wires sticking from their ears and no visible weapons stood outside. Kuma sensed the bulge of their handguns inside their coat pockets. He was certain that he could disable both of them in the span of half a second if he had to. Two punches to the throat. They'd never see it coming.

Pandora elbowed him. "Relax," she mouthed.

Inside the private room was a single table with five spaces, two of them occupied by a man and woman, neither of them appearing that much older than he was. Not even out of their thirties yet they were extremely wealthy. Ivan had dark hair that curled at the edges and a brooding look, even as he was smiling. The woman next to him wore a silver sequined jacket over a black dress that she'd squeezed into. She had thick, curly hair that framed her cherub-like face and while she wasn't smiling there was a friendly cast to her gaze.

Ivan was busy shoving a piece of shrimp into his mouth when they entered. He quickly swallowed, stood up, and offered his hand after wiping it on his pant leg. Kuma had few interactions with people above ground, but he'd watched enough internet videos to imagine Ivan as a kind of rich fraternity kid who spent his days lounging on his father's yacht. Given his role as the discoverer of faez crystals, he couldn't imagine that was entirely true, but the image stuck.

"The famous Duro Hernandez. I can't tell you how excited I am to meet you," said Ivan, grinning like a schoolboy who'd just found a porno magazine on the street. "I have to say you don't look anything like the fearsome waku that the mangas depict."

Duro inclined his head. "It's useful to not look like a waku at times."

Kuma wrinkled his forehead at the casual interaction with Duro, doubly so about the manga. He wanted to remind Ivan that Duro was the warleader of the Drops, not an old university friend, and should be treated with the proper respect. But Duro's reminder about Ivan's oddness stilled his tongue.

"This is Audrey," he said, gesturing towards the woman at the table. She muttered a greeting, but seemed to be observing them intently.

Duro slipped between Kuma and Pandora, putting his hands on their shoulders and giving them a squeeze. The familial touch seemed out of place, but given the circumstances, Kuma tried to relax.

"These are my young protégés. You may have heard of them. Kuma Santos and Pandora...well, let's just say, like all icons, she only goes by one name."

"Merlin's tits," exclaimed Ivan, grinning at Audrey. "They were the ones that fought that duel. The one from issue twenty-eight!"

"You've heard about that?" asked Kuma, incredulous.

Ivan clapped his hands together. "Read about it. Chitei Senshi Manga. How much of it was true?"

"I've never read it," said Kuma, a little dumbstruck by the exchange. He felt like he'd walked into a completely different world and if it weren't for the goofy grin on Ivan's face, he might have thought he was being made fun of.

"Please, sit," said Ivan. "I can't wait to hear about, well, everything."

A waiter came in and asked about drink orders. When Kuma hesitated, Duro ordered for him, choosing a beer that sounded like what he enjoyed at the Onyx. Pandora picked an aged whiskey. There were no prices on the menu, but Kuma had a good idea they wouldn't be paying, nor could they afford to.

As Ivan reached for his glass of amber liquid, a bracelet on his wrist was revealed. It had a familiar G&T logo.

"You own G&T?" asked Kuma.

"I do. Great and Terrible Industries. It's a bad pun about my twin sister and I. You've heard of my company?"

Kuma inclined his head, thinking about the time he'd raided a G&T warehouse with Deacon for the Eclipse elixir. "I have."

Drinks arrived right away. Ivan peppered them with questions about the duel, trying to determine how much in the manga was true. It occurred to Kuma that the reason Pandora had been brought along was for the two of them to impress Ivan.

"I would have given Invictus' dick to be there," said Ivan, shaking his head. "And I can tell you, it's huge, I've seen it."

Audrey pursed her lips as she rolled her eyes. "He hasn't."

"Come on, hun, I know you've done a little crotch gazing in your life. It's hard not to notice. That thing is a python hiding in cotton weeds. I think that's why he always wore robes, so we wouldn't notice."

"Are you talking about the Head Patron Invictus?" asked Kuma.

"*Former* Head Patron," said Ivan, putting his arm on the back of Audrey's chair. "Who knows where he's at now. Probably on a beach wearing a nut bag and drinking mai tais."

"Wait? You knew him?"

"Not well, but we met a few times. I wasn't technically part of the Order of Merlin, but my sister was." He picked up his drink. "I know Pi better, but she's impossible to get ahold of now. Poor girl. I don't think she knew what she was signing up for when she took the job."

It was Kuma's turn to be awestruck as he realized that the Pi he was talking about was the famous Pythia Silverthorne, current head patron of the Hundred Halls. During the infernal invasion, Razor clan had hunkered down until it was over, being completely outclassed by the creatures that had passed through their territory, but everyone knew the stories of Pi, her sister Aurie, and the others from the Order who had battled the demons across the city and killed the enormous dragon that had attacked the Glitterdome.

"I remember your brother when we briefly held him during that time. I'm glad that he survived his journey through the canyon of ghosts," said Duro.

"Ares always knew how to put his foot into it." Ivan brightened. "That's right, you're Niran's son. I met him once, I guess it'd be almost six years ago."

"You did?"

"We were hiding from my father's house manager and trying to find our sister." Ivan snapped his fingers. "My condolences about your father and Razor clan." He looked to Duro. "Is it okay to say that?"

"It's perfectly fine, no offense taken," said Duro. "Speaking of the Undercity, Kuma acquired a new stone lately, but we've been unable to identify what it does."

He gestured towards Kuma, who had to unbutton his shirt and

remove the ruby from his belly button. Ivan took an eye-scope from an inside pocket and put it up to the stone when he received it.

"A ruby? And no idea what it does?"

"I've tried a few things, but nothing works. It's like I'm lacking something when I use it," said Kuma.

Ivan pulled the eye-scope away from his eye, tongue resting on the tops of his teeth with glee. "Wait. Did you get this from another waku? Gave 'em the crimson smile? Was it a duel or just a fight, or no, a scrap, as you say."

Heat rose to Kuma's face at the thought of his friends dying to Deacon's guns during that day. The casual disrespect filled his mind with rage. Kuma smashed his fist onto the table, rattling glassware. Pandora placed her hand on his thigh under the table but he didn't slow his words.

"Many died that day. It's not a game, what we do in the shadows. Nor should it be written in some manga to be gawked at by lighters."

"Kuma. Get a hold of yourself. He doesn't know our ways," said Duro sternly.

"Hey, it's my fault," said Ivan, holding up his hands. "My mouth has a way of signing me up for all kinds of beatings. If you'd cracked me across the jaw, I would have expected it. I know I got it more than once from our creepy house manager because of my mouth. He weirded me out. Was better when my father administered the beatings. Not gonna lie and say I might not have enjoyed it, but that's another story that my therapist has heard a dozen times."

"Babe," said Audrey, "you don't have a therapist. You have a wife and a dog."

Ivan reached into a pocket, producing a small vial of black liquid. He put a few drops into his drink.

"I've also far too much access to alchemical modifications for my behavior, but what's a guy gonna do? Anyone want some?"

"No thank you," said Duro, waving his hand over his drink.

"Are we good, Kuma?" asked Ivan.

Feeling the intensity of Duro's gaze, Kuma bent slightly in his chair.

"May the shadows keep you safe."

Ivan tossed the ruby across the table and Kuma snatched it from the air. "Wish I could tell you something about it, but the only thing I know is that's a fine specimen for whatever it does. The faez crystals are like spells frozen in time, and using them accesses the magic inside. But for now, the only way to figure them out is to use them."

Dinner arrived and their conversation moved to safer topics. Ivan talked about the headaches of running his business while trying not to get stepped on by D'Agastine Industries. Kuma's anger receded during the conversation. While he didn't trust Ivan Charmer, he didn't dislike him either. The mistrust wasn't anything like Deacon or the Crows, but Kuma could tell Ivan acted on impulse and often without consideration for others. He lacked discipline, which seemed strange given the success of his alchemical business.

After they'd eaten and were waiting for dessert, Duro reached into an inner pocket and produced a folded piece of paper. He handed it over to a curious Ivan.

"I have one other request. It may seem unusual, but it's extremely important for my clan's survival. I wanted to know if you have anything that might help me get through this door," said Duro.

Ivan took the paper, unfolded it, and studied it as Audrey leaned over. They both seemed disturbed by whatever they were looking at. Kuma shared a glance with Pandora, who mouthed the word, "Door." There was only one explanation: it the door that they'd been working on during one of the challenges. Everyone had been speculating the purpose of the activity, that the Drops would be robbing a bank for the funds to hire Blackstone Security, or a private vault for powerful artifacts that would help them against the alliance, or it was for a hidden portal in the Undercity that could lead them to a secret realm where they'd be safe, or a hundred other ideas. Kuma thought the bank vault seemed most plausible. The cliff training could be a stand-in for climbing the outside of a skyscraper. He wasn't sure how the water exercises fit in, but he was sure that Duro had a plan.

"I'm sorry," said Ivan, suddenly serious as he tossed the paper into the middle of the table. Kuma caught a glimpse of a thick vault door on the schematic. "I can't help you with this. My days of selling drugs at parties and holding illegal raves is over. I've much more to lose now."

"The Drops looked the other way when you infringed on our territory," said Duro.

Ivan held up his hands. "I run a big alchemical business and have a poor reputation in the public eye due to a legal conflict with my father years ago. My business would disintegrate if it was known that I helped a notorious Undercity criminal gang. No offense, I love you guys, and this has been a special treat meeting you, but I have to pass on helping with a task that doesn't in the slightest bit look aboveboard. If there's anything else I can do, let me know, but this isn't one of them."

Duro folded the paper back up and shoved it in his inner pocket, inclining his head.

"I understand. I respect your decision. Thank you for your hospitality."

The quick acquiescence surprised Kuma. He'd thought Duro would have pushed the territory business further. The Drops had always been known for their ruthlessness, which made rivals fear interfering with the clan.

A muted cell phone rang. Duro pulled it out of his pocket and placed it to his ear. Kuma resisted the urge to listen with his amber, but he thought it sounded like Daraja's voice on the other end.

"My apologies, Ivan. I must head out right away for an unexpected meeting. I'm sorry that we couldn't work together, but maybe we can in the future." He turned to Kuma and Pandora, throwing a key on the table. "I'll have Dane take you back to the entrance. Head straight to the Pajot and tell Brazio to double the guards until I get back."

Duro rose and bowed, which made Ivan and Audrey start to rise, but the warleader was out the door before they made it to standing. Kuma got to his feet at the same time as Pandora.

"We should be going as well," said Kuma.

Ivan had a mixture of excitement and disappointment on his brow. He leaned over to a bag next to the table.

"Wait. I have one more request. It'll be quick, I promise." He produced a colorful manga and a black pen. "Could I get you to sign this? On the front would be perfect."

"Sure," said Pandora before he could decline.

The cover of the glossy manga depicted what Kuma could only assume was him and Pandora in the middle of their duel. They flew through the air at each other, feet forward, about to impact. Pandora quickly scrawled her name on the front, sticking to the single moniker. When it was his turn, he briefly flipped through the pages, seeing a rough outline of the events of that day, including the scorpic fights. He scribbled his name on the front and handed it back to Ivan, who accepted the signed manga with the exuberance of a six-year-old boy.

"Good luck with your scraps," said Ivan, thrusting the comic into the air as they left the private dining room.

Kuma could barely think until he'd thrown himself into the back of the SUV with Pandora.

"Did you know about the manga?" he asked.

She shook her head as the SUV pulled away from the restaurant. Dane glanced through the mirror.

"Oh, you didn't know?"

"No," said Kuma. "How would I?"

Dane chuckled as he turned the wheel. "Every big clan has one. Not run by the clan, but some fanboy editor. The clan always gets a cut though and has editorial oversight."

"My father knew about these?" asked Kuma.

"And Daraja, and the others. Hey man, it's a niche market. It's not like they're selling millions, but it's a great recruitment tool and makes some side cash for the clan."

"It was a poor representation of you," said Pandora. "You weren't that angry during the fight."

Dane let them off back at the warehouse. The key got them through the door. Before they entered the elevator, Pandora said, "What did you think that request was for?"

"The vault door? I don't know, but it had to be important for Duro to haul us away from training. You should have used your maetrie magic on him," he said.

Pandora crossed her arms. "I told you already, I don't have that."

"I'm sorry. My mind is a little fucked right now. Never thought I'd have dinner with one of the defenders of the invasion, someone that casually spouts off interactions with Invictus *and* Pythia Silverthorne in the same sentence. Or find out that I'm the star of a manga I'd never heard of before."

"Co-star," said Pandora with her mouth shifted to the side.

"Co-star." He wrinkled his forehead. "That didn't freak you out?"

"Of all the weird things in my life, no, it actually seemed kinda normal. It's easier to see the death and conflict when it's just a depiction on a page, not the real thing which comes with pain that never seems to go away. Not like losing your father."

He exhaled sharply and squeezed his hands to fists.

"I should have been there that day, not skipping around the Undercity playing hero. Maybe he wouldn't be dead."

"And if you had, then I wouldn't have found Brazio and we wouldn't have pulled the clans together, and we'd both be dead right now."

"You can't know that," he said sharply.

"It was the likeliest outcome. Kuma. Your father was brilliant. He led the clan for decades, navigating through countless wars, business decisions, the invasion, and the discovery of the faez crystals."

"Until your grandfather killed him," said Kuma.

Pandora looked away. "I never wanted that. It's only now that I'm realizing how much they lied to me."

That she hadn't refuted him or hit back stronger made him realize he was out of line.

"I'm sorry, Pan. I know that wasn't you. You've done your best to stop them, which has to be hard, going against your family."

"Family are the people that love and support you no matter who or what you are. What they did to me? That's not family. That's something else."

The fear in her black eyes surprised him. He'd always seen her as an unstoppable force without doubt or panic. Her lower lip quivered slightly before she clamped it closed.

"What did they do to you?"

"At first, I was living with my mother and learning the ways of the maetrie. They trained me with their children, who were stronger and faster than I was. They beat me and called me a mongrel. Or weak steel. Or the ugly dolgant. Or a million other insults. Once when I unknowingly disrespected one of the older trainees, they grabbed me in the middle of the night and shoved me in a box filled with faeila. I stayed curled in a ball while they attacked my flesh until someone heard my screams."

"Faeila?"

"Insects made of glass and concrete. Some can be quite beautiful, like a stained glass butterfly, but they're brutal and dangerous in large clouds. Can strip a person down to the bone in less than a minute."

"That's why you have those scars on your back," he said, understanding. "They were like flying piranha?"

She nodded.

"That sounds awful." Kuma stiffened. "At least I knew my father loved me and wanted me to get better as much for myself as for the clan."

"My father loved me like that. I wish he wouldn't have died." She hung her head. Kuma resisted the urge to pull her into an embrace for comfort. "After that my mother thought that I shouldn't train with the other maetrie children. There was too much difference between us and they would have probably killed me. She begged her father for an alternative. He set up a meeting with a maetrie that lives in the furthest reaches of the Eternal City, in a place even the maetrie fear to go. He was once the most feared warrior in the realm. A member of the Ebony court. At least until they lured him away and wiped out the entire clan in his absence. With no one to fight for, he left their society, went out on his own. They sent me to him. Hylakane. The Steel Sun. I spent less time there than it took me to reach him. I failed as his trainee. I was too weak, or too human to do what he wanted me to do."

"You were a child."

"In the games of the maetrie, there are no children. Only future warriors. They'd kill a child as easily as a grown man to prevent future conflicts. After I returned, my grandfather saw me as a liability, a weakness to be exploited by his enemies, so he sent me to their gladiator training school instead to show that he thought I wasn't worth their attention. I should have realized then what he thought of me. I foolishly believed he was protecting me."

Kuma held out a hand, and she stared at it as if it were a live snake.

"I'm glad you decided to side with us against your mother and grandfather. I can't imagine how hard that must have been. I knew only my parents' love for me."

She accepted his hand. Her palm was warm, and they kept shaking.

Pandora smiled wistfully. "When do we become our own people? Or are we always a product of our parents' decisions?"

"If you figure that out, let me know," said Kuma.

They collectively realized they'd been shaking hands the entire time and broke the grip. Kuma couldn't meet her searching gaze.

"We should get back. Duro's warning sounded serious."

"It did."

He followed her into the elevator cage. Without Duro there was more room, so they could stand across from each other without having to smash shoulders. She held her finger over the button that would send them back into the Undercity.

"I wish I could have met your father."

"I wish you could have met him, too. He was a good man, a great father, and an even better clan leader." He sighed. "I wish I could have met your father too."

Fourteen

Pandora sat on the end stool sipping a glass of watered-down orange juice while Triana worked the stove. The sounds and smells of sizzling chorizo filled the narrow kitchen. Choo-Choo and Navos were still in bed, and Vasy was out to borrow eggs from a neighbor.

"Is it true about the Razor boy?" asked Triana, looking over her shoulder. Unruly hairs slipped out of her ponytail, forming a wispy crown around her forehead. She didn't look like she'd been sleeping lately.

"They're Drops now."

Triana used the tip of her spatula to break up the frozen meat aggressively.

"Not that boy, or his uncle. I can't believe we let those killers into our home. How is it fair that Emilio has to train with them? What if Vasy runs into them on the paths?" asked Triana, her voice cracking.

"Your daughter is a strong and resilient kid. She'll figure it out," said Pandora.

"It's not right," muttered Triana as she increasingly smashed the spatula into the pan. Pandora slipped around the counter and gently pried the tool away from Triana.

"Why don't I help? Maybe you should have a glass while I cook," said Pandora.

Triana opened her mouth to refuse, but Pandora gently steered her to the stool, and she plopped down like a rag doll.

"We need them. I know it's hard, but every waku is important and they're two of our best scrappers. It's like we got a second Duro with Brazio."

"You should have slit his throat when you found him. He was weak. You could have done it. Emilio would have done that for me," said Triana quietly.

Pandora pushed the meat around the pan. The larger chunks were still frozen in the middle. She tried to squash one down, but it shot out and rolled across the counter, leaving a grease trail.

"Sorry!"

After getting it back into the sizzling pan, she tried again, but knocked two more pieces out. Pandora sighed as she used gentler force on the frozen meat, but she was so focused on the larger chunks she forgot about the smaller pieces until one of them started to burn.

"You've never cooked before?" asked Triana.

Pandora let her head hang down. "I remember helping my dad make eggs when I was little, but that's about it."

Triana appeared at her side. She placed her hand over Pandora's and guided her movements in the pan.

"You can't get too focused on one thing," said Triana. "You have to flit around the pan, keeping things moving to make sure the browning is even. The larger chunks will work themselves down, but you can't push too hard or they'll fly out of the pan."

"As I'm well aware."

Triana guided her for a half-minute with the spatula. The motherly attention was soothing. Pandora had never really wanted to cook, but she could see the appeal. At least for people you loved.

"I think you've got it now. Luckily you're an excellent student," said Triana.

"Thank you."

Triana gave her arm a squeeze before returning to the stool. Pandora managed to cook the remainder of the chorizo with minimal burning. Vasilisa showed up shortly after with a small basket of eggs.

"I think I'd better cook the eggs," said Triana, holding her hand out for the spatula.

Pandora took her spot on the stool next to Vasilisa, who was fidgeting with a bracelet on her arm.

"Heard you went into the city with Duro and Kuma," said Vasilisa absently.

Pandora noticed the way Triana froze over the pan. "I did. It was Duro's request."

"What would you need to be doing with that boy?" asked Triana harshly.

"I can't say," said Pandora. "But it was important. Duro's trying to navigate us out of this mess."

"I don't understand it," said Triana with a sigh. "We did nothing after the Crows raided us and thirteen of our clan were dead. We should have struck back, made them pay, and now they have you doing ridiculous tasks that no one will talk about, but I can hear Choo-Choo and Navos whispering about them sometimes."

"I don't know why they're having us do that either, but I trust Duro."

"I don't trust Brazio," said Triana.

Vasilisa gave Pandora an exasperated look with a shoulder shrug. She'd heard her complain about her mother's constant focus on Brazio's and Kuma's presence in the Pajot.

"How's school?" asked Pandora, hoping to change the subject.

Vasilisa snorted and pulled her glass near with her stump arm. "Half the time the teachers put us on self-study because they've been assigned guard duty, or something else they've never done before. I usually practice throwing my knives or doing push-ups. When all this is over and I'm old enough for the Academy, I want to be ready."

Heavy steps announced the appearance of Choo-Choo and Navos, who looked sleepy-eyed as they entered the kitchen.

"Pan? I didn't know you were here last night," said Choo-Choo.

"I wasn't, but Triana invited me for breakfast."

Navos slipped past after giving her a fist bump. He reached into the tiny refrigerator for the orange juice, pouring himself and Choo-Choo a glass. The pair jostled for the remaining stool, laughing and trying to knock each other out of the way until Navos stepped back and offered the seat with a gracious bow. When Choo-Choo tried to sit, Navos kicked it out of the way, nearly knocking his friend to the ground, but he managed to grab the counter to stay standing.

"Enough, you two," said Triana. "You'll break my nice things."

The pair smirked at each other and picked up the stool. Choo-Choo offered it to Navos, who knocked the hair out of his eyes and slipped onto the seat.

"What was with all the noise last night?" asked Vasilisa.

Choo-Choo smirked. "We were wrestling."

Triana turned slightly with the spatula in her fist. "Did you know Pan and that Razor boy went into the city together?"

A shadow passed across Choo-Choo's face. "I know. I was there when Duro got them."

"How can you train with him? Or his uncle?"

Choo-Choo's expression blanked. He stared at the counter. "I want to keep you and Vasy safe. That's all."

"I just don't understand," Vasilisa said quietly.

"You'll understand when you're older," he said.

"I am older. But I guess I'll never understand because I can't be a waku," she said, holding up her stump. "I'd be able to help if they let me. I'm just as good as the others."

"I know, Vasy. I know," he said.

The eggs were finished shortly after. The mood was somber and conversation revolved around the harvest while they ate. With more mouths and everyone stretched thin with guard duty or other tasks related to the defense, there were fewer edible yields. The plants that made drugs were mostly at target levels, but they were having trouble getting them to market in the city. Without the cash flow, everything in the Pajot would grind to a halt.

Pandora stayed mostly silent, offering occasional thoughts, but letting Choo-Choo and Navos drive the conversation. Whenever Triana added her opinion, underlining anger came through, even when the topic was nothing to be mad about. Choo-Choo kept checking back to his mother, his frown deepening the entire time while Navos kept a cheery and oblivious expression. Vasilisa watched silently, keeping a flat smile, but Pandora could tell that she was bothered by her mother's frustration. By the end of breakfast, Vasilisa was pushing bits of eggs around her plate while her mother ranted.

"Time for training," said Pandora after they'd helped Triana clean up the kitchen. She gave hugs before she left, twice as long for Triana and

Vasy, heading back to the Academy ahead of Choo-Choo and Navos to have time to get ready.

Fifteen

Kuma rubbed the bruised flesh under his arm where he'd gotten shot with a rubber bullet on their last attempt. They'd tried to run behind a single shield, but the shooters had fired at the ground. The bullets had bounced up and hit them repeatedly until someone in the front tripped and the entire group fell into a pile. Instructor Nikolai's comment about their attempts getting worse stung.

"Come on," said Pandora, on her feet and clapping her hands encouragingly. "We've got ten minutes until we try again."

Xylos was sitting cross-legged on the ground. "Can't we just do the push-ups and take another twenty minutes of break time?"

"I'm all for another attempt," said Tick. "But only if it's something that might work. That last one was a disaster."

"It would have worked had Einar not tripped," said Yara.

"I only tripped because someone stepped on the back of my heels," said Einar, stroking his mustache.

Grumbling and muttered curses followed. The mood had soured.

"Come on, everyone," said Kuma, stretching his side. "Maybe we should do that one again. It could be the right idea, but just poor execution."

"I didn't trip. I was tripped," said Einar, glowering. "It's a big difference."

"That might have been me that did it," said Kuma, holding his hands up. "I'm one of the people right behind you."

"Figures a Razor boy would be the one to screw things up," said Choo-Choo.

Heat rose to Kuma's face but before he could step forward, Pandora stood between them.

"There's no Razor here. Only Drops," she said.

The tension was thick until Camina said, "What if we split up into multiple shields rather than trying to fit behind one?"

"I don't see why it would hurt," said Pandora. "We have four topaz—put one with a shield? Two groups of two and two of three?"

"Dibs on Adrena," said Xylos as he punched her in the arm.

The heavily pierced Adrenalynne rolled her eyes. "I'm always carrying you."

The others split up as Kuma expected: Choo-Choo with Navos and Pandora, Yara grabbed Camina, which left Einar to hold the shield for him and Tick. The makeshift barriers had improved over time, with sturdy handholds and reinforcement from the constant barrage of rubber bullets.

Kuma took the left side of the shield next to Einar, who would be carrying most of the weight as the topaz while Tick tucked in behind them. Pandora had been calling the start, so everyone looked to her in the center group behind Choo-Choo and Navos. She counted down, holding three fingers, then two, then one.

"Go!"

The rubber bullets came in a barrage, thudding against the wooden shields. Splinters flew into the air like sparks. Kuma kept his left arm tucked in as he ran beside Einar. The topaz moved faster, causing the barrier to tilt slightly, so Kuma made himself light so he could keep up, but doing so only encouraged Einar to run faster. He was outpacing Tick, whose stones gave him no extra physical abilities.

"Slow down!" said Kuma, but Einar leaned forward and churned his legs faster. The shield was at a forty-five-degree angle. The shooters focus-fired on them, and a collective cry of pain to his left announced that Choo-Choo's group had gotten hit multiple times.

Kuma managed to catch up to Einar when he leapt with Lightness but then Instructor Nikolai called out, "Time!" They let the shield clatter to the ground to see they were about two-thirds of the way across and they were the team that had gotten furthest.

"Close but not close enough," said Einar, shaking his head.

Kuma reached down to pick up the shield when Tick called out a warning. He turned to find Choo-Choo barreling down on him with murder in his eyes.

"You fucking did that on purpose, deflecting those bullets into us!"

Kuma put his palms up but seeing Choo-Choo's fists, he brought them down to defend himself.

"I wasn't—"

Choo-Choo's punch had the power of a topaz. He managed to block it but the force knocked him to the ground. Flooding himself with Lightness and leaping away kept him from getting grabbed by Choo-Choo. The others were shouting for them to stop, but Kuma had to move quickly before a relentless Choo-Choo had him. It was like trying to keep a boulder from rolling down a hill, except that he was always in its way no matter how he moved.

There were times that Kuma saw opportunities to counterpunch, but he didn't want to make Choo-Choo any angrier. His bald head was covered in a sheen of sweat as he threw head-crushing roundhouses. Kuma switched between Heavy and Light; the rhythm of the fight kept him constantly moving.

"Stop now!"

The shout was given with authority and Kuma slowed, thinking it'd been an instructor, giving Choo-Choo a chance to close the distance and grab hold of him. Kuma was in the middle of switching back to Lightness when Choo-Choo flung him by the arm as if he were throwing a hammer for distance. Kuma flew through the air, trying to orient himself for the landing. He smashed into the wooden wall that was the target of their exercise.

A little disoriented from the impact, Kuma popped to his feet unsteadily as Choo-Choo continued his assault. Before he reached the wall, Pandora grabbed him by the arm.

"Stop! Stop it now! Emilio!"

The use of his real name broke him out of his trance. Choo-Choo halted with his fists up, looking around as if he were expecting to be attacked. Kuma had his hands up in case he changed his mind.

"What the fuck, man?" asked Xylos.

"He got me shot up on purpose," said Choo-Choo.

Navos tried to put his hand on his arm, but Choo-Choo knocked him away and paced around the area, looking like he was talking himself into resuming the fight.

Kuma was so focused on Choo-Choo he wasn't really paying attention to Camina, who was trying to get everyone's attention. As Choo-Choo started moving towards Kuma, she stepped into the middle of them.

"Everyone shut the fuck up and sit the fuck down for a moment." She pointed at Choo-Choo. "You, over there."

"Don't get in my—"

"You can have your tantrum after I'm done, but I had an idea about how to get across the field after watching you two idiots." The entire group turned their attention to Camina. Once she realized she was in the spotlight she exhaled. "Maybe we're approaching this all wrong. We're all trying to get across the field in the ten seconds by running. What I just saw was that Choo-Choo threw Kuma about thirty feet in half a second. Maybe we could launch the emeralds to the wall and they could take out the shooters, giving the rest of us a chance to cross without getting shot. If we don't have to use the shields then we can go much faster."

The explanation was like a bomb going off in everyone's heads. Kuma couldn't help but grin at his friend even as he rubbed his shoulder.

"Ain't no way I'm letting anyone throw me," said Einar, puffing up his chest.

"I will," said Kuma. "Choo-Choo can throw me again if it gets us past this challenge."

"You can throw me too," said Yara.

All eyes fell upon the mustached waku, who deflated as he gave Kuma the stink-eye. "Fine. If it helps."

"Great," said Camina, clapping her hands.

"Question about one part of the plan," said Xylos. "When we're taking out the shooters, what does that mean?"

The entire group turned to Nikolai, who seemed surprised by the sudden attention. After a moment of thought he answered them.

"For the purposes of the exercise if you can reach through the window and touch the shooter, they will be dead and no longer fire," said Nikolai.

With the judgement finalized, the group gathered together to discuss details. They only had two topaz to throw people, since Einar was both. He couldn't throw himself. Adrenalynne would throw Kuma, while Choo-Choo would toss Yara.

Once everyone was ready, Camina gave the countdown.

"Go!"

The six other waku burst into a run using the smaller shields they'd made for individual protection. As the bullets impacted against their protection, Adrenalynne grabbed Kuma's arms.

"Ready?"

He'd been keeping himself Heavy until he could no longer hold it. He switched to Lightness.

"Now."

Adrenalynne gave a half-spin, launching him high into the air like a human frisbee. Without gravity's hold he soared above the others, rotating uncontrollably from the launch angle. A few shooters aimed at him but his speed and angle made him hard to hit. As the ground rushed up towards him, about twenty feet before the wall, he tried to orient himself so he could hit the ground running, but he landed awkwardly, tumbling head over heels. A bright burst of pain in his back announced his death. He heard the older woman say, "Got 'em."

Kuma looked up from the ground to see Yara at the wall. Two of the shooters had dropped their weapons since they were dead. He checked behind to see Pandora and Navos bounding across the field using sapphire Pushes. Kuma pumped his fist as they reached the wall a moment before Nikolai called, "Time!"

The entire group erupted in cheers, even the shooters. After days and days of attempts, being shot countless times with rubber bullets, and doing thousands of push-ups, they'd finally gotten some of their team across the field in the allotted time. Instructor Nikolai came over to them with a grin on his lips.

"While you didn't get the whole team over, three out of ten is a good start. For every member that reaches the wall, I'll knock off twenty push-ups." He placed his hands behind his back. "Additionally, if you can knock out all the shooters, then you can cross the field in any amount of time."

After completing their push-ups, Kuma approached Choo-Choo, who'd just climbed to his feet and was dusting off his palms. The bald waku tensed as he approached.

"Great job with the throw," said Kuma, holding out his hand. "We couldn't have done it without you."

Choo-Choo looked like he was trying to figure out where the insult was hidden. He accepted the handshake, giving a single pump before pulling away, his face never breaking from its somber confusion. When Kuma turned back, he noticed the rest of the team had been watching quietly, clearly expecting a second blowup by their hunched foreheads.

"Okay, everyone," said Kuma. "Who has ideas on how we can improve?"

Sixteen

Duro had only been in the clan leader's private quarters twice, and both times were vanishingly brief. He wasn't forbidden to enter them, but he'd always respected Daraja's request for privacy. She'd wanted a separate place away from the responsibilities of the clan.

The visit was upon her invite. Brazio and Nikolai were already there, sitting on wooden benches next to a rock garden, sipping tea. The sound of water trickling from a fountain soothed Duro's troubled mind.

"I'd think I was back in the Machi," said Brazio, leaning back in his chair while next to him Nikolai was stiff and looked like he was afraid to disturb a single mote of dust in the clan leader's private quarters.

"Daraja spent time in Tokyo as a young woman. She has fond memories of those times."

"I do not have fond memories," said Daraja, entering from the back. She wore a gold and black patterned dress that hung to the floor. She carried invisible weights, and the bags around her eyes couldn't be hidden by makeup. "But it was an instructive time. The practice of meditating in a rock garden, however, was thoroughly implanted into my soul. Whenever I have a thorny problem vexing my every thought, I spend time here until a solution appears."

"Is that why you've called us here? Do we have a thorny problem that needs to be solved?" asked Duro as he poured himself a cup of tea.

Daraja pursed her lips. "Don't patronize me, Duro. You're not very good at it."

"I wasn't patronizing. I'm just optimistic that our current direction is correct, despite the overwhelming obstacles laid before us," said Duro.

"We're nearly out of money, your little group is barely progressing in their goals, Dominion has brought in some outside help that has me quite troubled, and I'm fairly certain we have a spy in the Pajot."

"Is that why it's only the four of us?" asked Duro.

"Yes, though I would have had Luscious attend had he not had an important meeting in the city. Before you ask, no I will not elaborate, but I did send Helena with him as extra protection."

Nikolai frowned. "Not sure it's wise that a former Razor is here. No offense, Brazio."

The former warleader of Razor lifted a shoulder.

"I invited him because Duro trusts him," said Daraja. "And that's good enough for me."

Brazio inclined his head. "I'm honored."

Duro winked at him. The other waku was like having an older brother. He'd enjoyed the time working with him.

"The team is progressing," said Duro as he set his cup on the table. "They managed to solve one of the tasks yesterday."

"Not solved based on the parameters you gave me," said Daraja. "Progress. But too slow. Our time is running out."

"What are you suggesting?"

Daraja paced away, stilling near the rock garden like an ancient pillar. She stared at the field of white rocks, carefully brushed into patterns that suggested waves. Duro wasn't sure if she was breathing anymore.

"In my estimation, we have two choices. Either make a full-on frontal assault on the Crows, which is an option we all know will only weaken us even if it's successful, or pack up everyone in the Pajot and either scatter to the winds or relocate somewhere else."

"Dominion won't let us live peacefully," said Brazio, lifting his chin. "I don't know the maetrie well, but I know enough about them to know that. We won't be able to stay in the city, and even another city wouldn't be far enough away to keep them from coming after us."

"I've enough favors to cash to get us a portal to somewhere far enough beyond their reach to make it not worth pursuing us."

Duro stiffened. The Pajot and the Undercity had been his home his entire life. While he wanted his clan to live a peaceful existence, he didn't like the idea of running either. Nor learning the landscape of an entirely new realm.

"How long have you been planning this?"

The frown on her lips was cut with sympathy. "Longer than you'd like to know. But I had to consider all options, especially once Razor fell."

"Options like that don't magically appear," said Duro. "You've been planning that for some time."

"Not planning," said Daraja. "Exploring options, which it seems we might need now."

"Where would it be?" asked Nikolai.

Daraja looked away. "We'd be under the protection of a being who has no love for the maetrie and has the power to keep them from bothering us. That's all I'm willing to say right now."

"You forgot an option in your list," said Duro, stepping forward. "The team can be ready in a few weeks. A month at the latest. We might not have the numbers, but we have the best waku in the Undercity."

"A month is a lifetime," said Daraja with a sigh in her voice. "Even two weeks is too many. Every day I expect them to come crashing down on us like a tsunami that's been traveling across the ocean unseen. If your team was making faster progress, I might consider them, but they're going to be too late. Much, much too late."

The news was a blow to Duro. The answer was just out of reach. He could feel it.

"I can speed up the timetable. I'll need money to find answers quicker. The final obstacle isn't going to be easy to solve."

"I already told you we're nearly bankrupt. The Crows have shut down our operations throughout the city. We have product but we can't sell it. The only thing we have left of value is our stones, and we need those."

"We've none left to sell?" asked Duro, surprised. He'd been so busy he hadn't been able to read the recent business numbers.

Daraja gestured in the direction of the Pajot. "Our mines have been closed for weeks and even when they were working, we rarely pulled out the kind of stones that earn the big payments."

"Then give me what money we have that's extra and a few more days. If we don't progress, then I'll agree to whatever plan you think is best," said Duro.

While Daraja stared back at him unblinking, Nikolai asked, "What about the spy?"

Daraja hung her head. "I'm not entirely certain, but some details of our inner workings have gotten to this Dominion Thule. My source in the alliance is fairly sure that we have a spy."

"Or the spy is double-dealing and they're trying to sow doubt," said Brazio.

"A plausible analysis, but I have no way to determine the truth right now."

"Daraja," said Duro, "give us more time. I swear the team will come through for you."

She flared her nostrils. "A few days, no more than a week. Whatever you're going to do, you'd better do it fast, because once I give the word we must leave quickly and only with what we can carry on our backs. I don't want the spy to get word back to Dominion. He'd hit us when we were trying to leave the Undercity. It'd be a bloodbath."

"A week," said Duro. "You gave me a week."

"At most," she said, shaking her head. "Don't push it. We're almost out of time."

Seventeen

The seventh ward was not unknown to Helena. When she'd been a young soldado in Razor clan, her beat had included the canal district in the ward. It'd been easy work, shaking down drunken out-of-state college students in the city to enjoy its many distractions. If Invictus PD tried to apprehend her, she would disappear into the sewers and make her way back to the Goblin Romp where she could disappear into the Under-city. It'd been easy work—almost fun.

Because of her experiences she was well acquainted with the interesting features of the seventh, so she was immediately put on guard when Luscious Gaunt, the resident mage of the Drops clan, told her their destination as they drove in the city.

"The Glass Cabaret was the one place in the ward we were told to avoid," Helena told him as she turned onto the ring road.

Luscious' sour expression was barely different than his normal resting appearance, but she could tell he wasn't happy about her pronouncement.

"Daraja has asked me to pursue any and all avenues in regard to the clan's predicament. While I agree with your caution, I happen to know the owner is a source of valuable information, especially about our new foe."

Helena drummed on the steering wheel. "Fine. Obviously you don't need my permission, but I'm coming with you."

"I'm afraid that's not how the owner works. In fact, it'd be best if you waited in the vehicle while I made my inquiry," said Luscious, absently tapping the briefcase in his lap.

On more than one occasion, she'd mentally confused Luscious for a lawyer by his attire even though he was an alumnus of Coterie of Mages. She'd heard he'd gotten into trouble for using forbidden magics and had fled to the safety of the Undercity and eventually to the employ of the Drops.

"You're not making it easy to guard you," said Helena as she pulled into a parking spot on the street across from a ubiquitous Wizard's Coffee. Hall-aged students came and went through the door, the out-going clutching colorful paper cups of steaming coffee.

"I won't need guarding in the Glass Cabaret. Radoslav's presence is enough to dissuade any interference," said Luscious as he slid out the door. He paused with it open, completing his thoughts. "I won't be more than an hour. Try not to cause a scene."

Helena rolled her eyes after Luscious left.

"Pompous mage," she muttered, flinching when he turned his head her direction as if he'd heard her through the glass.

The Glass Cabaret was half a block from her location. It was easy to spot as it was the only bar that had a bouncer outside day or night. She'd never understood the purpose of the bouncer given the nature of the owner. As a maetrie exile, he was more than capable of handling himself.

She started to turn on the radio, hoping to catch the latest hits. Since they'd been chased out of the Machi, she hadn't had time to relax or enjoy new music, which was the one thing she treasured about coming into the city. She'd heard there was a new Garbage Kings album due soon and was hopeful that it was on the radio. As her fingertips brushed the dial, the hairs on the back of her neck rose as if she'd sensed someone watching her. Helena checked all the mirrors, spotting no sign of being observed.

Despite the temptation of the radio, she remained in silence, keeping a wary eye on her surroundings. If the alliance had followed them, it would be easy to set up an ambush. Helena climbed out of the SUV, feigning a bit of stretching on the sidewalk while she scanned the area.

She was sure someone was watching her, but she couldn't detect them. It was maddening. As a two-stone waku, she'd long ago gotten over not attuning to an amber, but this was one time she wished she had the sensing stone.

When the visit passed the hour mark and then the second, Helena grew worried, but she reminded herself that he was a capable mage and the Glass Cabaret would be a terrible place for the alliance to hit. Besides, the bouncer hadn't moved since her arrival, which meant everything was good inside. Around the time she'd convinced herself she needed to enter the jazz bar, Luscious appeared with his briefcase and his trademark sour expression.

"How did it—"

"Get in. Drive."

The tone was stern but not urgent. She hurried around to the driver's seat. After pulling into traffic, she drummed her fingers and raised an eyebrow.

"How'd it go?"

Luscious stared straight ahead with the briefcase on his lap.

"Do you have your blades?"

"What kind of question is that? Of course I do."

The older mage let loose a sigh, which confused Helena. He wasn't the type to express sorrow or frustration. She frowned.

"While you were inside, I kept getting the feeling someone was watching me."

He reacted as if it was news he'd been expecting. He checked the side mirror before shaking his head lightly while his fingers rubbed the thick gold bracelet on his wrist.

"It might help if you explained what you're thinking, Luscious. I know we haven't been clanmates long, but both our asses are deep in the shadows here. I'd like to know what you're thinking, what you're worried about, because you've been rubbing that bracelet of yours, which I assume is enchanted."

Luscious checked down, frowning at himself.

"The visit was short," he said. "Radoslav made me wait even though the bar was relatively empty. He knew why I was there and told me what I'd been planning on asking even before I had."

"That's great, right?" asked Helena, bunching up her forehead. "I thought this guy required favors for an answer."

"He declined to help, but informed me that we were being followed."

"Great, so I wasn't losing my mind. Did he say who? We got a bunch of alliance or Crows?"

"Neither, which is why he declined to get involved no matter what I was willing to promise. I had come ready to offer anything he asked to help save the clan." Luscious rubbed the leather briefcase. "The individual who is tracking us is a notorious maetrie assassin named Kavano."

"Individual?" asked Helena, sighing. "I thought it was a whole team after us. The two of us should be able to handle anything even if they are a maetrie."

The way he looked at her jettisoned the idea from her mind.

"There could be no worse person after us. If he means to kill us, then there's little we can do. Make peace with your maker if that's a thing you must do," said Luscious.

"Then should we go back? Should we drive away? Or find somewhere safe in the city to hole up?"

Adrenaline filled her limbs with the desire to fight. She breathed shallowly as she navigated through traffic as they headed to the opposite side of the city by way of the ring road.

"No. Kavano is like the incarnation of death. If he means to kill us, then we'll soon be dead. Better to face it head-on and hope that it's not his intention."

"I'm not just lying down to die," she said.

"Neither am I. I plan on unleashing everything I'm capable of, even the things frowned upon by the Halls, should it become necessary." He gestured towards a cross street. "Take us to the entrance in the third. He might expect us at the Lazona one."

"Third? I don't know the one in the third."

He gave her a description of the location, which she only knew vaguely, but enough to reach. When she hit the cross street, she gunned it, racing past cars and buses at high speed. If they got pulled over and throw in jail, it'd probably be a welcome break from what she might expect from the next few hours. Helena drove evasively, as if she were trying to shake a tail, even though she'd never seen one. She cut down alleyways and side streets.

"Pull over here," he said.

She skidded into a parking spot outside of a bookstore called Left Tower Books. An older gentleman carrying a bag with the store logo hurried down the street, glancing backwards as they stormed out of the vehicle.

"This way," said Luscious, scanning the area as they ran to an alley that stunk like old piss. Halfway down on the chipped brick wall, concrete stairs went down to a boarded-up door.

"Would you?"

Helena kicked through the barrier, revealing an old basement. Dust motes drifted through the air and she spotted a dead rat near a pile of empty beer bottles. She flipped on her headlamp and went inside.

"There's an entrance here?"

"Partially blocked, but I'm sure we can get by," said Luscious.

She passed an old boiler, clearly out of use, and found the door that led into the Undercity.

"Go ahead. There's concrete and steel bars at the base of the stairs you should be able to break through. I'm going to leave a trap here, in case he's still following," said Luscious.

Helena hurried through the passage, finding a set of stairs leading into the darkness. At the bottom, she found the barrier that he'd described and, using her topaz, managed to break through the wall with a dozen hard kicks and then some yanking to move the steel out of the way.

She made it wide enough to slip through, guessing Luscious could as well given his tall, lanky frame. In the room beyond, a metal spiral staircase descended below. She hit the stairs, hurrying down them for the long journey to the bottom. A minute after she started down she felt the stairs vibrate with a second person, which she hoped was Luscious. A half hour after she entered the spiral stairs, she came out into the Undercity. She scanned the area for potential ambush sites, slipping behind a set of stalactites with her blades out to see who was following.

When Luscious stumbled onto the rocky ground, she stepped out and he raised his hands as if he were going to cast a spell. He looked pale and sweaty.

"Someone entered the stairs when I was halfway down," he said.

"I don't know this entrance, you have to lead."

Luscious took them through a narrow tunnel, while Helena kept glancing behind them. If the person was halfway down, then they had a good twenty-minute head start. Maybe they could reach the Pajot before he caught them.

When they entered a huge cavern lit by bioluminescent fungi, Luscious smiled. Which while unpleasant, was a sign that they might make it back.

"Almost there."

Halfway across the cavern, he turned his head. The bracelet on his wrist was glowing crimson and his smile faltered.

"Go. Fast as you can. I'll try to slow him down."

"Wait? Are you sure?"

"Go," he said emphatically and opened his briefcase on the rocks.

As she hurried across the cavern, she heard him speaking atonally. Ghostly lines formed from his hands, creating a webbing across the cavern. She thought he was creating a barrier, but then the network collapsed around him and she heard a guttural roar. Though he was partially blocked by a rocky formation, she saw that he was much larger than he was before, with twisted horns and a shadowy aura surrounding him.

Helena left the cavern at the same time she saw their pursuer enter on the far side. She caught a glimpse of his awkward gait and the sword in his fist. There was something primal about his appearance that left her shaken. After that, she ran full out, oblivious to the dangers that might be ahead because they could never be as bad as what was behind.

The scream rose like a wailing wind, marking Luscious Gaunt's death. She hoped she would make it back to the Pajot to be able to in-form them of his sacrifice and have a drink or ten in his honor.

She started recognizing the tunnels as ones that led to the northern entrance near the canyon of ghosts. It was the passage that went from the Terreno to the Pajot. She thought about trying to confuse him and heading the other way, but decided he'd be able to find her regardless. She didn't know much about the maetrie, but their powers far exceeded most humans'.

As she turned the corner, she heard a foot scuff from behind. Kavano stood in the shadows, shoulders tilted, sword hanging from his fist. An eerie hum emanated from the blade, making her sick to her stomach. He spoke in the silk and gravel language of the maetrie, which sent shivers down her spine.

"There's no point in running," said Kavano with an odd smile. "I promise I'll make it quick."

"I won't make it easy."

"Come now, we both know that's not true," he said as he approached with a deliberately slow pace.

Helena held out her blades and growled under her breath. "I am the shadows, the fist that does not unclench, the blade that does not bend. I am a waku of the Drops clan. El Clan Eto Vas!"

She took two steps. He'd been at least fifty feet away, but then he was right there, as if he'd teleported. She'd seen a faint shimmer of his passage. He was faster than anyone she'd ever seen before—even

Duro. Helena didn't realize her throat had been cut until the warm liquid splashed against her chest. She fell to her knees while holding onto her blades. She wanted to die with them in her hands.

Helena looked up to find the maetrie assassin, Kavano, standing above her with a smile that was neither kind nor pleasing. He lifted his blade, the peculiar hum like a drill against her soul, and swung—

Eighteen

Pandora found Duro outside the ladders talking to a group of soldado. He frowned at a pair of blades in his hands, handing them back when he spotted her approach.

"Come on," said Pandora, leaning back and grabbing Yara's sleeve to pull her along. She looked a lot like her cousin, Kuma, except she was more slender and their eyes were complete opposites. Kuma had a faint crinkle at the corners, the kindness of a child who'd grown up with loving parents. It wasn't that Yara probably hadn't had a similar experience, but she looked like she was angry at the world for an injustice she'd never gotten over.

"It's a dumb idea," said Yara. "I should have never brought it up."

"It's a great idea and we're talking to him."

Before Yara could slink away, Duro waved them over. He had flecks of blood on his hand, which he wiped on his pant leg.

"I hope this isn't about a duel with Brazio," said Duro.

They both shook their heads.

"Then what did you want?" he asked harshly, making her flinch internally. Gone was the intense warleader, replaced by a lingering sorrow.

"Tell me."

"You know how we haven't been able to beat the cliff challenge. Maybe we get a quarter or halfway up and then someone knocks a pebble off the wall, or we scuff a foot and then we have to start over," she said.

"I am aware," he responded flatly, making her hesitate to continue.

"Yara was checking things online and found something that might help us."

Duro raised an eyebrow at Brazio's daughter. Yara reluctantly handed over her phone, which was opened on the *Herald of the Halls*, the main newspaper in the city. Duro read the screen silently with his lips pursed.

"Tinker's Hall, huh? You think this device would help us?" he asked.

"We watched the videos of its use. They shot guns within its radius, and noise detectors never picked up a thing. It won second prize in their competition," said Pandora breathlessly. She'd been excited the moment Yara had showed it to her. "They have it on display outside the hall. It's not that well guarded. If we left now, we could be in the city by nightfall.

We could be back by morning with the device and our noise problems on the cliff solved."

"Yes, I see," said Duro even as he looked like he wasn't paying attention at all. He kept glancing towards the eastern entrance as if he were expecting someone to come through it.

"Can we go? I was thinking we could take a small group. I promise we'd be back as soon as possible."

"Yes, we can go, but I'm coming with you. The Undercity is much too dangerous right now." He frowned. "Go back and tell your father, Yara. I need to grab some things for the trip. Pan, you visit Elani and ask her for eight quarter-sticks of explosives and the proper trigger mechanisms."

Pandora started to ask a question, but stopped when he said, "Do it."

The harshness of his tone surprised her. In over two years, she'd never known him to show anger. Pandora sprung away towards the maintenance shop. She found Elani behind her desk, studying documents.

"You don't work here anymore," said Elani without looking up. Her face was etched with exhaustion. The entire clan was under pressure but some bore it more than others. She'd been tasked with building defenses and adding additional sensing equipment. Their best chance against the combined forces of the alliance and the Crows was to know when they were coming and act accordingly.

"Duro sent me. I need eight quarter-sticks of explosives and the trigger mechanisms to go along with them."

Elani squeezed her pen at the warleader's name. She didn't move for two long heartbeats before nodding and climbing to her feet with the dread of someone on their way to the gallows. The explosives shed was away from the main building. Elani unlocked it with a key from around her belt.

"Our stores are low..."

"We wouldn't ask unless it was important."

Elani opened the door but didn't head into the shadows. "We?"

The head of the department didn't know exactly why Garret had been killed, just like the rest of the clan, but Pandora was well aware that she blamed her.

Pandora squeezed her eyes shut. "I'm sorry, Elani. He was a good kid."

She spun around, anger contorting her face. "Then why is he *dead?*"

"He got mixed up with the wrong people. He was taking money to pass information and other things," said Pandora, not wanting to tell Elani about the attempted bombing. "I tried to warn him, but he was too far gone."

Elani stared back blankly before a quivering exhale came out. It turned into sobs. Pandora quickly collected the older woman into her arms, letting her cry on her shoulder.

"No one told me."

"I'm sorry."

After a few minutes, Elani broke away and disappeared into the shed. She came out with a satchel and handed it to Pandora.

"Do I want to know?"

"Trying to find a way out of this mess," said Pandora.

Elani blew out a breath. "Be careful. The shadows do not lie."

Pandora gave her a two-finger salute on the way out. On the way back, she swung by her quarters to change. The place was empty and she could hear them training in the assembly yard. The Drops had great waku, especially with the infusion of Razor, but would it be enough? She switched into clothes more suitable to the city. Yara and Duro were waiting for her at the main area. The warleader headed to the east when she arrived, taking long strides.

"Not the Lazona?" she asked as she hurried to keep up with Yara on her tail.

"It's being watched."

The gruff tone told her not to ask any more questions. She stayed in his wake as they hurried through the Pajot. When they left, the darkness took on a different quality. She felt like every corner was an ambush, even as she could see with her sapphire radar and knew that Duro's powerful amber was scouting ahead for them.

Duro moved unusually through the caverns—at least unusually compared to their previous trips together—stopping frequently to listen, or hurrying ahead, forcing them to use their stones to keep up. It felt like they were being followed, though she couldn't detect a tail.

After a two-hour journey to the southeast, Duro seemed to be searching as they circled through the same cavern more than once. Eventually, he found a partially hidden passage that led to a circular chamber. At the center was an obsidian pillar surrounded by runes etched into the smoothed floor.

"Don't touch it," he said.

"That's a portal stone, right?" asked Pandora.

"The mages built it to move around the city easily. Without inherent faez and the password, you can't use it, and some of them have traps to keep people from testing them."

Pandora had traveled through portals, but the ones the maetrie used were quite different. Some didn't even require obsidian to travel, using other magical means.

The passage led further to the south for another ten minutes until they reached a concrete wall. Duro held out his hand, so she gave him the satchel. He set three charges hooked to a trigger and ran the line into the tunnel about fifty feet away.

"Pray to the shadows we don't cause a collapse, or we'll have to take a more dangerous path."

He toggled the box, and an earth-rattling explosion sent a wave of dust through the tunnel. Pandora closed her eyes and tried not to breathe until it was past. After the cloud dissipated, they found the concrete wall had been demolished, leaving a narrow gap that they could slip through.

"You two head up, there are stairs ahead," said Duro, crouching by the wall and removing more explosives from the satchel.

"What is he doing?" asked Yara.

"Keeping anyone from following, I think," she said.

The stairs were hewn into the granite for the first two hundred feet and then they turned to old wooden ones that looked partially rotted from age.

"These okay?" asked Yara, pushing her toe into a plank that had split in half.

An explosion rocked the earth, sending dust streamers onto them and the wooden stairs into a sway. Pandora grabbed the rock wall to stabilize, but the shaking ended quickly.

"I hope these stairs go all the way up," she said.

"If not, then we'll have to climb," said Duro, who appeared below them. "Let's move."

"Is someone following us?" asked Pandora.

"I'd rather not find out," he said.

The climb to the city took longer than expected because there were multiple gaps in the stairs requiring them to climb the rock wall, but it wasn't a problem for the three of them and they reached a clean basement through a locked door that Yara kicked open. The sound of people working and talking filted down to them from the main floor.

"Where are we?" asked Pandora as she spotted shelves full of wine in velvet catches. A walk-in freezer was on the back wall.

"I don't remember," said Duro as he moved up the stairs.

Pandora followed him into a big kitchen. A couple of the white-coated chefs gave them a worried glance as they arranged food on white plates.

"City inspector," said Duro with a wink as he headed through the swinging doors.

The restaurant was filled with middle-aged couples and families dining. The room was modern arcane with copious amount of black wood with etched glowing runes that were probably for show, rather than actual magic. The appearance of three people covered in dust and carrying satchels brought a lot of worried glances, but they quickly moved through the room and onto the street.

"We're right outside of the city limits," said Duro as he checked to the horizon. The Spire was visible, as the setting sun still glowed on the top quarter, but the rest of the city was cast in shadow.

Duro pulled out his phone, stared at it for a moment, then said, "Yara, call us a taxi."

"Not calling Dane or Phillip?" asked Pandora as Yara pulled out her phone. "Or are you worried they're being watched?"

Further conversation was cut short when a taxi went past and Duro waved it down. The three climbed into the back.

"Tenth ward."

The bearded driver looked over his shoulder. "Anywhere in particular?"

Duro went silent for a moment. "The Wax Museum."

"You know it's closing soon, right?"

"That'll be our problem," said Duro.

"Whatever," mumbled the driver, turning up his radio. The music had a thumping beat and wailing guitars. Pandora might have enjoyed it more, but the tense travel through the Undercity had given her a minor headache.

Duro paid the driver after he dropped them off. The sun no longer reflected off the top of the Spire, and streetlights flickered on.

"It's about eight blocks from here. We can warm up with a brisk walk."

The air was cool, refreshing on her skin after the long climb. She figured it was September, but it could be early October for all she knew as the calendar in the Undercity meant much less than above ground, where the seasons kept people informed.

The ward was packed with corner bodegas and apartment buildings.

A few times older vehicles with tinted windows slowed down to check them out, but none of them stopped. A noisy bar flashed neon lights onto the street as college kids in dayglow outfits lined up to enter. Half of them had lips stained blue or purple, suggesting either a trend or the latest psychedelic elixir.

"We're here," said Duro when they stopped on a corner.

Ahead of them was a brightly lit square in front of a colorful old warehouse. The outline of the building was staid, but the murals and bright lights made the place look like a carnival. Tents in the front were well-lit and had people wandering through them to examine the gadgets designed by the Tinker's Hall students. Pandora vaguely remembered a show-and-tell that had been set up similarly when she'd lived in Chicago with her father. It'd been for the older kids, but she'd wandered through with wonder in her eyes wishing she could have had a booth like them. It was one of those things she'd expected would happen eventually—until her father died.

"Split up and check it out. Remember we're tourists. Meet back here in an hour."

Pandora made sure she had no more dust on her clothes. She approached the tents cautiously, trying to remember what it was like to wander without purpose. She felt like a stranger in their world. The urge to check over her shoulder was strong, but she kept her face neutral.

The tents were filled with families or students checking out the displays, which were contained within glass cases. There were more than a dozen gadgets within the tents. Pandora marveled at the designs. A trio of smooth metal blobs climbed over each other like living things, their shiny surfaces morphing as they moved. A camera-shaped box with a lens on the front would brightly flash and then an illusionary critter would "crawl" out of the glass and wander around the box until it disappeared. In another tent, a silvery crown was placed on people's foreheads and had their eyes lighting up as if they were watching fireworks. No one explained what the person saw, and Pandora wasn't sure she wanted to risk any adverse effects.

She made her way to the sound-dampening device in the third tent. It was a simple box with a few toggles on the side. A board explained how it worked while a video played showing the device in action. A girl with short, curly brown hair in a wheelchair watched as Pandora examined the device through the glass case.

"Did you make this?" asked Pandora.

"I did," said the girl, grinning and adjusting her glasses. "It's not my best work, but it does the job pretty well. I had the idea when I couldn't study for a test because my neighbor was blaring their music on Mach ten." The girl rolled her eyes. "But it didn't work as well as I would have liked because trying to study in absolute silence was worse than the noise."

Her exuberance about the work reminded Pandora about how different her life was from that of most people her age. There were stickers on the girl's wheelchair signaling all sorts of interests of which Pandora had no recognition. It was a life she'd never been given a chance to choose.

"Which Hall?"

"Huh?" replied Pandora.

"Sorry, I thought you were a student. You look like one."

The comment got her heart racing. A reminder of the life she could have led had things gone differently. Pandora put up a fake smile and shrugged. "Never tested."

"Really? How? Everyone gets tested," said the girl.

"Moved around too much, I guess." Pandora gave her a short hand motion, desperate to get away from further questions. "Good luck with your schooling."

Pandora left the area immediately. She was standing with her arms crossed when Yara appeared.

"Something wrong?"

"Did anyone from the clans ever enter the Halls?" asked Pandora.

The corners of Yara's eyes creased. "Why? Those mages are everything wrong with the world. Magic has ruined everything. Look what happened during the invasion."

"You don't consider the stones magic?"

"They're not the same. Limited use. There's no stone of ruining the world," said Yara.

"I guess you're right."

Further conversation ended when Duro appeared. "Viewing ends in forty minutes. After that, they take the items into Tinker's Hall. I need one of you to make a distraction and I'll grab it. We can meet back at the Wax Museum."

"I'll do it," said Yara right away.

"I'll keep watch for the PD, I guess." Pandora put her hand on Yara's arm before she moved away. "Don't hurt the girl in the wheel-chair."

Yara screwed up her face. "I ain't no wayhos."

Pandora took position at the corner, watching down the streets for random police activity. She checked back to the tents to see Yara in the first one with the weird blobs. A sudden cry and a crash was followed by people running out of the tent. Yara was picking herself up after trip-ping into the box, knocking it over and sending the living gadgets onto the concrete.

A crowd formed around the commotion. Pandora tried not to get distracted, checking the third tent for signs of Duro's approach. The girl, unfortunately, hadn't moved to the other tent to investigate.

A blur shot out from the corner building. Someone screamed and when Pandora checked back, the glass case was on the ground, and the girl was pointing down the street.

"He stole the Mute Box!"

Pandora thought that would be the end of it, but then the girl hit a button on her wheelchair. She shot out after Duro, flying over the concrete steps and racing down the sidewalk. The wheelchair bounced and rocked but never tipped over.

"Shit."

Using her opal, Pandora raced after her, hoping to detour the girl before she caught up to Duro and got herself hurt. The wheelchair was faster than expected. Duro was a hundred meters ahead. When Pandora caught the girl, she tried to put her hand on the wheelchair to slow her down.

"Be careful. You don't want to get hurt," she told the girl as she grabbed the armrest.

The girl shrieked and said, "You're with him!"

Before Pandora could react, the girl pulled a short tube from an inner pocket. Pandora didn't recognize the danger until the end of the tube exploded, throwing her through a plate glass window of a bike store. She landed in a pile of display bikes, the handles sticking painfully into her back as alarms blared.

Nineteen

Lights flashed and sirens roared. An unbroken piece of glass lay on her lap while a bike handle stuck painfully into her rib cage. Pandora rubbed her chest where the girl had hit her with that explosive tube. There'd been no gunpowder. The explosion had been magical, but it still hurt like hell.

Glass crashed and broke around her as she climbed out of the store while red and blue flashing lights reflected around the corner. People were running towards her from Tinker's Hall.

"Not good, Pan."

Shaking off the pain, she decided neither direction was appealing. The cops had mages in their employ, and any one of the people heading towards her could be from Tinkers.

"Time to fly."

She Pushed off the concrete, expecting to lift into the air so she could land on the roof, but she barely rose two inches off the ground. Pandora feared the explosion had somehow robbed her of her abilities, until she remembered the sapphire required faez-soaked objects with which to interact. Her sapphire was mostly useless in the city.

Pandora broke into a flat run, using her opal to coax her muscles and lungs to maximum speed. She headed away from the Hall, but towards the flashing lights. Three Invictus PD vehicles skidded around the corner. The first two passed without slowing and she thought she would make it, but the third slammed on its brakes, sending up a cloud of rubber. Two hulking officers leapt from the car.

"Freeze! Stop running!"

She ignored the command. The crack of a shot followed. A web of electricity wrapped around her, sending her into convulsions. She slammed onto the concrete, quivering with pain, her muscles held in stasis. As she fought the effects, the two officers sauntered over with their hands on their belts. They were laughing.

"Looks like we caught some tunnel trash," said the first.

The second officer leaned into her face. "I think you're right, Ron. Pale, pasty skin." He grabbed her hand. "Look at these calluses. I bet she's in a clan. Probably has some faez crystals on her somewhere. Let me see if I can find them."

He started pulling up her shirt as she fought to move again but her muscles were made of concrete.

"Well, lookie here, we've got a pair, and ain't that cute how she keeps them on her belly button. Gonna have a grand ol' time with her at the station."

He started fussing with the catches, trying to remove them from her stomach. Spit formed on her lips as she tried to tell him that she was going to shove her blades into his gut, but her tongue didn't work.

A shape landed behind the standing cop. He made a noise before a fateful gurgle made him drop to his knees. The kneeling cop looked up in time to catch a foot to the face. Yara followed up with a heavy punch to his forehead, knocking him out cold on the sidewalk.

"What happened to you?"

Pandora couldn't answer, so Yara picked her up and put her on her shoulder. As she ran away, Pandora saw the first cop was alive, but holding his throat where Yara had punched him. Two blocks away, Pandora felt like her muscles would allow her to move again.

"Let me down."

Shaky legs made her feel like a newborn foal, but the act of using them was better than being a sack of potatoes.

"I can run."

She was slow at first, but as the blood pumped through her muscles and she used her opal to work through the worst of the effects, she managed to hit a good stride. They met Duro at the Wizard's Wax Museum. The girl in the wheelchair was slumped over.

"You didn't...?"

He shook his head. "I put her to sleep. She was feisty." He held out his arm, which had an angry bite mark. "She'll wake up in a few minutes with an awful headache."

Sirens whirled in the distance. Not close enough to make her worry.

"Back to the restaurant?"

"That way is blocked." He frowned as he turned his head, checking the empty street. "Fuck. We have to go. Now. Follow me."

Pandora shared a worried glance with Yara as they broke into a sprint. With her limbs warmer, Pandora was able to mostly keep up. She kept checking behind, seeing nothing, but feeling a worrying itch at the center of her shoulder blades. Duro led them east towards the ninth ward, not bothering to slow when vehicles passed, as if whatever was following them was worse than being spotted by the cops.

The landscape grew familiar as they winded through the streets. Duro stopped outside a place with a glowing neon sign in front. Freeport Games. Before he reached for the door, he turned his head.

Pandora followed his gaze to a figure at the end of the street. She couldn't see him, but there was something familiar about the way he stood. An awkward angle to his shoulders that left her shaken.

"Come on," said Duro.

Inside the shop, the noise was intense. Dozens of kids sat around tables playing games with boards and dice and little plastic figures. In a booming voice, a tall, pink-haired girl wearing roller skates was explaining some imaginary scene to younger kids. As they passed the front counter, an older man with wiry gray hair and bushy eyebrows that could have been caterpillars held his hand out. Something about him sent a shiver down her spine.

"I thought we were done," said the man behind the counter in a deep gravelly voice.

"I need another favor, Hemistad."

The old man sniffed the air. His expression curled into itself with anger.

"How dare you lead him here?"

The words were spoken low enough no one should have been able to hear him, but the entire room quieted and heads turned their direction as if they sensed the power being revealed.

"I had no choice. He won't bother you. He's after us." Duro bowed at the waist. "Please. The lives of my entire clan are at stake. I offer you anything you wish."

The old man growled beneath his breath. Pandora had the impression of a great beast lurking beneath his skin. Hemistad jerked his head towards the hallway at the back of the store.

"Go."

Duro burst away and Pandora followed. They reached a cage at the center of a square room. A pit went into the darkness below. Inside the cage, Duro hit a button and it lurched into motion, descending at a pace entirely too slow for Pandora's taste.

"Who's chasing us? And who is that man that let us back here?" asked Yara, uncharacteristically shaken.

"I don't know the name of the one chasing us, only that he's a mae-trie assassin and that even the three of us combined would be no match for him."

"Kavano," said Pandora, suddenly remembering. She'd never met him in the Eternal City, but had seen him once at her grandfather's estate. The others at the party had whispered tales of his prowess. There was no deadlier assassin alive.

"Kavano," said Duro, tasting the name. He turned to Yara. "The owner of Freeport Games, Hemistad, is an old acquaintance. If there's anyone who could stand up to Kavano, it would be him."

"Who is he?"

"What is he would be a better question."

Pandora banged on the railing. "Can this thing go any faster?"

Their journey back into the Undercity was longer than any before it. Pandora kept expecting the maetrie assassin to come sliding down the wire and land on the top of the cage. A few times, Duro's head snapped up as if he'd heard something. His hand went to his blades, but he never pulled them.

When the cage broke into a huge cavern, the final leg of their descent, Pandora's heart thudded with hopeful relief. She kept tapping on the railing and mumbling to herself.

"What are you counting?" asked Yara in a whisper.

"It helps me stay calm."

When the cage was fifty feet from the bottom, Duro said, "He's climbing down the wire."

"Can we outrun him?"

Duro shook his head. "When we land, I want everyone to get out as quickly as possible and we're going to try and pull the cage and pulley system off the ceiling. I don't think he can survive a thousand-foot fall."

When the cage was nearing the floor, they each jumped out. As it landed, they climbed onto the top and each grabbed a section of the wire. Pandora was less use without a topaz, but she gave it her all, using her opal to enhance her muscles. The three of them strained and yanked, trying to dislodge the pulley system, which had been designed to hold great weights.

"Ahhh!"

Duro was yelling when the wire finally gave. There was suddenly no resistance.

"Jump!"

They hurried off the cage, scrambling into the cavern. A few seconds after they got away, a heavy piece of machinery crashed into the cage, crushing it. They each looked up towards the hole. There was no sign of the assassin.

"Let's move. Hopefully he had to jump to the wall and he's climbing back up."

"And if he's not?" asked Yara.

Duro didn't answer. He took off along a gravel path. Pandora gave Yara a shrug and followed. They ran at a good clip. The whole time Pandora kept expecting Kavano to appear in their way, but they made it back to the Pajot in good time and with the sound dampener. When they arrived, the exhaustion from the day set in. It was early in the morning and training would be starting in a few hours.

"Get some sleep. I'll see you both on the Night Wall."

He held up the Mute Box before disappearing down the path towards his home.

"That was too close," said Pandora with a sigh. "Thanks for saving my ass on the street."

Yara squinted. "How did you know the name of the assassin following us?"

"I heard it somewhere. Maybe one of the old gangs I ran with that did business with the maetrie." She gave a hesitant smile. "Like a ghost story. Someone to make you afraid. It might not even be his name."

Yara seemed to accept the explanation. They headed back to the Academy, climbing into their bunks in the deep hours of the night. She saw Kuma spot her. He gave her a long look before rolling back into his covers. When Pandora lay down, her mind raced with the adrenaline still running through her system, keeping sleep at bay.

"Shit."

Twenty

Pandora watched Xylos and Navos sparring playfully on the training grounds while they waited for Instructor Nikolai to show up. The lanky bleached blond used his sapphire to tug on Xylos' limbs when he tried to make contact with his kicks. The pair were circling around each other while the rest of the team watched. She checked Choo-Choo to see faint amusement. A marked difference from the previous week, but yesterday's successful climb on the Night Wall had put everyone in a good mood.

Across the concrete pad she caught Kuma staring at her, which brought warmth to her chest. He quickly looked away, feigning an adjustment to his uniform, but she knew what she'd seen. If they happened to survive the war with the alliance, she hoped they could rekindle their relationship. She knew it'd been mostly physical and they barely knew each other, but she wanted the chance to try under normal circumstances.

A covert whistle announced the instructor was on the way. Everyone hurried into their lines, stiff with attention. Two lines of five waku. To Pandora's surprise, it was Duro that appeared, followed by Brazio and Nikolai. The warleader made a low gesture—permission to relax—and Pandora shifted into a broad stance.

"The shadows are pleased with your success," said Duro as he paced before them. "As am I and the other instructors. You've solved the wall and the field and have proven yourselves in combat and in physical ability in the lake."

His lips flattened. He strode the length of the line twice before stopping.

"I'm afraid it might not be enough. The final obstacle, the door, is currently beyond our reach. I'm afraid unless we can find a way past it, our time in the Pajot is nearing the end."

Pandora shared a glance with Yara on her right. The rest of the team was doing the same. She felt emptiness in her heart. They'd worked so hard, risked so much, and now they weren't going to go through with whatever plan they'd been withholding from them?

"We're leaving?" Pandora blurted out when the ache grew to be too much. The rest of the team added their supportive nods, but the weight in Duro's gaze gave her pause. Whatever he was going to say wasn't going to be easy for her to hear.

"Not yet. Which is why I wanted to explain why we've been putting you through so much with your training. The entire point of this exercise has been to prepare for a hit on the alliance. We believe that if we could take out the leadership of the clans, including their head, Dominion Thule, then their partnership would collapse in the scramble for power."

She tried to hide the impact of his comment, but it staggered her. Pandora gripped the edges of her uniform and counted the cracks in the concrete. They were asking her to kill her grandfather, and while he'd ordered awful things to be done to her, hearing it made her head swim.

"In the alliance caverns, which used to be the home of the Demon Dogs before Dominion took their leader's head, they have a remote headquarters building, high upon the cavern wall. Our way in is through the power plant located adjacent to it. By climbing this cliff in complete silence, and then crossing the field quickly to take out their defenders before they can raise the alarm, we can have access to the main area. The problem is there's a door that we cannot get past. It's made like a vault. I'd hoped to find help in bypassing this obstacle, but there's no one left who believes in our cause. If we'd been able to, then we could have hit the clan leadership, wiped them out, and then escaped through the waterfall on the opposite side. With a little luck and a lot of breath holding, we could come out on the other side of Canter's Folly with the war over."

Silence fell upon them like a weighted blanket. The reason the instructors had been pushing them became clear, and now that they were one step away from being able to complete it, to find out that it currently wasn't possible left them confused and frustrated. For Pandora it was worse as she was left wishing for something she wasn't sure she truly wanted.

"We can figure it out," said Choo-Choo. "I know this team. We beat the other challenges, the field, the cliff. I even let Kuma beat me on the dives."

The entire group laughed, even Kuma, who bowed towards his former enemy. Choo-Choo bent at the waist equally. When he returned to standing, Duro approached and put a hand on the bald waku's shoulder.

"You've performed admirably, coming together as a team in a short time frame and solving challenges that no one thought possible. If we had another few weeks, a month, not much longer, we might have found a way, but Daraja wants us to pack up and leave the Pajot in two days' time. We believe the alliance and the Crows are preparing to hit us not long after. I'm afraid we've run out of time."

A thought struck Pandora like a bolt of lightning. She should have seen it the night they had dinner with Ivan Charmer, when she saw the vault door. Had she known what it was at the time, she might have made the connection. But once she admitted who she was, and what she knew, no one would look at her the same way. It was an irrevocable step as if she were leaping from a high cliff in hopes there was a net below.

"I have an idea," said Pandora, stepping forward. The look Kuma gave her was pure heartbreak. He gave her a tiny shake of the head, sensing what she was about to say.

"Go ahead," said Duro, gesturing.

She squeezed her eyes shut, checking back to the warleader before letting out a quivering breath.

"Is this something you need to speak to me in private about?" he asked.

"No. I think that everyone has to know the truth or they won't believe me."

The tension thickened on the training grounds. She could feel dozens of eyes upon her. She'd never been so nervous in her life, but everything she'd worked for up to this point could unravel and there'd be nothing she could do about it. She was trusting that her friends—her family—would understand her motives and reasonings.

"I know who we can find that might know about the vault. She was probably in charge of its installation. He wouldn't trust anyone else with a task that important. That critical to his protection, which he's always been paranoid about. It's what she's always done for him."

"Pan?" asked Duro, mouth shifted to the side. He stared at her with sympathy. The other instructors looked equally subdued, because they knew what she was about to admit, though not the why.

"Selena would know. If we can find her, we could extract the information we need. I doubt she's at the Terreno anymore. Probably wherever Dominion has made his home in the city."

Choo-Choo stepped closer to Pandora hesitantly, as if she were a living bomb. Kernels of betrayal formed wrinkles on his forehead. He sensed the deception like a dog sensing a dishonest traveler.

"What are you trying to tell us? Who is Selena and why would she know this and why do *you* know this?"

Pandora's eyes glistened with wetness, making it hard to see. She swallowed. "Because she's my mother, and I am Dominion Thule's granddaughter."

It sounded like an explosion went off. Everyone was speaking at once, looking to each other to see who already knew. She saw Einar reaching for his blades and though he did not draw them, the act was as if he'd stabbed her in the chest. Worse yet was the way Choo-Choo stared at her as if she was contagious. He took a step back, accusations poised on his lips. She wanted to tell him to stab her and be done with it. The urge to bare her chest for the blade was overwhelming.

"Silence!"

Duro stepped forward. "Before your theories grow too wild, or someone acts rashly, know that the leadership of the Drops clan has known about her relationship to our enemy. But I can assure you that we trust Pandora. Without her, we'd already have been overrun. She has been our biggest asset in this shadow war."

The comment silenced the worst of her critics, but the weight of their gazes destroyed the fragile shield she tried to put up.

"How do we know we can trust her?" asked Camina, smudged eyes creased with anger.

The others clamored for an answer. Murmurs of *traitor* or *spy* were thrown around easily, words she'd heard before, but she'd never been so affected by them. Choo-Choo had stilled with his arms at his side. Thoughts and questions flowed through his eyes as he stared at her, but he seemed too distraught to speak. In the chaos of her reveal, she looked to Kuma, not for any reason other than she knew he was one of the few people that supported her. He gave her a weak smile.

When Kuma stepped forward, her heart climbed into her throat.

"I trust her," he said. "The reason we were able to bring our two clans together was because she revealed Dominion's plans to recruit the Blue Daggers with a batch of Eclipse. Myself, Camina, Tick, and Pandora took them down, stopping the Blue Daggers from joining the fight during that critical time. That was information she stole from her mother and gave to us. If she were working for them, she would have never done that. They could have ended the war right then. There's not a single doubt in my heart."

More shouting followed and she kept expecting someone to brandish a blade or knock her down. She would have welcomed it, if only to get it over with.

"Quiet!" said Brazio, stepping forward. "I know my new clan does not know me well, but for the others, you know me very well. I can tell you I trust Pandora unequivocally, even though I barely know her. I know this because she saved my life when Dominion's gang was hunting me down and I was too weak to fight. She protected me when she would have no other reason to do so."

Pandora turned to the team, though she faced Choo-Choo specifically. The ache in his eyes broke her heart. She'd betrayed his trust, even if it'd been for good reasons. She could understand if he never forgave her.

"I'm sorry I've been keeping this secret from you, but I feared what you might think and some of it might be true. I was sent here to infiltrate the clans on behalf of my grandfather. I thought I was going to be turning on ruthless criminals, but that's not what I found. Your honor, your dedication and discipline, and most importantly, your love for each other changed my mind.

"They trained me in the Eternal City. The maetrie know no love for each other, only how much they can get away with. Every day is a battle for survival there, and every friend is really an enemy. I thought the Undercity was going to be a smaller, human version of that. But I was wrong."

She stepped close to Choo-Choo. Her hand quivered at her side as she desperately wanted to reach out, feel his touch as a friend. To know that all their time together hadn't evaporated under the hot gaze of truth. She clenched the hem of her uniform if only to have something to grab onto. As if she might fall off the surface of the world into a void of her own making.

"It was you and your family's acceptance of me that taught me that. I was friendless. An outcast. But you invited me into your home. Seeing you and Triana and Vasy interact with each other. Seeing your love and willingness to do anything to protect each other. It's what taught me that what I'd come to do here was a mistake."

He stared back with a deep frown, leaving her gasping for understanding. For life. When Choo-Choo bowed his head with his eyes closed and gave a tiny nod, the tension in her body broke loose. He opened his arms and she collapsed into them, the embrace bringing shuddering relief to her soul. When their hug was finished, Choo-Choo put his hand on her shoulder.

"I stand with Pandora. I stand with all of you."

The fever of betrayal broke with his pronouncement. The other members of the team crowded around her, patting her back or giving her their support. Kuma went last.

"Thank you," she whispered.

"No, thank you. Without you, none of this would have happened."

They filtered back into a single line rather than two separate ones, with Pandora at the center, taking relaxed positions as Duro stepped to the front. He seemed to be searching for words.

"A return to the city would be dangerous at this juncture. Especially after our recent raid. But if the team thinks that we must exhaust all options and pursue Selena Thule for the slim opportunity at breaking through the vault, then I'm willing to take that chance." He looked across the team. "If you believe in this plan, take a step forward. I will only accept a unanimous decision."

He barely finished speaking before the entire team took a step in unison. Pandora's chest filled with pride.

"Okay, then. Brazio, I think the team is ready for some real action. Shall we prepare another raid?"

"I think that sounds excellent," said Brazio, his eyes glittering with amusement.

"Then it's decided. We'll return to the city, but this time as an entire team. This raid can serve two purposes, one to find the information we need to bypass the vault, and the second is a last chance to solidify the team."

"Is it really going to be that difficult?" asked Tick. "Aren't we talking about one person? I know it's Pandora's mother, but that doesn't seem so hard."

Duro frowned. "For one, we don't know what obstacles we'll encounter when we find her, but the bigger problem is that we don't have a safe way out of the Undercity."

"We don't?"

"The Lazona is being watched heavily, and I ruined the only other two passages I know to get out."

Tick screwed up his face. "Then how are we getting out?"

"We're going through the fifth well, the place the Invasion started, and the area the mages who watch it call the Chamber."

Pandora had heard of the Chamber, but never thought much about it because it was something the mages of the Hundred Halls cared about. The location was near the center of the Undercity, almost directly beneath the Spire and not too far from the Terreno.

"Shadowmaster Duro," said Einar, "wouldn't it be more prudent to fight our way out at the Lazona rather than deal with Hall mages?"

"Not if we want to maintain our surprise. The alliance will never expect us to go out that way, and the mages at the Chamber won't know we're coming. They guard the spirit well, observing it for signs of an infernal awakening, but they do not watch the Undercity except to keep critters away. They won't expect a team of waku passing through their area." He looked over the group. "If there are no more questions, I want you to return to your quarters and gather your things in preparation for the raid. Bring two sets of clothes. Wear your shadowed gear, but bring something to wear in the light that will not mark you as different."

On the walk back to the dormitory, Pandora went slow. The prospect of seeing her mother again after everything that had happened left a hole in her heart. She hoped she could somehow persuade her mother to help their cause, and if she wouldn't, Pandora knew the repercussions would be painful for both.

Twenty-One

Kuma was one of the first to finish preparing. He was standing on the training grounds when Pandora arrived in the shadowed gear the clan used during raids. Her face was smudged with patterned grease, making the whites of her eyes stick out. Her jaw pulsed with thought.

"That was brave," he told her. "Braver than a scrap with a dozen Blue Daggers."

"I couldn't keep that weight hanging over me. Not when there's a chance to save the clan. Save our families."

"Are you ready to confront your mother?"

Pandora squeezed her lips white. "I've been ready for a long time. I can't keep avoiding my past. Eventually I have to deal with it. Who I am.

What that means."

"And?"

Her expression broke with laughter tinged with madness. Pandora had always been solid as a rock, the best waku in the Academy: someone who had survived the worst and came out swinging. But she looked on the verge of breaking. Shadows passed across her eyes.

"I wish I knew. Every day is like going through a portal and not knowing what's on the other side. Family isn't always the people who you were born from, and it's taken me a long time to figure that out."

Their quiet conversation was interrupted when Choo-Choo approached, chest puffed out like a bull's. Kuma stiffened. Their relationship had improved since the fight on the shooting field, but that didn't mean they were suddenly friends.

"Hey, Tiny Bear," said Choo-Choo gruffly.

"Yeah?"

"You ever figure out what that ruby does?" he asked, jutting his chin.

Kuma leaned his head back, trying to understand his angle. "No. Not yet. Why?"

"You'd better if we're going to have a chance at surviving all this crimaza shit at the Chamber."

He grinned ferally with all his teeth and extended his hand. Kuma met his grasp at the wrist, hiding his relief. When they were finished shaking hands, Kuma gave Choo-Choo a deep bow, which was returned by the bald waku.

"It's nice to see you two being friends," said Pandora with a hand on Choo-Choo's shoulder.

He pursed his lips. "We're *not* friends. But we are clanmates and that makes us family. I must respect that, even if my mother won't understand."

"What changed?" asked Pandora.

"Your sacrifice. What you revealed in your little speech, knowing that we might all hate you for it. Or worse, killed you as a traitor. But your courage shamed me. You gave up your flesh-and-blood family, turned your back on them, to save mine."

Kuma watched as Pandora curled her arm around Choo-Choo's neck and pulled him in, forehead to forehead with her eyes squeezed.

"*You're* my family, Emilio. That's the thing the maetrie don't understand. They'll use anything and anyone for advantage. I wish I'd seen that before."

"Someday after all this, you're going to have to tell me about the Eternal City," said Choo-Choo.

Pandora smiled, but Kuma had a good idea she wasn't looking forward to that explanation. The pain of what her mother had put her through was reflected in her black eyes.

The rest of their team filtered onto the grounds, joining them in a knot of discussion. Everyone took a moment to touch Pandora or give her an encouraging word, which gave Kuma hope that they would survive this trial. When the instructors arrived, they wore similar clothing and had the same shadowed camouflage painted on their faces.

"The team will go with me," said Duro. He nodded his head to his fellow instructors. "They'll be providing a distraction so no one follows us. If the alliance finds out we're not in the Pajot, they might find reason to attack. This trip must be quick. It's morning in the city. I want to be back here in twelve hours, which would be not enough time for the alliance to return. If you can't move quickly, I will leave you behind."

Duro quietly gave Brazio and Nikolai instructions. After they left, the group headed towards the passage that led to the Terreno along the canyon of ghosts. The pace was quick, forcing Kuma to cycle his emerald to keep up. He occasionally pulsed the ruby, hoping to discover its purpose, but felt no noticeable difference. A few of his teammates seemed to notice something, suggesting the effect was outside of himself, but he wasn't willing to risk slowing them down to learn more. As they left the Mouth, he focused on keeping up.

Since he'd been a member of the Drops, he hadn't been to the Terreno. His only knowledge was from the time he'd followed Pandora and they had to escape to the canyon to avoid detection. Kuma wondered how business was with two clans worth of waku and soldado no longer attending. Was Leesa still working at the Onyx? He guessed the Umbra, the Poinsettia, and the other businesses related to the two clans no longer existed.

Duro led them northwest when they neared the Terreno. He slowed their pace, making it easier to keep up. The passages still had scars from the Invasion: claw marks in the stone, the bones of demons that had perished in interspecies fights, broken horns. The place they were headed had been the epicenter, the location the demons had broken through. They'd flooded east towards Big Dave's Town and eventually came out into the eighth ward. The Goblin Romp had been destroyed when demons too large to fit through the brick archways had surfaced. Kuma had been in the Machi when it happened. They'd felt earthquakes, which had been growing more frequent during that time, and then reports of the demon army had reached him. He'd worried that the end of the world had arrived. Luckily, the mages of the Halls had repelled the invaders and closed the portal that had been opened at the fifth well.

Duro halted at the edge of a cavern, holding his fist up to signal the stop. He waved Tick over, which meant the warleader needed his tiger's eye stone. Kuma was in back, so he couldn't see what was happening. Tick stayed at the corner of the tunnel, concentrating on his task, while Duro disappeared. A minute later, he returned, gesturing for everyone to move slowly and quietly.

A man and a woman in enchanted armor were lying on the ground. Not dead, but their tongues hanging out suggested that Duro had knocked them out. Duro removed a badge from the woman and waved it at a piece of rock that looked no different than the others, but a faint glowing line appeared in the shape of a door, which opened, revealing a wood-paneled hallway. Duro disappeared inside while they waited.

He waved them through once again. Kuma tried not to gawk at the symbols etched into the wood walls, pulsing with faint eldritch light. The stones on his nipples and belly button warmed as if they were waking to the wards.

A long hallway ended in thick double doors that looked built to withstand a nuclear blast, but Duro didn't lead them that way. He took them through a separate door that led to an elevator. Kuma silently hoped the car would hold the entire team. He hated the idea that they might be split up, but when the doors opened up, he saw there was enough room for twice their number. The elevator climbed to the sur-face smoothly, making Kuma wonder if they were really moving at all.

"Change into your street clothes." Duro started stripping out of his shirt. "I don't know what to expect at the top, but be ready to move fast. No killing. We don't want to become enemies of the Halls."

The group change was awkward in the tight space, making Kuma glad the elevator was as large as it was, otherwise they would have been elbowing each other the entire time. He tried not to look at Pandora when she was in her underclothes. She shot him a sly grin when she caught him. Their state of attire wasn't unusual since they shared a dormitory and frequently changed together, but the tight space made it a collective experience.

When the door opened, it was like a starting gun had gone off. Two guards were posted outside in similar gear to the ones that had been in the cavern. Duro delivered a single punch to each in the span of an eyeblink, while Choo-Choo and Navos caught them before the crashed to the ground.

At the end of the long hallway, a hidden door opened into a grocery store. They were in back by the freezers, which had a variety of dumplings, frozen seafood, and ready-made meals. An older Korean lady behind a glass case who was reading a book with a scantily clad couple on the front startled when they appeared. Duro put a finger over his lips and slid a stack of bills through the slot in the glass.

"No one's dead," he told her. "We just needed a way out of the Undercity. You can tell them we won't be coming back this way."

When they stepped out into the daylight, Kuma was immediately impressed by the towering statue at the center of the square. The area was filled with tourists gawking at the depiction of Invictus. There were a few protestors with signs like: "Mages Will Destroy the World!" or "Down with the Halls!" But it wasn't like the first couple years after the Invasion when the square was packed with people protesting the Hundred Halls.

Walking with the group made it easier to be outside. Kuma didn't feel like he was going to get sucked into the sky, and risked craning his head at the skyscrapers feeling like a bug wandering around a field of steel grass. At a corner, he spotted a glass gondola floating through the air on invisible wires, high above the buildings. It was the first time he'd seen one since he was a kid.

They headed due east towards the Spire. Kuma wondered if they were going to enter it, until they veered around the base where endless parking garages were built. On the other side, right at the edge of the first ward, Duro stopped where the cars were entering.

"We're headed into the first ward and into the financial district. We have intel that Dominion keeps a suite in one of the buildings and that Selena has been seen coming and going. I've already sent a message to Dane and Phillip. They're going to meet us nearby with a vehicle. If we spot her, a small group of us will grab her and take her back to a hideout we've never used before. Once we grab her, I want everyone who isn't in the vehicle to head to the Lazona entrance."

"I thought you said it was guarded?" asked Camina.

"It is, but like the mages at the Chamber, they won't expect us to come from this direction. We won't be using the elevator though, but heading down the stairs, but I don't think that's an issue for all of you," he said with a wink. "You'll wait for us near Gamemakers Hall. There's a lot of weird stuff that goes on around there, so no one will notice a few more people wandering around."

The financial district of the first ward felt like an entirely different world than the other parts of the city he'd been in. Men and women in expensive tailored suits walked with bodyguards, or were obscured with shimmering fields that made them anonymous. Brands of vehicles Kuma had never heard of zipped past, oblivious to the police officers patrolling.

The entrance to the building that they were watching had metal detectors, but also a single mage with a small furry mammal on his shoulder that everyone was forced to pass by. Kuma was stationed next to Adrenalynne, who had chosen a worn beanie to hide her neon green stubbled head.

"I feel like I'm in a different world," said Kuma, feigning playing with his cell phone while Adrenalynne acted like she was looking for a ride.

She snorted. "It is a different world. Even amongst the mages of the Halls, there are classes. This area is the home to the super-rich. Not far from here there are gated neighborhoods with yards as big as the old main cavern and houses with more space than all ours put together. If you're rich enough—and especially if you're a mage—you can do just about anything."

The morning passed without sign of Selena Thule. They moved locations occasionally so no one would get suspicious. He never saw where Pandora was set up, but it made sense that she wasn't in plain view where her mother could spot her.

Traffic in the area never let up, even as the morning wore on. Kuma watched self-important men and women yell into their phones about margin calls or short sells—terms that made no sense to him. But it felt like everyone was in a hurry or intensely angry about something that was happening due to a shift in the financial markets.

Sometimes Kuma had wondered what it would be like to live in the city. There were places that drew his interest, or curiosity at least, like the illusionary battles that happened over the second ward. The financial district was not one of them. It reminded him of a colony of insects climbing over a carcass of rotting meat, lashing out and biting anything that got near in hopes that it might be food.

As the sun climbed into the sky and over the tops of the skyscrapers, blaring down on the streets, which were like great canyons, Kuma caught signals from the others of his clan. He spotted the target, a woman surrounded by a shimmering privacy field walking along the street. A black SUV started rolling up, so Kuma crossed the busy street as the light changed, avoiding the slowing cars. He heard Adrenalynne call his name, but he ignored her. Whatever was going to happen between Pandora and her mother, he knew he needed to be there. As Duro and Choo-Choo leapt out of the SUV and grabbed the obscured woman, tossing her into the vehicle, Kuma threw himself into the back seat next to a surprised Pandora. The door slammed and the SUV sped away.

Twenty-Two

"How do we know it's her?" asked Choo-Choo from the back seat as he held her shoulders.

Pandora sat next to the shimmering obscuration field. The woman inside of it wore a navy blue patterned skirt and black high heels. They were all that was visible outside of the field. She could have been any financial analyst or hedge fund manager on the street, but Pandora knew it was her mother. There was a push and pull between them like two opposite magnets spinning wildly on their axes.

"It's her."

The woman sat between Pandora and Duro while Choo-Choo and Kuma—who had surprised her by leaping into the SUV at the last moment—sat in the far back seat.

Duro grabbed the bracelet on the woman's wrist, unclasping it. The hum of an enchantment dropped, revealing Selena Thule. The bone and gold half of her face shone like polished mask while her hair was combed over the human side of her face. She glared back with the intensity of a lightning storm.

"You're fools if you think this will do anything," Selena said, scowling and maintaining eye contact with Pandora.

Duro stared at the back of her head with heavy-lidded eyes before turning to Dane in the passenger seat.

"Anyone on our tail?"

"Clean as Invictus' butthole. The moment we pulled up, a flock of pigeons descended on the sidewalk, scattering those rich assholes. No one saw us grab her. At best, the security cams might have caught it, but they won't know anything for days."

The SUV headed through back alleyways and underneath raised roads. Pandora barely noticed their passage through the city as she hadn't broken eye contact.

"You know she's a traitor," said Selena. "I sent her to the Undercity to spy on your little clans."

"I told them everything, Mother."

Selena sat back against the seat, fidgeting with the bone-and-gold arm that she held against her chest. They eventually pulled into a parking garage in the ninth ward. Phillip backed the SUV up to a loading dock on the lowest floor. Once inside, Duro hauled Selena out and led her into the elevator. The seven of them ascended into the building. The apartment overlooked a park where families were lunching on blankets and throwing frisbees for their dogs.

"Your entire clan is going to be wiped out soon," said Selena as they bound her to a metal chair with enchanted cuffs. Both wrists and ankles were immobile.

"Maybe," said Duro, sitting on the table before their captive. "But you'll answer some questions first."

Selena spat on Duro's leg. He ignored it as he pulled a blade from inside his jacket.

"No," said Pandora right away. "Not like that."

Duro turned his head. "You know she'd do the same to you."

"That's why I can't. I can do just about anything, but not that. It would make me like her."

Selena smirked. "It's that human weakness shining through. Maybe it was good that you betrayed us. You would have been like a flaw in the steel."

"Why do you toil for him, Mother? Why do you hurt your own daughter on his behalf?"

"You know the game he plays. Any weakness would be exploited by his enemies. If you cannot win, you die. You know this," said Selena.

"All too well," said Pandora as memories from her years in the Eternal City bubbled up like tar. The constant fear, the push to excel, and trying to figure out everyone's motivations in case they were out to kill her. "For a time, it broke me. Robbed me of my humanity. It wasn't until I joined them that I understood what I was missing. It's the mae-trie that are weak. They lack the bonds of true family. It's what makes humans stronger."

She smiled weakly at Choo-Choo and Kuma and Duro. It was hard to have her defects exposed in front of them by her mother. Her mind was too wrapped in the chains of her mother's comments to tell if they agreed with her. She was afraid her negative thoughts would affect how she read the blank expressions on their faces.

"You might as well kill me," said Selena. "I'll tell you nothing. Not just because he would punish me, but because I believe in his cause. The Undercity should be ruled by one clan. You're squandering your opportunity by squabbling amongst yourselves. The rest of the world is only just waking up to the opportunity in the shadows. The faez crystal trade must be controlled, and soon, or it'll be taken away. My father, *your* grandfather, is only doing what should have been done years ago."

"He doesn't love you," said Pandora.

"What does love have to do with anything?" spat Selena. "This is about winning."

The urge to storm away burned in her limbs. She stayed because she didn't want to show weakness in front of her mother, but the words wouldn't come. If she gave in to Duro and let him torture Selena, that would only be proof of what her mother had said. She'd trapped herself by making that demand.

"Look how weak she is," said Selena. "You would not call her a clanmate if you could have seen her in the Eternal City, how she failed to live up to the promise of her blood. How she was kicked out of the school when maetrie half her age outshone her. How after I begged for a second chance, injuring my own prospects, she failed again when I sent her to a special teacher. One better suited for a weak-willed human.

"When things got too rough, she would come to me, bloody and bruised, begging to return home. What she could not understand is that training would make her stronger if she would just commit. Instead, she lay in her own piss and vomit, complaining about the way she was treated, as if we all hadn't gone through the same struggles.

"When it was clear that my kindness was only holding her back, I bribed the other students to punish her. They put her in the box with the faeila. I hoped the creatures would strip away her weakness, reduce her to a base being that could be reformed into something stronger. Something more maetrie, less human."

The admission that her mother had been behind the box was like a spear to the heart. Twenty-three links in the cuffs. Eleven bars on the window. Seventy-one dimples on the glass lamp.

"See," said Selena, laughing. "She's counting. Whenever she gets overwhelmed, she counts primes. Poor little Pandora. You know that comes from your maetrie blood. So when things get too overwhelming, you're not falling back on your human traits. You weak, simpering little worm. If you'd just forget them, shed your human skin, embrace your maetrie blood, you could be great. You have that in you, daughter."

Every inch of Pandora's flesh burned with shame. She hadn't realized she'd been rocking on her heels, counting primes, until her mother had called her out. Normally she could control it, or at least hide the fact that she was overwhelmed, but her mother had exposed her in front of her clan.

"Pan—"

Pandora shot her hand out, cutting off Duro before he could speak. At first she fought the tears bunching up in her eyes. Then she let them flow, streaking down her cheeks defiantly. She'd let her mother do it to her again, put her on the defensive, make her forget why they'd even captured her. For a moment there, Pandora felt like she was back in the Eternal City getting yelled at by her mother for not being better. Weren't the tables turned? Shouldn't it be her turn to interrogate her mother?

"You're not immune to his disappointment either, Mother. Look what he did to you when you failed him."

"He scraped away my humanity so I could be improved. I thanked him afterwards, just like you should be thanking me. Those scars on your back should be a reminder of the weakness leaving your body. After that week in the box, you were much better, Pandora. You were almost mae-trie. A weak, crippled maetrie, but there were signs of your greatness. It was the only reason your grandfather agreed to send you to Hylakane."

"You don't think that he won't get rid of you once he has control of the Undercity? He only kept you around because you were useful to him in this human world. Not to be his emissary, but his lacky, to run errands or build things for him he wouldn't stoop to do himself. You're not his daughter, you're his shitty human project manager, who ruined his plans for hitting the Drops by letting the plan slip to your traitor daughter."

Pandora knew she'd erred the moment her mother broke into laughter.

"This human world? My father knows it better than I do. That's why he was ready to take control of the Undercity. He's been here a long time. Do you think that he brought my mother to the Eternal City and conceived me there? No, he's been in the city for a long time, studying the mages, the super-rich, learning their ways in preparation for the time when he can assert control. Your grandfather has long vision. Even lon-ger than the maetrie queens and their worthless Courts. They rule over an empire of ashes. They do not see as far as he does, and that will be their downfall. Everyone's downfall. The Undercity is just a beginning. It's not the end. That's why he'll do anything to take control."

Pandora had hoped to trick her mother into revealing something about the work she'd done in the alliance, but instead she'd only proved how little Pandora knew. She'd had no idea that Dominion had been in the city of sorcery for a long time, because she'd seen him in the Eternal City on a regular basis and assumed that was where he'd made his home.

"I know what you're trying to do, Pandora. You're after information about the headquarters I built for him. You want to trick me into revealing details." The others in the room stiffened with recognition. "I won't tell you anything about what I built, the traps, the little surprises, the vault door. Because he saw what you would plan. Dominion knows you'll eventually try to come for him, thinking to take him out in one blow, keeping the Undercity for yourselves. You can torture me all you want, take my limbs from me, leave me a ruined ball of flesh in a tiny box— and still I'll tell you nothing. Because you're all nothing to me. Even you, Pandora. Once I had high hopes, and then I just wanted you to be a part of the family, but now I see you for what you are—a failure. And a human one at that."

It might have been Selena bound to the chair, but the entire room was devastated by her announcement. Even Duro looked discouraged. They'd come to turn the tables on the war, only to find out they'd been anticipated. More than that. Expected. It was like waking up to find the sky wasn't real. The ground beneath her feet had shifted. The idea that they should flee, leave the Undercity and escape to somewhere far away had taken hold in her mind. Why risk an attack when he was expecting

them? It'd be a slaughter. Somehow they'd lost even before they'd started. And it was all her fault. Pandora had only proved what her mother
had just said. She was too human, too weak to count. Everything she'd
done and learned in the Undercity was for nothing. And capturing her
mother would only announce their plans to her grandfather.

"I see it in your eyes, Pandora. You want to run away just like you
always do. When things get too hard you crumble. Do you need to
count primes? Do you need to cry again? You don't even know what
you are, but I do. You're a failure as both a human and a maetrie."

"No."

Pandora said it out of instinct. She said it because it was the only
way to stay standing and not curl into a ball. But just the simple act of
defiance kept her mind turning. Whirling. She'd been in the Undercity
so long she'd forgotten the ways of the maetrie. If someone punches
you, you hit back harder. Use their weaknesses against them. Turn their
strengths to disadvantages. Her mother had been doing that to her—and
to the others in the room.

"No. I'm not a failure. And you're not fooling me. You might have
put in the vault, but there are no traps, no hidden surprises. You've de-
duced what we're going to do." Duro rose to his feet, but she waved him
off. "You're right, Mother. We're going to hit the alliance, kill Dominion
and his little group of subservient clan leaders. Even his pet mercenary
Titus Cabone.

"And you're right, we brought you here to find out about the vault. You see, that's the part we haven't been able to figure out. We don't know how to get through it. But you made a mistake. You revealed something you should have never said. I know that you won't tell me the codes, or anything about its installation that might help, but I know someone who will. Someone I didn't realize until today shared a hatred for my grandfather."

She turned to Kuma and Duro, who stared at her with confusion on their brows.

"We had dinner with him recently, and until this moment, I had no idea that my grandfather had been his house manager. He's been living in Invictus for decades, learning about the super-wealthy, the mages of the Halls, everything. He said something at the dinner that until this moment I didn't understand, but her words helped me make the connection."

Repeating her mother's words brought enlightenment to them. Kuma spoke the name that was firmly in her mind.

"Ivan Charmer."

Twenty-Three

The SUV ride into the tenth ward was silent except for the rumbling of the engine. Kuma sat in the back seat next to Pandora while Duro drove. Dane and Phillip had stayed back in the apartment to watch Selena Thule. The truths revealed from the interrogation floated around the vehicle like smoke. He wasn't sure what he was more surprised about, the way her mother had treated her during her childhood, or that Dominion Thule had been the house manager for the Charmer family.

After they'd made the connection, it was easy to find the truth on the internet. His name wasn't listed in any article, so the Charmer family, or Thule himself, had suppressed the information, but there were a few pictures in dark corners about it. The Charmers had been a huge part of high society. The father had an empire of influence that had spanned multiple arenas of business until he got into a legal war with his children and then he disappeared. There was a lot of speculation about what happened and if he was still alive, but the damage had been done. As far as they were able to learn, only three of the six Charmer children were still alive. The youngest, Andromeda, who worked in the Mystique traveling circus; Kitty Charmer, who lived in Asia somewhere; and Ivan, who ran his alchemical company G&T Industries.

His house in the tenth ward was right next to his little factory. There were other production facilities in the city and elsewhere, but he used the one next to his house as a place to build out experimental mixtures in his laboratories.

Next to him, Pandora had her head down and her hands resting in her lap. Kuma wanted to reach out and show her support, but he was afraid the gesture would be misinterpreted. She caught him looking and the corners of her eyes creased with what he hoped was acknowledgement.

He gave her the hand signal for "What's the situation?"

She responded with the two-finger salute that said, "All good here."

Kuma knew it wasn't true. She looked raw from the encounter. Pandora had been fidgeting with the hem of her shirt, rubbing the threads with her thumb. Her mouth had been moving as if she were counting when she stared out the window at the city. He wished he could see inside her head. Before the interrogation, there'd always been a part of him that worried about her past, her connection to her mother and grandfather. This despite all evidence that she was on their side. After the Crows' betrayal, it was natural to have kernels of doubt lurking in his mind. No longer. It was inconceivable to Kuma that she would ever go back to them after learning what they'd done to her. They'd treated her like a fighting dog, worse than one, keeping her in a cage, letting those faeila, whatever they were, flay her flesh. He remembered the scars from their tryst in the back rooms of the Onyx. He'd had no idea how awful their origins were.

"Will this guy talk to us?" asked Choo-Choo from the passenger seat as Duro turned a corner.

"Knowing what we know now, I hope so," said Duro.

"He will," said Pandora tightly. Her hand was squeezed into a fist on her thigh as if she would make him talk whatever it took. Kuma didn't think it would require that, but it was clear she'd invested her soul into this final chance to make the plan work.

Kuma reached out to take her hand and unclench it, but he pulled it back before he crossed the gap between them. She caught the movement and turned her head slightly.

"The bigger question is, *can* he help us," said Duro.

"Everything we read about him suggests he's capable of it," said Kuma.

He was less sure in his head, but he wanted Pandora to believe that her sacrifice had been worth it. Her head still hung low.

Choo-Choo had been thumbing through the loaner phone Dane had given him. He was sitting in the passenger seat. "Celesse D'Agastine, the head of Alchemists Hall, called him a genius at a recent industry conference. That has to mean something, right? She runs one of the biggest companies in the world."

"Or he might not want to risk his empire on petty revenge," said Pandora. "Or because he knows my grandfather, he knows how much he would be putting himself in harm's way by helping us."

"Enough speculation," said Duro as he pulled onto the street. "Now we have to focus on convincing him."

The house they'd pulled up to didn't look like it belonged in the area. The brownstones on the opposite side had chips in the paint and tufts of weeds in the yard, while Ivan's house looked like it had been featured in an architectural magazine. Next door, a huge warehouse had been converted into a laboratory ringed with high fencing and barbed wire. Pulsing runes on the poles signaled the additional enchantments.

Two security guards in heavily runed gear stood outside the entrance to the house. Kuma wasn't sure if they were the same ones that had been outside the room at the restaurant. While getting past them wouldn't be an issue, they didn't know how many others were in the area.

"Go away," said one, a big guy with an automatic weapon held to his chest menacingly. "There's no trick or treating here."

"We're here to talk to Ivan," said Duro, inclining his head respectful-ly. "We met with him recently, but have new information. He'll want to talk to us."

The guy leaned forward, ignoring the signals from Duro with a scowl on his lips. "I said. Go away. He's not here anyway. In Budapest for a meeting with investors. You'll have to contact his press secretary if you want another meeting."

Kuma tuned his amber until he could hear the beating of the securi-ty guard's heart. In the middle of the city, a thousand sounds came into focus, which was overwhelming. The hum of the electric lines, the cluck-ing of chickens from nearby, the slam of a car door, and people talking near the entrance to the laboratory. Turning his attention to the house, he heard the whistling of a teakettle and the soft speech of someone speaking to a pet.

"He's inside," said Kuma. "Talking to his dog, Barkley."

Duro gave him a nod as he rolled up the sleeves of his shirt with methodical surety. "We're talking to your boss. Send someone inside to get him, or I'll make him regret hiring you."

"I told you, fuck off," said the guard, nodding his head as he turned the barrel of his weapon towards them.

"Are you sure you're willing to risk it?" asked Duro, opening his hands. At that distance, Kuma knew there was no way the guard could fire before Duro had disabled him.

Duro cracked his knuckles by squeezing his fists. The faint smile on his lips was a warning the guard should have taken, but he lifted his chin and sighted down his gun. The second security guard stepped to the side, never lifting his weapon.

Kuma detected the guard's muscle clenching a moment before Duro blurred forward. Two cracks of fists on skull echoed in the entryway and then the guard slumped to the ground without the weapon in his hand. The second guard rotated his weapon, but Duro held his hand up.

"We just want to talk to your boss."

At the peak of tension, the front door wheezed open until the curly haired Audrey peeked out.

"What's going...oh, it's you," she said, eyes darting. The door swung wide. "Come in. Ivan's upstairs working on a compound."

The four of them stepped over the fallen security guard. Audrey gestured to the second and said, "Harold, would you do something about him?"

"Yes, ma'am."

The interior was an open floor plan with doors to a bathroom, the backyard, and the stairs being the only exits. Framed posters of a Mystique performer Kuma quickly recognized as his younger sister Andromeda were on the wall along with paintings of events he assumed were from the invasion. A helix-like multicolored tower on a strange plain was the feature of the largest painting.

"Let me get him," said Audrey, heading up. A brown-and-white dog came bounding down the stairs, ears flopping. The dog, Barkley, ran right to Pandora, who seemed surprised by the attention. She crouched down and scratched his ears. He leaned into her and then unceremoniously plopped at her feet. A moment later, Ivan Charmer strolled down the stairs in a white lab coat.

"He's great therapy," said Ivan. "Barkley, that is. He always knows who's having the worst day."

Audrey made a face and pointed to his back as if to say it was always him.

Duro bowed low at the waist. "Thank you for seeing us, Ivan. I'm very sorry about having to handle your guard outside. Our matter is urgent and he seemed reticent to let us through."

"See, Audrey. Reticent. None of the gangs in the city would be so eloquent. I really should have visited the Undercity more. It's a whole 'nother world down there." He turned to Choo-Choo, who had been studying the strange tower painting. "Like that? I had it commissioned after you know what."

"What is it?" asked Choo-Choo, staring at it as if it were a live bomb.

"It's the infernal realm. Yeah, I know it doesn't look like what you expect, but if you can imagine, that place is closest to the birthplace of magic and the universe, which technically speaking, I think are the same thing," said Ivan as he went into the kitchen.

"Coffee or tea?"

"Tea please," said Duro.

As Ivan rummaged through his cabinets, producing a box of various tea and an electronic pot for heating water, he turned his head.

"Are you Choo-Choo?"

The bald waku startled, giving a short bow in reflex. He seemed surprised and nervous by the question. "I am."

"I knew it," said Ivan with a hand on his hip and his mouth cocked. "I recognized your physique from the manga."

"What?"

Duro cleared his throat. "I'm sorry to interrupt, but we wanted to speak in confidence to you about the topic I brought up before."

Ivan was filling water for tea. "I was hoping this was a social visit. Maybe you could show me some of the fights from the manga. Or maybe I could commission some new ones, but with more detail about what actually happened, not just the artist's rendition. You know, pick up the little details like the sexual tension between Kuma and Pandora that had to be there. It's so obvious from everything I read. But maybe I'm misreading it. Am I right?"

Kuma felt his cheeks warming and checked back to Pandora, forgetting Choo-Choo's presence. He stared at them with his jaw open.

"Babe," said Audrey from her stool by the counter. "That might be a little too much speculation."

"Right, sorry," said Ivan, pouring the cups of tea. He pulled out a little vial of brown liquid from his coat pocket and dripped it into the cups. Duro held out his hand to stop him.

"Oh, don't worry. An additive that I really enjoy. It helps the tea steep faster and enhances the flavor. I crafted it myself. But we can talk while we wait for the tea."

Duro inclined his head again. "We wished to speak to you about the vault door."

"Merlin's hairy balls, man, I told you, I can't get involved with that. Too much risk as much as I want to be a part of it, but you know, my adventuring days are over. I'm a businessman now, or at least that's what Audrey reminds me about on a daily basis."

She smiled. "If it were up to him, he'd be making experimental potions that make you fart bubbles, or be able to see the inside of some-one's skull."

"I don't even recognize myself anymore. Not the same kid who once held an illegal rave in the Glitterdome." He paused as he removed the tea bags, tossing them adroitly into the garbage can. "Sorry. I can't shut up when I'm nervous. But like I said, I can't mess with the vault."

Kuma stepped forward before Duro could speak. "I believe you might be interested in our cause based on a common enemy."

"And that is?"

"Dominion Thule."

A cup slipped out of Ivan's hand, crashing to the counter and spilling tea across the floor and onto Duro's pant leg. Audrey immediately popped up to help clean, but the fear in their eyes was unmistakable.

"He was your house manager," said Duro. "And now he's the head of the alliance clans and he means to wipe us out."

The stunned Ivan kept looking around as if he were expecting a purple rhino to come crashing through the wall. Choo-Choo reached for a cup of tea, but Ivan reached over and knocked it out of his hand.

"Don't drink that. I drugged it."

"What?" asked Choo-Choo, clenching his fist.

"Nothing harmful. Well," he said, rolling his head, "it would make you very suggestable for a short period of time. I wasn't going to do anything crazy, mostly I wanted to make sure you didn't kill me." He spread his hands. "Sorry."

Duro frowned. "You know this Dominion Thule."

Ivan hung his head. "Of course I know that creepy fucking bastard. It was like living with a ghoul. You'd be headed down to the kitchen for a bite to eat and bam! He'd be right there in your way, staring at you as if he knew that you'd been jerking it for the last hour to some Weird Circus porn."

"How could he be your house servant?" asked Choo-Choo.

"You have to understand my father was one of the most powerful people in the city that you'd never heard of. Possibly the world. He could snap his fingers and have a dozen different people in Beijing killed. You'd never know it was him, but he had that power. That's why Mr. Thule worked for him. He wanted those connections and some other things." Ivan leaned on the counter looking like his morning had been ruined. "What does he...? No wait, I don't need you to answer. Of course, it's the faez crystals. He wants to control them."

"He can use the stones to make powerful warriors," said Kuma.

Ivan chuckled. "I don't think he cares about the stones that you care about." They all looked at each other incredulously. "Don't get me wrong. You can do some badass shit, but it's the ones you don't want, the battery stones, that on the whole are more valuable. Sure, the ambers and emerald and all that are cool as hell, but there are only so many to go around. But there are way more of the other stones that mages are only waking up to. With magic weakened by the infernal realm no longer bumping uglies with ours, those stones are a way for mages to make up the difference."

"Then you will help us."

Ivan swallowed. He looked like he was going to pass out. "If word gets back to him..."

"We would never say a thing," said Duro.

A little laugh slipped out of Ivan's lips. "That slimy bastard has ways of finding things out. For all I know, he's got one of his lackeys waiting outside to slit my throat after you're gone." He leaned against the counter. "And don't think my guards will stop them. They're just for show. To keep the curious away. This place has been broken into more than once. His pet assassin Kavano sliced right through my unbreakable safe with his stupid sword."

Ivan made air quotes around *unbreakable*.

"You know this Kavano," said Duro, his jaw pulsing.

"Merlin's sweet and spicy butthole, you've got to be kidding me. He's back? Oh, Audrey, we're so fucked. We shouldn't even be talking to you right now." Ivan pushed his hand onto his forehead, sweeping his hair back in a brown wave. He was breathing heavily.

"What can you tell us about him?" asked Duro.

"Assassin by hire. As far as I know, there's no match for him unless you're bringing demon lords into the equation, but since the Invasion, that option is out. If you see him, run, but that's not going to help you either. Probably best to drop to your knees and hope he makes it quick."

"I am aware of his prowess," said Duro calmly.

"Prowess," said Ivan with a laugh. "That's like saying the Duke of Dong had a decently sized package."

"Babe," said Audrey with a furrowed brow.

"Sorry."

A car turned down the street with thumping bass making him flinch. When he looked back to them, Kuma stepped forward.

"You should help us because it's the honorable thing to do. Opposing Dominion Thule is good for the city. If he's the person you say he is, and I believe you, then stopping him now before he's gained too much power is what's most important right now. I know you're an honorable person based on your role in the Invasion."

"I spent that entire time being shamed into action. What I really wanted to do was stay in our bunker and drink myself to death in the bowels of the apocalypse."

"If not honor, then don't you want to stick it to him?" asked Kuma.

"I wish my twin was here. She would help you." He sighed. "She fought him once. Kavano. Barely survived. The only thing that saved her was...never mind."

Audrey collected Ivan's arm. "Shouldn't we help them? I remember the pain Mr. Thule caused your family. I hate to see you get hurt, but you know he won't stop with the Undercity. And once he's got control, you can be sure he'll come after you whether you help them or not. And besides, why else have you been working on it?"

Ivan placed his forehead against Audrey's. "This is why I love you, babe." He nodded. "Come on. I've got something for you."

"You do?" asked Duro.

"After our conversation, I started working on it despite myself. It was a problem. No, wait. An itch. A little fucking gnat in my brain and I had to get that bastard out either by making it, or putting a drill to my skull. Anyway, two of you can come up with me. The place is a bit of a mess and I don't want anything broken. Could kill us all in a haze of deadly gas."

Duro gestured to Choo-Choo, and the two of them followed. As they left, the dog Barkley trotted to the door and Audrey grabbed a rubber ball and headed outside, leaving Kuma alone with Pandora.

"Did you know anything about your grandfather's relationship with the Charmers?"

Shadows passed across her eyes in a haze of pain. "Of course not. I was being tortured while he played nursemaid to a bunch of rich socialites."

"I'm sorry, Pan. I didn't mean to ask it that way. It's just, what's going to happen if this plan works and you come face-to-face with him?"

"That's what you're worried about?" she spat back.

"I worry because I don't understand. I had caring parents that pushed me to be the best, but also respected me. What they did to you, your mother and grandfather, I don't even know how to comprehend it."

"If you want to know if I'm broken or not, I think you can guess the answer."

Her mouth was bent into a crooked line. Her eyes were unfocused.

"When we were in the canyon of ghosts and we wandered into the patch of lantern fungus, it was the most frightening experience of my life, but I would do it again if I had to."

"Why?"

He ran his hand through his hair. "It was the first time I let my walls down. Yeah, I know, it was the fungus doing the brick breaking, but during that time, I clutched to you like a lifeboat in a storm. So I know you're not broken. A bit fucked up, sure—not as bad as our host, but you know what I mean."

The corners of her lips curled slightly. "You know how to compliment a girl by calling her not as crazy as Ivan Charmer."

Kuma chuckled despite himself. "Yeah, not exactly poetry."

He approached and took her hand. The warmth between them sent shivers down his spine and sent tingles across his face as he faced her from only a foot away. The fact that she hadn't pulled back was a minor miracle.

"I'm sorry for what I said back when we started training. Accusing you of manipulating me. I made your problems all about me, and that wasn't fair. I see now what a shit-show you've been dealing with since you came to the Undercity. I can't imagine how much it hurts to have your family turn on you like that. But know that I'm here for you, whatever happens. I've got your back."

"I'd be honored to fight by your side." Her gaze narrowed. "You were talking about scrapping, right?"

He released her hand, placed his hands at his sides, and bowed deeply. Pandora's mouth rounded and she started to take a step forward when the door opened. The brown-and-white dog bounded in with a ball in its mouth, Audrey right behind. Barkley placed himself between them, so they both crouched down to scratch his back.

The others from upstairs appeared right after. Duro held a duffle bag over his shoulder.

"Remember, don't get it in your eyes, or well, you won't have any left," said Ivan, following them down.

He led them to the front door.

"Thank you, Ivan Charmer," said Duro with a deep bow. "Your help is invaluable to our cause."

Ivan looked unsure of his situation, leaning on one foot and scratching the back of his head.

"I get first dibs on the manga when all this is over. Issue one. Signed and numbered of course. By all of you."

"Of course," said Duro.

When they reached the SUV, Choo-Choo checked back to the house.

"Are all city mages this insane?"

Duro frowned. "In their own way, yes. Power has a way of warping one's soul if you're not disciplined against its effects. But this Ivan is more than the others. Significantly. But in his own way, he seems the most sane too, because he acknowledges the truth of his being. Come on, we have a directive to fulfill."

Twenty-Four

The journey across the Undercity wore on Gregor's bones. His feet and knees ached and his knuckles were scraped from climbing through the rocky tunnels like a common criminal. He wished Dominion would put in an easier access near the alliance caverns, but he was paranoid about being attacked.

"We're not far, boss," said Laird.

Gregor took a handkerchief from his pocket and dabbed the sweat from his forehead as he leaned against the wall. The tunnels were humid and warm. "If I'd wanted a sauna I would have fucking joined one. Why haven't one of you lazy fuckers handed me a bottle of water yet? Deacon would have if he were here."

Laird quickly handed over a bottle, which Gregor uncapped and chugged even though he knew it would hurt his stomach. He couldn't believe how much he missed Deacon. He'd been a constant thorn in his side, but now that he was gone, Gregor understood how much he relied on him.

The next cavern was the alliance headquarters. Gregor couldn't believe how much had been accomplished in a short amount of time. Before Dominion had taken over, the clans had spent their time squabbling and scrapping amongst themselves. He'd seen homeless camps in better shape, but now the place was looking like it might someday rival Big Dave's Town or the Terreno.

"Eleventh Gonka," muttered Gregor. "What kind of bullshit name is that for a bar? Laird, you're with me. The rest of you fucks can get a drink there, if they have anything that's worth drinking. Probably bottled maetrie piss that they're selling for three times the rate."

It wasn't just the environment that had changed. The alliance clan members weren't lounging around or drinking in public like some of his louts. The entire place looked industrious, which was a minor miracle to Gregor. He wouldn't have given two shits for the rabble that had existed here before, except for a few of their disciplined multi-stone waku, and now they were buzzing around like tattooed bees.

After the elevator, two guard stations, and a vault door that could have been in a bank, he finally found himself in the meeting room where

Dominion had cut off the Blue Dagger's head. Gregor threw himself

onto a chair, sweat making his shirt stick to his back.

"Get me a fucking beer, Laird, before I pass out."

While he waited, Gregor stared at the painting on the wall. Little

details stuck out from the landscape: a woman getting murdered in an

alley, an old man throwing bags of cats into the river, horrid creatures

lurking in the forest. The longer he looked at it, the more he wished he

was anywhere but that room. His inspection was cut short when the

gray-skinned maetrie entered.

"Dom, ol' friend, you've really spruced the place up since I was here

last. Though I have to say, you should find a better wall hanging than this

monstrosity. Don't know what it is, but it creeps me the fuck out."

Dominion Thule never took his eyes off Gregor. Nor did he make

a face, nor say a single word, but Gregor had the sudden feeling that he'd

made a mistake. He sat up tall and spread his meaty hands wide.

"Sorry. I'm a little worn out after the journey. My mouth got away

from me."

Dominion slid into the seat at the end of the table. Gregor re-

pressed the urge to wipe the sweat from his forehead.

"The Drops are planning on attacking this site," said Dominion.

"What? Really? I thought they were smarter than that. With your

crew, you'd slaughter them wholesale, a sight I'd like to see."

"You'll get your wish, Gregor. I want you to stay here for the time being and send for a large contingent of your best warriors. We're in a sensitive time right now. I cannot have anything go wrong."

"How large? You know I gotta keep my borders tight too. I'm stretched at the moment."

"Then you will become more stretched. I need your men right away," said Dominion with the surety of a general giving orders to his subordinates.

"How sure are you that they're going to attack?" asked Gregor.

"My spy tells me they've been planning something, but none of the details. They've kept their actions well-disguised, but I know enough that the focus of their planning is this location."

"Which is like a fucking fortress."

"Nevertheless, I want your men. They'll be used for patrols, bulking up our guards, and a few other specific requests."

"The extra waku gonna stop 'em?" asked Gregor.

"Those aren't my only adjustments. In addition to resources brought in from the Eternal City, I've relocated some particularly dangerous creatures into places that make an additional complication. While I'm confident that our defenses are robust, there's no time for complacency."

"Hey, if we need more waku, why not send for Deacon? I miss that scoundrel more than I ever thought I would."

Dominion's nostrils flared lightly. "Deacon will not be joining us in the near future. His training is going well, but he has much to learn before he can be as effective as I'd like him to be upon his return. But be assured, he will be coming back, hopefully sooner rather than later, but this threat is much too immediate."

"Understood." Gregor's fingers twitched. "What is it you want me to do? I could bloody a nose, break an arm when the time called for it, but these waku are a bit out of my league."

"You'll be in charge of the defense. Monitoring the guards, the outer door, elevator, that sort of thing. Making sure nothing unexpected happens. I recognize this is below you, but I need someone who under-stands attention to detail. I assure you that once this threat is past and we've dealt with the Drops once and for all, consolidating the Undercity, you will be rewarded handsomely."

Gregor winked. "I appreciate the confidence. I'll make sure they don't get inside. It'll be my head on the block as well if they do."

Dominion snapped his fingers, and the door behind him swung open. A clan member rushed in with two ornate boxes that were wide but flat. The first was large enough to hold a suit jacket. The second was no bigger than a data pad.

"These gifts from the Eternal City will make you a more effective warrior should the need arise. You'll want to put them on after our con-versation to give yourself time to adjust."

"Would be nice to crack some skulls myself like the old days," said Gregor, opening the smaller box first.

Two gold-and-bone bracers sat in the velvet catches. "What's this? I ain't exactly into jewelry, if you know what I mean?"

"Should the need arise, they'll allow you to access the portal wall and enter the Eternal City. It leads to a hidden garden of my making, so you'll be safe there, but do not leave the premises until one of my servants can collect you and bring you to my enclave. I cannot protect you on the streets."

Gregor pushed the box to the side and unclasped the larger one, pushing up the lid. The bracers from the first box had been easy to recognize. His mind didn't immediately understand what he was seeing in the second one. It looked like a long piece of curved black metal with jagged barbs sticking out. Smaller pieces of metal curled out from the main structure as if it were the spine of a snake with the flesh peeled away.

"What's this—"

Words fell short when he realized Dominion was no longer in the room. *Creepy bastard.* He was smart enough to know not to say it out loud, even if the pale-skinned maetrie was no longer in the room. The metal structure in the box made his skin crawl. It was one thing to put on the gold bracers, which would make him look like a rich socialite at the country club. The larger device looked like something out of a medieval torture room. He almost expected a rack to be on the wall, which reminded him that the strange painting of the olden forest was up there.

Gregor picked up the metal spine. It felt both sturdy and light, but he couldn't identify the material. If he had to guess, it was a type of steel but there was something glossy and black that made him think it wasn't metal at all.

"How do I put on this thing?"

He lifted it over his shoulders, measuring the length in relation to his arms. He had no intention of wearing it, since it seemed like it was meant to go under his clothes, but as the middle section bumped into his meaty shoulders, the entire length clamped onto his arms.

"Gah!"

The surprise had him trying to pull it off, but when it didn't budge he calmed. Laughter flitted to his lips as he thought about the spectacle he'd presented when he reacted to its touch. Gregor caressed the section along his forearm. The curved parts held his sweaty shirt to his skin. He looked for ways of removing it, but the structure held fast. Gregor reached back to his neck, looking for a clasp or button which might release it, when he felt a sudden heat from the material. The first touch was almost pleasant, like the beginning of a massage when the warm blanket was laid over top. The reminder got him excited because his massages always came with an exciting ending.

"I just need—"

The words cut short when pain ripped through his body. The first touches became bright fire across his shoulders and neck. It felt like metal barbs were sinking into his flesh, and as he screamed and tried to yank the device off, he watched as it cinched tighter around his arm. His shirt melted away, leaving no barrier between it and his skin. Gregor fell to his knees, the agony leaving him gasping for breath. He was sure he was having a heart attack, because he knew his body couldn't manage the strain. The not-metal was imbedding itself into his body. He could feel tendrils wrapping around his bone. It wasn't a device, but a living creature, and he'd never be able to remove it.

Twenty-Five

The weight of the earth above Kuma's head felt real after he returned from the city. He wasn't sure if it was an acknowledgement of how different each world was from the other. On the streets, the sky went on forever, while his life was bound by walls and ceilings that never moved. Or maybe it was the fact that their plan had taken shape and now they would have to carry it out. The challenges, while painful and frustrating at times, had been exciting and interesting. But they'd all been theoretical. Now they would have to embark for the alliance territory and put them into action.

"We're going to go over this one more time," said Brazio, standing at the front of the team. The Academy grounds had been vacated by the other students, who were sent to guard duty or other parts of the Pajot. Three separate muting boxes had been set around the area to prevent listening from a distance with an amber.

The entire team groaned. It'd been hours of constant drilling on the details.

"I know it's agonizing, but when we're in the thick of it, I don't want you to think about what to do. Only act." Brazio placed his hands behind his back. "One."

The entire team repeated at the same time in a droning singsong voice: "Leave home through the old maintenance tunnels so no one can see us."

"Two."

"Move fast and quiet. Kill anyone we find. Approach from the west."

"Three."

"We climb. Adrena and Choo-Choo in the lead. Pan and Navos scout. No sound. We make it to the top."

"Four."

"Cut the wires then cross the field. Yara and Kuma in the box, then the others cross when it's safe. We're inside."

"Five."

"Tick and Xylos to the elevator. Let no one up."

"Six."

"Duro and Einar to the door."

"Seven."

"Camina and Nikolai cut the power."

"Eight."

"Brazio breaks the door."

"Nine."

"Everyone but Tick and Xylos through the door."

"Ten."

"Let the killing begin."

"Eleven."

"Leave a surprise and head to the east."

"Twelve."

"Big breath and take a dive. Hope you survive."

"Thirteen."

"Regroup at the Great Arch."

"Fourteen."

"It's over. Return home."

Brazio winked. "Good." He looked over the group. "Now what happens if Tick gets shot and can't guard the elevator?"

Camina raised her hand. "I take his place and drop the charges."

Brazio snapped his fingers and pointed to Navos. "What happens if you fall off the cliff?"

"I do two hundred push-ups because I'm an idiot and catch up to the others, but only if I'm in the radius of the sound blocker. Otherwise, I make my way around to the front and try to lead the guards near the front away to distract them."

"You can save the push-ups until you return to the Pajot, assuming you make it there alive."

The alternative scenarios went on for another twenty minutes until Brazio checked back to Duro, who gave them a solemn nod.

"I think we're good."

Duro joined Brazio at the head of the team. "Everyone finish your final preparations. We'll be leaving in five hours. That should be enough time for you to eat and get a short rest. Hopefully we'll be back here in about twenty hours with the leadership of the alliance dead and the war over. If not, then Daraja will take the clan out of the Undercity. May the shadows keep them safe until they reach their new home."

"May the shadows keep them safe," muttered the entire group, knowing they wouldn't be joining them. For the team, it was either victory or death.

"Any last questions before we go?"

Xylos raised his arm enthusiastically, which made Brazio chuckle.

"Xylos...is this a real question?"

"Absolutely. Since this might be the last time we're all together and alive, I wanted to know...well, the entire team would like to know who would win in a duel between you and Duro? We've sorta got a lot of money riding on the answer, and since..."

The two waku glanced at each other with mirth on their lips.

"How much money?" asked Brazio, bringing laughter from the group.

"More than is sensible," said Xylos, wincing.

"Should I tell them?" Brazio asked the warleader, who lifted both shoulders. "We already fought your duel in a cavern far south of here."

Everyone sat up tall. Kuma studied both waku for signs of the winner.

"And?" asked Xylos with his palms up.

Brazio smirked. "It was a robust fight. We both learned new techniques on using our stones."

The entire team groaned.

"You're seriously not going to tell us?" asked Xylos.

"When we return to the Pajot after a successful mission, we'll tell you who won. Might even schedule a rematch," said Brazio, which had the entire team laughing. "Now, get out of here. Go rest, or whatever you need to do in preparation."

As everyone filtered out, Kuma caught Pandora coming up from the side, so he slowed so he could talk to her.

"Hey."

"Nervous?" he asked.

Pandora looked like she was being held together with a piece of string.

"We've been training like banshees for weeks, preparing for this day, and now that it's here, I can't think about anything but what my mother said to me. It doesn't help we've been sitting and talking for the last few hours. I'm used to being in motion."

"Want to do a little sparring? Enough to erase the jitters? I know I could use it. My legs were bouncing the entire time."

Pandora smirked. "I could use a rematch."

Kuma checked over his shoulder to see the others entering the main building.

"Use the training grounds in back?"

"Meet you there."

She burst into a run, forcing him to use his emerald to catch up, but her sapphire made it easier for her to pull ahead. When he reached the back grounds, which were tucked between the wall of the cavern and the generator building for the Academy, she was standing with her curved blades out.

"Not even gonna let me get warmed up, are you?" he said.

Pandora sprung into an attack, blades like a blender. His legs were tugged forward while he was pulling his weapons out to block. He cycled Heavy and when she relented, leapt to the left with Lightness. She followed, arms pinwheeling. The sound of blades singing through the air followed. They bounced around the grounds, using the walls and rocks as springboards, never clashing except for passing blades.

"No stalactites for you here," she said, crouched low like a tiger on the prowl.

He opened his mouth as if he were going to speak and leapt high with Lightness. On the way down, he cycled as Heavy as he could manage to keep her from knocking him off course with a Push. The maneuver was risky, but it would force her to flee, fight, or get knocked down.

He felt the Push against his chest like a heavy wind, but his weight made dislodging his arc impossible. Her eyes went wide as he landed atop her, using an "X" attack to knock away her blades. Before he could get the tip of his weapon against her throat for the win, she kicked out his knee, forcing him to roll over.

The ground was just another battlefield. They fought on their sides with kicks and blades, the clash of steel ringing through the air. Kuma cycled between Light and Heavy rapidly, leaving no room for her to use her sapphire. It was a technique he'd been working on, but hadn't applied to a scrap yet.

Feeling confident and curious, Kuma triggered the ruby when he cycled to Light and kicked off the ground to regain his feet. Pandora anticipated him, hitting him with a Push, but instead of sending him away spinning, they exploded apart like two opposite magnets.

He bounced back to his feet at the same time as Pandora, but paused as he tried to understand what had just happened. Kuma dropped the ruby and planned another arcing attack, when Pandora's gaze shot over his shoulder.

"What are you two doing?" asked Tick, who'd run up. His face was blotchy red.

"Blowing off some steam," said Kuma. "What's up?"

Tick pursed his lips, reticent to speak. "We're leaving now."

"Now? I thought we were getting some rest?" he asked.

"They caught a spy, and Duro's not sure if he got word out before they grabbed him."

Pandora joined him at his side.

"A spy? Who?" she asked.

The frown told him that it was going to be bad. He hoped it wasn't Brazio. "Better see for yourself."

As they followed the smaller waku towards the front of the Academy grounds, she said, "What did you do back there? I wasn't expecting to fly apart like that."

"I used my ruby, but I don't know what it did," he said.

"It felt like I was really light, like I had an emerald."

He slowed as the implications hit him, but he didn't have a chance to speak, because he spotted a familiar figure kneeling before the war-leader with a blade to his throat. It was Natsuo Torres, the former fixer and business manager of the Razor clan. He had tears running down his cheeks as Brazio glowered at him.

"How could you?"

Brazio backhanded Natsuo, leaving him curled on the ground.

Kuma came up next to Camina, who stared at the spectacle with abject horror.

"Brazio found him hiding behind a wall in the kitchen with some sort of communication device, but it burnt up before they could examine it."

A pit formed in Kuma's stomach. Their plan was over before it began. If Natsuo had sent their plans, which they'd been repeating over and over, to someone outside the Pajot, then it would only be a matter of hours before they knew about the attack.

Natsuo climbed back to his knees, hands shaking as he held them up.

"I have a secret family in the city. I thought no one knew. Dominion told me he'd kill them if I didn't spy for them."

Brazio grabbed him by the shirt and lifted him off his feet, barking in his face.

"You've been spying on us this whole time? Even in Razor?"

Kuma couldn't believe it when Natsuo nodded. He'd been a member of the clan for decades. Niran had trusted him explicitly.

"I only gave a little at first, but he kept asking for more, threatening worse things. I wanted to say something, but I couldn't. They were watching her and my kids. That gray-skinned bastard would rip their hearts out."

"So instead you sold ours to the highest bidder," said Brazio, dropping Natsuo to the ground.

"Brazio," said Duro, flatly. "We don't have time for this. The damage is done. We have to act."

The older waku nodded absently. He pulled out a blade and grabbed a shrieking Natsuo.

"You're lucky we have to leave or I'd cut you into pieces and put you back together for the next five years."

"I promise—"

The rest of the words never left his lips as Brazio pushed the tip of his blade into Natsuo's chest. The gasp of surprise was followed by a gurgle and then a slumping to the concrete. Brazio wiped his blade off on Natsuo's shirt before returning it to its sheath.

"Grab your things," Duro said to them. "We're leaving in ten minutes."

"But the spy," said Navos.

"If he got word out, it'll take time for them to get back to the alliance area. They won't expect us to carry out the plan so soon and might not be hurrying."

"But if they are?" asked Navos.

"Then we're walking into a trap." He looked out over the group. "If any one of you wants to back out, now is the time, but I'm leaving in ten minutes and I hope you're all with me."

Kuma checked to his teammates, hoping no one would leave. Duro examined them all one last time, before giving the signal for "Be ready." He stalked away towards the Academy building where their gear was waiting. No one spoke. Then everyone followed.

Twenty-Six

Travel across the Undercity was made in silence. The training, the stakes—everyone seemed to be repressing even their breathing as Duro led them through endless caverns. Until three years ago, Pandora had never stepped foot in the Undercity, but now it felt like home. Maybe earlier in her life, she might have clung to the faded memories of Chicago, when her father would cook her pancakes and bacon before school. But she couldn't remember the details anymore, except for the creases around his smile and the way the bacon sizzled on the grill. The Eternal City had been a horror show. Only looking back did she understand how awful it was. During that time, she'd been so intent on impressing her mother and grandfather, becoming the warrior they wanted her to be, that she hadn't realized how much of her humanity they'd been stripping away. Which left the Undercity and the Drops as the first real home she'd experienced in her short life. She wasn't just risking her life to save herself, but for Triana, and Vasy, and Elani—and everyone else in the Drops clan. It was the main difference between humans and maetrie. The city elves sought control over others and were willing to do anything to achieve it. Humans, for all their flaws, wanted community, wanted family. Pandora thought of it as the difference between her sapphire Pushes and Pulls. The maetrie thrived when they could tear bonds apart, while humans were best when they pulled together. It was a strategy older than time, one they were employing in the shadows of the Undercity.

For the first time in weeks, she didn't feel the need to count primes. Whatever happened in the next few hours, either she'd be rid of her grandfather, or she'd be dead in a hole without a thought in her head. Ahead of her, Kuma ran next to Choo-Choo, their previous animosity buried by the needs of the clan. If that wasn't proof of the superiority of the human condition, then she wasn't sure what was.

The muted grays of her enchanted vision made the tunnels and caverns seem washed out. Duro had given them elixirs to help them see in the dark. It wasn't the first time she'd used such potions, but they made her eye sockets feel like they'd been dipped in cold water.

During a brief rest when Duro gave them a chance to empty their bladders, grab a bite to eat, and shake out their limbs, Pandora spotted

Choo-Choo looking pensive as he stared at an unusual knife in his hands. She approached him, catching that the hilt was etched with words, but he slipped the weapon away before she could see what it said.

"You okay?"

His mouth twitched even as his eyes were dead. "Thinking about Valeria."

The memory of his sister was unusual in a time like this. Pandora glanced back to where Brazio was standing.

"Emilio..."

He lifted a shoulder in forced casualness. "I don't want to lose Vasy or Mami. That's all."

"Good," she said. "Focus on that. We're doing this for them and everyone else in the Drops."

Choo-Choo nodded but she wasn't entirely sure he was being honest with her, but further conversation ended when Duro signaled for the journey to continue.

A short time later, they entered a large cavern with a body of water at the center and a tall cliff on the opposite side. Thirteen waku stared at the first obstacle that they'd been training to defeat for months. Three instructors and ten students. The plan made perfect sense in the safety of the Pajot, but standing outside the alliance caverns, the idea that only thirteen of them could end the war seemed ludicrous. Too many things had to go right for them to succeed.

Duro had given the signal for silent communication a half hour before, so he made the sign for a single-file line to circle around the water. The listening devices weren't yet in range, so they didn't have to active the mute box, but no one wanted to make an errant noise and give away their approach.

Pandora happened to be third from the front as they snaked around the small lake. It wasn't more than a hundred feet across, but the stone around it sloped precipitously, suggesting it was deeper than it looked. The black surface was mirror smooth. A ledge went around the side. Pandora noticed she wasn't the only one staring to their left, expecting something to come bursting out of the water to drag them below, ending their plan before it began. She checked back to Tick, who was three people behind her, to see him staring intently as if there was something lurking below. When a bubble of air came up at the center of the lake, the pace of travel increased.

On the other side, there was about thirty feet between the cliff and the water. The entire crew stayed near the wall, even though there was no indication that anything lived in the lake.

Preparations for the climb began when Nikolai pulled out the black box they'd stolen from Tinkers and set it at the base of the cliff. When the green light switched on, the silence hardened. They'd only trained with the mute box a few times, but Pandora found she abhorred the effect. It made her feel like she didn't exist, but it was the only way up the cliff without triggering the sensors near the top. The field of sound negation was pointed upward. When they'd learned the device was powered by uncolored faez crystals, they were able to swap out the original crystal for a larger stone, giving it much more range.

Unlike the others climbing, Pandora didn't wear a harness. She'd learned she could fall from just about any height in the Undercity without injuring herself. The other sapphire, Navos, hadn't managed falls more than thirty feet. The difference was being able to slow herself from a higher distance using the cliff as a braking device. As long as she was within ten feet of stone, she was confident she could stop herself using angled Pulls and Pushes.

Duro held up three fingers and Pandora heard their collective voices in her head: *We climb. Adrena and Choo-Choo in the lead. Pan and Navos scout. No sound. We make it to the top.*

She found right away that the rock was different on this cliff. The Night Wall was mostly granite, but this one had softer stones. Within the first ten feet, she grabbed a jug hold only to have the piece break away. Thankfully, she was able to drop it safely to the ground, then she signaled the rest of the team to be careful.

As a scout, she climbed twenty feet ahead of the lead climbers, Adrenalynne and Choo-Choo, looking for problems that might cause delays. She had a piece of glow-in-the-dark chalk that she used to mark the route. It was only faintly visible from up close. She climbed faster than Navos, who was lower to her left. At the middle section of the cliff, there were uneven shadows that she hadn't been able to see from below. She knew there were large patches of obsidian which required careful passage, or outright avoidance, but that wasn't what she was seeing.

As she neared the blotches of shadow, she realized they were depressions in the wall. She couldn't tell if they were caves or just sections that had fallen away in years past. During the pre-invasion times, she'd heard there were frequent earthquakes that had broken loose rock structures that weren't well connected.

From twenty feet below, she realized they were caves. Not only that, but she spotted white goo hanging off the edges that looked like guano, or bat feces. If there was a large colony of bats in the caves, that might give them away should they come flying out. Especially because the mute box would inhibit their sonar, making them fly erratically. She made her way to the edge, taking care not to put her hand in the slick guano. Pandora was about to pull herself over the edge when she spotted anchor bolts in the wall beneath the cave. It wasn't unusual to see, since the alliance clans had probably explored this section of their territory in the past, but the bolts looked recent and much larger than what would be required for climbing. She spied at least three along the base, and then more above the caves, leading towards the top.

The team was about forty feet below her and working their way up quickly. Avoiding the caves wouldn't be difficult, especially with the pre-sunk anchor bolts to use. The bigger question was, why were they on the wall at all? She examined the bat feces. She wasn't an expert, but it was dried out and appeared old. Had they relocated the bats because they were setting off the sensors? That would make sense given the larger anchor bolts. A large cage could have been lowered down to collect them, but why bother with a colony of flying mammals? She would have imagined they would have just thrown a grenade into the hole and eliminated the problem quickly.

As she stuck her head above the edge, she used her sapphire radar to probe the interior of the largest cave, glad that the field of silence wouldn't affect her ability. There was something odd about the interior of the hole. It wasn't the shape she expected. Most caves had been created by water or other erosion, which gave them a certain feel, but this one seemed to be filled with curved pipes in back, which were much too smooth to have been created by natural phenomena.

Navos had almost reached her position, but she waved him off, wanting to examine the interior for problems before the team had to make its passage. Pandora pulled herself onto the uneven ledge, peering into the darkness. It seemed to resist her enchanted vision. If she could hear herself, she'd know that she was breathing heavily, but the absence of sound made her feel like she was floating through deep space.

Pandora reached into her side pouch, producing a headlamp and switching it to the dimmest setting of red light. A bit of motion to her left had her startling only to find that it was Navos pulling himself to the ledge. He must not have seen her signal, but now that he was there, his presence made her feel better. She clicked on the crimson light and pushed it into the cave, revealing the collection of black curved pipes she'd expected from using her sapphire radar. The muscles in her chest relaxed when she realized they were benign. Pandora was reaching to turn the light off when the pipes shifted toward her, forcing her to re-evaluate what she was seeing.

They weren't pipes.

They were tentacles.

Before she could step towards the edge, a tentacle slammed into her chest, throwing Pandora off the cliff.

Twenty-Seven

Kuma was in the middle of the pack and to the right of Choo-Choo. The loose stone was making for a slower climb. No one wanted to knock a piece onto another climber. They hadn't thought to bring helmets since the Night Wall was made of granite.

They were a third of the way up the cliff and about forty feet from Pandora, who seemed to be investigating a cave higher on the wall. Kuma signaled to Yara on his left to give him more slack in the rope. He hated being tethered to everyone else, but his emerald made him an ideal anchor should something happen to the rest of the group. His job was to find cracks in which to jam pitons to use as stationary ledges. If someone slipped, he could push himself against the wall and switch to

Heavy to keep the entire team from getting pulled down.

While they'd practiced climbing in the silence of the mute box, it unnerved him. He'd never realized how much he used sound to understand what was going on around him. It wasn't the same to jam his foot onto a ledge and not hear the scrape of his shoe. Even the thump of his heartbeat was absent.

Kuma leaned back, holding onto the latest piton to see how Pandora and Navos were progressing. He could no longer see Pandora, as she had stepped into the cave, but the blond-haired waku was leaning on the edge watching her. A shift in Navos' body language had Kuma sending his amber upward. He wasn't sure what he was seeing when a shape went flying out from the wall, plummeting past them. It happened so fast, he didn't realize it was Pandora falling until she'd flown by on her way to the ground. His gut knew that she was too far from the wall to slow her descent as she'd done so many times during practice.

He reached behind to grab a blade and cut himself loose from the harness when Brazio signaled upward. A glistening black tentacle had Navos around the waist and was bashing him against the stone wall. Kuma checked below but saw no sign of Pandora, so he cut the harness, put the blade in his teeth, and began climbing upward.

Safety went out the window as he scrambled upward, using his Lightness at difficult moments. His uncle Brazio beat him to the ledge, hung on with one hand, and attacked the tentacle that had Navos. Other appendages snaked out and tried to grab him, but Duro reached the ledge next, and the two warleaders managed to hold off the tentacles.

The absence of sound made the fight feel like it was in slow motion even as it happened frighteningly quick. Tentacles writhed around the entrance to the cave, fending off their attempts to rescue Navos, who was looking battered from the constant smashing. The blond waku was using his sapphire to keep from being pulled into the cave, so the tentacles were trying to dislodge him. If he was knocked unconscious, it would be the end.

Kuma looked for Tick because of the tiger's eye. The creature looked similar to the one in the lake that had pulled them into the depths. He hadn't been able to stop it, but maybe he could convince him to let Navos go. Tick was about fifteen feet below the ledge, holding a clawed hand upward as if he were trying to impact the creature, but it was too much for him. The others were trying frantically to reach Navos, but the tentacles were faster than even the strongest waku. Having to fight on a vertical surface was limiting their abilities. If only Pandora hadn't fallen. Her sapphire was strong enough to hold the tentacles at bay. When he checked below, he saw her swimming back to shore, but too far away to affect the fight. They needed to rescue Navos soon, but that would require another sapphire.

The fight with Pandora when he used the ruby gave him an idea. He maneuvered to the left, being careful not to get knocked off by anyone else. When he was close enough to Navos, he activated his ruby.

The sensation was overwhelming. He nearly let go of the wall. Vertigo slammed into him, followed by heady rushes of power. The powers of every stone in use around him was flowing through his body. He felt elated and sick at the same time. The same effect seemed to be hitting everyone nearby, as their attacks slowed. Kuma almost stopped using the ruby, especially when Yara was knocked from the wall to his left, but her emerald would keep her safe for landing.

Kuma gripped the wall with the strength of a topaz. He reached out with his borrowed sapphire, Pulling on the tentacle to keep it from smashing Navos against the rocks. Xylos noticed what he was doing next and added his own Pull. The rest of the team picked up on what was happening, and before long, the tentacles moved in slow motion, giving Duro a chance to gain the ledge.

The distraction gave Kuma a chance to join Duro. He almost regretted it when he saw inside the cave. An enormous beak stuck out from the center of the tentacles. The creature was pulling itself out to use its mouth since they'd stifled the tentacles. Kuma slashed out at the curved beak, but the hard material resisted his strike.

Choo-Choo and Brazio joined them on the ledge. The former helped Duro free Navos, while his uncle fought the tentacles with blade and stones. The creature kept edging forward, using its tentacles to push against the wall, while they tried slashing the soft flesh around the beak, but even that was so thick they could barely split it with a topaz-powered strike.

As the creature moved out, there was less room on the ledge. The others on the wall were using their borrowed sapphire to keep the tentacles at bay, but once the ledge was gone they'd have no way to fight it. Kuma motioned for the others, signaling as best as he could to Push the beast back into the hole, but he couldn't get the message across while trying not to get his arm ripped off by the snapping beak.

Then everything happened at once.

Brazio slipped to the side, finding less protected flesh around the back of the head. When his blade struck true, the beak spread wide as if it were in a perpetual scream. The creature pushed forward, forcing Kuma to throw himself to the right, barely grabbing a crack and jamming his foot inside to hold onto the wall. But the creature's momentum continued, spilling the other waku from the ledge, right as they were freeing a nearly unconscious Navos.

The trajectory of the beast had Kuma screaming for everyone below to get out of the way. It was trying to escape from the cave, but in its haste and pain it'd forgotten it was high on a ledge, and the sapphire Pulls were continuing its momentum.

The creature slipped over the edge with Navos still in its grip. Choo-Choo grabbed hold of the blond waku as Duro hammered at the tentacle. They were the only anchor keeping the beast from tipping.

Then it released Navos.

The creature fell like a meteor, slamming into the base of the cliff. In the chaos of the moment, Kuma couldn't tell if anyone had been taken down with it. He reflexively started to call out when he heard his throat gurgle and the heavy breathing of his fellow waku still on the wall. The meaning of the return to sound left him frozen. The mute box had been smashed by the creature's impact. They would have to climb without making a single sound.

Twenty-Eight

The infernal creature had almost fallen onto Yara's head. She threw herself out of the way as it crashed into the rocky ground, its beak cracking from the impact. As she climbed to her feet, the sudden return of her heartbeat had her freezing with concern.

To her left, Pandora had been climbing out of the lake, soaked and dripping. She'd frozen too. The beast had smashed the mute box, leaving them without a critical piece of their plan. Even worse, she spotted the mustached Einar lying beneath a clump of tentacles that looked like a plant that had gone too long without watering. She'd never really connected to the older Drops member, but he was a member of her clan—and that's all that mattered.

Yara checked up the cliff to where the rest of the team was located. They clung to the rocks or stood on the ledge. No one was moving because they knew to make a sound was to give their position away. At least they'd gotten Navos away from the tentacle before it'd fallen or they'd be down two members of their team.

She signaled up to her father, who was peering over the ledge.

What do we do?

Her question was met with a shrug. Did this mean they had to abandon the plan? As soon as the words entered her brain, her hands turned to fists at the thought of losing a chance to kill Deacon. Yara had never gotten over the way he'd used her. When he'd arrived at the Academy, he'd been like no one else in the clan, and that had been part of the appeal. She'd always been in her family's shadow. If it'd only been her uncle, Niran, and her father the warleader, she might have been able to deal with it, but Kuma had always outshone her from up close. It was like trying to light a match near a bonfire. She'd hated him for it, which was why she'd hooked up with Deacon in the first place, to counter Kuma's friendship with the Crow. But she'd found herself attracted to Deacon despite herself. If he'd stayed the arrogant bad boy, she could have seen herself getting tired of the act, but he'd been incorporating their ways, making himself a hybrid of the Crows and Razor. She'd found it hard to resist.

So the day she woke to her uncle carrying her after Deacon had drugged her, she'd wanted to murder him. He'd clearly been planning on trying to convert her after the betrayal, which almost made it worse. How could he think that she would follow him after he wiped out her family? How could he think that she would do that? And did anyone else? It'd made her realize that he'd never truly learned the lessons of the Razor clan during his time at the Academy. He'd taken what he wanted and discarded the rest. Which was why she couldn't wait to drive a blade through his skull.

But that would never happen unless they could make it up the wall. No one was moving for fear of making a sound.

Yara stepped back and signaled to the others about Einar's demise. She received a nodded fist as acknowledgement. They'd expected that not all of them would make it, but not that they would lose someone so soon.

As she stared at the wall she knew they couldn't climb as they had planned before. They'd never once not made a sound requiring them to start over. Her arms still ached with the memory of push-ups after each failure.

But maybe they didn't all have to climb.

Yara signaled to her father to drop a rope. There wasn't enough room on the ledge for everyone, but she needed to explain her idea. After a few minutes of configuring, a rope was slowly lowered to her location. She clipped into the harness and let them lift her to the ledge, where she immediately put her lips to both Duro's and Brazio's ears to explain.

"Only one needs to climb. There are caves all the way up. We can use them like steps and then make the final push from there."

The two warleaders conferred silently. The abundance of ambers made it easy to whisper without triggering the sensors at the top of the cliff. Once they'd agreed and informed the rest of the team, her father started putting on a harness and coiling up a rope, but paused when she touched him on the arm and pointed to her chest.

I want to climb, she mouthed.

Her father's eyes creased with understanding then he nodded. Yara wanted to believe that she wasn't driven by the faint smile of approval, but she knew in her heart that she craved it. The needs of the clan had superseded hers, and she'd always understood, but it never made it easier.

As Yara approached the wall with the rope hooked to her belt, she knew that she wasn't the best climber of the team. It wasn't that she was bad, but there were better members to accomplish the task. But she didn't care. It'd been her idea and she wanted to be the one to make it happen. For too long she'd been in their shadows. No longer.

A crack went up the wall from the right of the ledge. Yara jammed her hand in the gap, and with her toes firmly on an edge, she pushed upward. Her topaz made it easy to grip and the emerald provided a boost when she needed to make herself Light for difficult sections. She made it to the next cave, about forty feet above the one she'd left. Yara dropped the rope and then leaned against the wall to brace herself to allow Choo-Choo to climb.

Once he reached her location, he took the rope and she continued climbing. The next section proved more difficult as it was mostly obsidian and they'd learned it was best to avoid the smooth rock if possible. She found herself stuck beneath a large field of the glossy black stone, and was traversing to her left when the hold broke. Yara was in no danger of falling as her other hand was firmly lodged in a crack, but the rock would bounce and trigger the alarms.

Yara snatched the piece out of the air before it fell out of reach. Hanging by one hand, the rock in her other, she exhaled slowly and shoved the piece into her pocket before continuing up the wall.

Using the caves as a series of ledges, she managed to lead the team up the cliff. When she reached the final cave, one that was barely big enough for one person to stand, she knew there wasn't going to be a way to get everyone up without being spotted or triggering the alarm. The amber stone helped her pick out the noise sensors because they hummed faintly with electricity. There were two, one on either side of the cliff, pointed downward so they didn't pick up sound from the alliance area.

Putting her knife in her teeth, she climbed horizontally until she reached the first sensor. As carefully as she could, she sawed through the wire until the little red light went out. When no alarm sounded, she breathed a sigh and crossed to the other side. When the second sensor was clipped, she risked driving an anchor into the wall using her topaz strength and dropped a rope down, which allowed the rest of the team to reach her location.

Twelve waku clung to the wall. Once they stuck their heads above the edge, they only had a short window to reach the other side and disable the soldados with automatic weapons on the other side before they were gunned down. But for the moment, it didn't matter to Yara, as she'd gotten them up the wall without incident.

Twenty-Nine

*F*our. *Cut the wires then cross the field. Yara and Kuma in the box, then the others cross when it's safe. We're inside.* The words echoed in Choo-Choo's head even as he stared at Brazio. He hated that those words were in the old Razor warleader's voice because he'd been the one to drill them. Camina tapped him on the shoulder, giving him the *hurry up* sign. He was assembling the person-sized box while he hung from an anchor bolt by his harness. The other Drops were arrayed across the bottom edge, preparing their parts of the plan.

Choo-Choo moved slowly, taking care not to drop a rod or connection device. The contraption required all the pieces to work. But he couldn't help but be distracted. Not for his own life. He checked back to Navos, who caught him looking and gave him a wry grin, a wave of blond hair hanging in his eyes.

The angle bracket took longer than he wanted to connect to a rod because it'd been bent slightly during the fight with the tentacled creature. As he worked it straight using his topaz strength, he noticed the tattoo on his inner forearm. VS-VS-TS. The initials for his mami and two sisters. He missed his older sister, Valeria, and would do anything to keep Vasy and his mother safe. If the plan failed, they'd have to flee the Undercity to a realm secret enough that Daraja had told none of them where they might be going.

Thinking about Val made him glance at Brazio again. He'd been the one to kill his sister in a duel, an event that Choo-Choo couldn't bring himself to forgive him for. He reached into his shirt to pull out the special blade he'd prepared for this day. On the hilt, he'd etched his sister's name: Valeria. When the opportunity presented itself, he planned on driving the blade deep into Brazio's heart. If he struck fast enough, there'd be no time to activate his black diamond, or heal him with an opal. He wouldn't do it before the attack was complete, but once Dominion was dead, Choo-Choo planned to strike. He put the short blade back in his shirt and refocused on the task.

As he pushed on the bracket, the iron snapped at the bend. The noise startled everyone nearby. He held up the broken section. The rod would have to be connected another way. He reached into his bag to pull out the remaining pieces to find one of the rods had been broken in half.

"Shadows below," he whispered, shaking his head.

The box was meant to protect Yara when he threw her across the field. He'd practiced for the last week, watching videos on Olympic hammer throwers to improve his technique. He'd been able to get her all the way across the field in a single throw, but that wouldn't be possible without the hexagonal box.

Choo-Choo peeked above the ledge using a mirror. The space was almost exactly as Duro had planned it. The opposite side was three hundred and fifty feet away, give or take a few. A wooden wall with open windows provided an easy shooting lane, and four soldados stared into the dimly lit area with rifles in their laps. The only difference between their practice field and the real one was a cluster of stone pillars near the left side that held up the dome-like cavern; otherwise, it was a perfect match.

The plan had been for both Kuma and Yara to be thrown in their protective boxes. Then it would be their task to get out of their containers and eliminate the shooters before they could sound the alarm, which was a set of buttons on the back wall behind the soldados. Reaching them would take the soldados a few seconds at best. The hope had been that the team's sudden approach would put them in a split-second decision of using their weapons or getting off their seats to hit the button. It wasn't possible now without a second box.

He signaled Duro that the box was unrecoverable. They'd have to find another way to cross.

Nikolai unslung a rifle from his shoulder. They'd brought a single weapon as a backup, but two shots, three hundred and fifty feet through a small window, was marksman-level shooting, and most of them were a spray-and-pray kind of gunman. If they couldn't take out the shooters, it'd be a bloodbath trying to cross the field. And if they couldn't cross the field, the plan was finished. He couldn't let his sister and mother down, nor lose his chance to kill Brazio. Not after all the tragedies that had already befallen their family. Honor demanded his revenge.

The entire team seemed disheartened by the problem. It was already going to be hard enough and now it seemed impossible. Too many things had to go right for them to cross the field without the alarm being tripped. The only way they could make it was if there was a distraction.

With an idea forming, Choo-Choo unhooked from his anchor and crossed horizontally to Tick's position, where he explained his plan. The scrawny waku nodded, so Choo-Choo moved to the warleader's position. No one disagreed, so the new strategy was spread amongst the team. He caught Navos staring at him after he learned what was going to happen. Choo-Choo tapped on his chest over his heart, receiving the same gesture from Navos.

It took Tick a half-hour to return from the bottom of the cliff after a quick descent on the rope line. A cloud of biting insects circled around him, but his tiger's eye kept their mandibles at bay. When everyone confirmed their readiness, Tick sent the insects across the field. The soldados didn't notice it until they were about a hundred feet away. They pointed at the cloud but made no move towards their weapons or the alarm. Choo-Choo could hear laughing and joking about the approach, which grew to concern as the insects continued their passage.

When the biting insects entered the first window, pandemonium ensued. Three of the soldados were no longer staring across the field, but slapping the bugs that were feasting on their unprotected flesh.

With the distraction in full swing, the team made their move. Without a teammate to throw, Choo-Choo was first over the edge, running straight for the lone shooter. His topaz gave him a good lead while Brazio filled in for Einar to throw Kuma in the box. The gunman lined up on Choo-Choo as he ran across the field. He was bracing for the impact of the bullet to knock him off his feet, and hoped that the injury wouldn't be fatal enough that an opal couldn't heal it.

The gunshot made him flinch. When he realized he hadn't been shot he looked up to see the shooter no longer in the window and the box containing Kuma landing near the wall. The other soldados were still fighting the bugs as they tried to make a run for the alarm, but Kuma burst out of the box and threw himself through the window. Three non-waku were no match for his blades, and the threat was eliminated. Everyone slowed to a walk, reaching the other side with the guards dead.

"Well done," said Duro, gesturing to Choo-Choo. "But the shadows do not care if we succeed, so keep your guard up. We lost Einar, so Choo-Choo, I'm going to need you at the door with me and Brazio."

The news sent a wave of conflicting emotions through Choo-Choo. He'd have the chance to kill Brazio that he'd always wanted once they were through the door. The hardest part of their mission was getting into the protected area, and Choo-Choo had no doubt that their waku, even without Brazio, could easily clean up the alliance leaders.

"Okay, everyone, five, six, seven. Go to it," said Brazio, signaling with a twirl of his fingers.

As everyone split up, Choo-Choo's gaze drilled into Brazio's back. They moved through the hallways until they reached the elevator, where two guards barely looked up in time to find Duro's blades slicing through their throats. Tick took position at the top of the elevator with his cloud of biting insects like a halo around his head, while Xylos took out a screwdriver to disable the power to the elevator.

Below them in the wide cavern, the place looked like another version of Big Dave's Town. Alliance clan members moved through the newly formed streets, and buildings were being erected in all the open spaces. The neon sign of a bar near the elevator glowed with purpose. No one below had detected their intrusion, and if everything went as well as he hoped, they'd be diving into the waterfall soon enough.

Choo-Choo joined the two warleaders at the vault door. The silvery surface was imposing as was the red line painted on the floor showing where they couldn't cross without triggering defensive measures. A big wheel was fixed on the front, but it was only used for manual openings— the door was normally triggered by an inner control center. The only cameras in the area were focused on the bottom of the elevator, which they'd bypassed by coming up the cliff.

Brazio handed him a gas mask, which brought them face-to-face. Choo-Choo didn't grab it right away, but his sister's killer never noticed. They'll drilled this part of the plan a dozen times, but it'd been on a makeshift wooden version that had none of the real protections. Unlike the other training tasks, they wouldn't be able to confirm that it would work until it had.

"Fifteen minutes to power cut, better get spraying," said Duro as he went to check on the lookout at the elevator.

The nozzle spray was Brazio's job, while Choo-Choo took the pump. The elder waku shot a green liquid at the circular handle, forming a cloud. It started working right away, eating through the enchanted steel as if it were butter, but even as rapidly as it was working it would still take time. He kept up the pump with a piston action until they'd burned through the outer layer, then Brazio focused the spray until it was a beam, filling up the interior section with the alchemical acid.

With the spraying complete and the cloud dissipated, Brazio yanked off his gas mask and motioned for Choo-Choo to do the same.

"Now we wait," said Brazio, checking his watch. They had five minutes until the power was cut. "Wasn't sure this was going to work like that mage said, but damn if his estimates weren't dead-on."

The older waku shot Choo-Choo a curious glance when he said nothing. Brazio crouched away from the red line while rubbing his jaw. He pointed to a scar on his cheek.

"You know, your sister gave me this. First time I'd ever been cut."

Choo-Choo growled under his breath and looked away. He couldn't stand hearing Brazio talk about Valeria, but was afraid if he said something it would only trigger his unresolved anger at the worst moment.

"No one had ever pushed me like that. Not until I dueled the war-leader. Your sister was special. I wish we'd never had to scrap and then Valeria could be here with us. I would have been honored to fight at her side."

"Do not speak her name."

Brazio rose. He seemed to take up a larger space than his size. He got in Choo-Choo's face but his expression wasn't one of challenge but sadness. He put a finger in Choo-Choo's chest, right where the blade was hidden.

"After this is over, if you want to duel me, warrior to warrior, without stones, I will fight you. I don't want to. Your mother has grieved enough, but I do not want to deny you your revenge should you desire it. It is your right. But know that this will not soften your heart. When I was a young warrior, I fought like a demon, killing anyone who dared to hurt my clanmates. My thirst was unquenchable."

He held up his hand, which was marred with white lines.

"These hands are soaked in blood. I offered a duel at the slightest provocation and my mouth was cunning enough to ensure they would fight me. Even when they did not, I found reasons to incite battles which we invariably won.

"But that ended the moment my blade went into her chest. I had admired her from afar. She was a warrior like no other, and after it was over I realized the damage that I had inflicted. You would not know this but there was a time that our two clans were closer. My brother tried many times to sow peace in the Undercity, using words rather than blades. Had I listened to him and not fought your sister, we might have been one clan years ago. This made us both weaker, and when the stones were discovered, things changed so quickly that it was almost too late."

Brazio gestured to the world around them with his eyebrows.

"*This* is my fault. And it's why I started listening to my brother, because he was wiser than I. Don't let your anger, your hatred, destroy what you're trying to build. What *we're* trying to build. But if you must have your revenge, I will accept your duel. After."

The standoff ended the moment Duro came back. He gave them both a flat-lipped glance before pointing to his watch.

"One minute. Prepare the chains."

Choo-Choo helped Brazio remove the thick enchanted chain from the duffle bag. Runes had been etched into the links. It took two throws, but he managed to hook it on the metal wheel affixed to the vault door right next to the smoking hole where the acid had burned away the inner mechanisms. He was going through the motions like an automaton, the previous practice carrying his actions, but his mind was stuck on what Brazio had said. It made Choo-Choo furious to think about being lectured by his sister's killer, using her death as some sort of lesson that he was supposed to buy. How could he dare? How *dare* he!

"Emilio?"

His true name startled Choo-Choo out of his thoughts to find Duro staring at him with a hunched forehead.

"I'm good."

"You don't look fucking good."

Duro glanced at the hallway where Brazio had gone to grab an extra piece of explosives from Tick.

"He killed my sister."

The corner of Duro's lip twitched. His intensity faltered briefly.

"You don't know, do you?"

"Know what?" asked Choo-Choo.

Duro shook his head slightly. "You can't ever tell anyone."

"Tell anyone what?"

The words came out harshly. If they'd been at the Academy, the warleader would have smacked him in the head for his insolence and he would have deserved it.

"Brazio killed Valeria because she'd killed his wife six months before. She wasn't a warrior. Not a soldado. Just a woman he loved dearly. But she got caught in an ambush on the way to the Terreno. The two clans weren't at war at the time, so they thought they were safe and only had the denizens of the Undercity to worry about."

"Val wouldn't do that," said Choo-Choo.

Duro frowned. "She was as ruthless and bloodthirsty as Brazio. The two of them were the same, and had things happened slightly differently, it would be Yara wanting her revenge against Val."

"I don't believe you."

"The truth exists whether or not you believe in it and will eventually return to equilibrium. Usually with a reality debt. The paradox of the warrior is that he fights best when he's not fighting at all. To throw a punch in anger is to betray the very principles of what you've trained to be. We're not warriors because we're tough or we want to kill. We're warriors to protect the people we love. So ask yourself, if you accept his duel, will you be protecting Triana or Vasilisa? Or will you be indulging your revenge fantasies?"

Duro's eyes shot to the left as Brazio returned in his white hazmat suit holding an industrial drill.

"Grab that chain. We've got a door to break."

The two of them wrapped the chain around their forearms. Duro was in front, right outside the red line. While they waited for the power to be cut, Choo-Choo reeled from Duro's words. Was he being selfish about his quest to kill Brazio? Or was he keeping the honor of his family? The conflicting responsibilities left him unsure.

Choo-Choo almost missed the signal because he was lost in his thoughts, but then he realized the lights in the hallway had gone out.

"Pull!"

Choo-Choo yanked on the chain, straining with every effort. The links bit into his palms and his muscles bulged, but the door didn't move. When it was clear the door wasn't moving, Brazio stepped over the red line with his drill.

The *pop-pop-pop* of gunfire startled Choo-Choo as holes opened up in Brazio's suit, but the elder waku kept walking. Choo-Choo didn't understand until he remembered the black diamond. The steelskin was protecting him from the defensive fire. When Brazio reached the door, he shoved the tip of the industrial drill into the hole and revved it. Dust and green smoke spit from the hole.

"Pull!"

Choo-Choo put his back into it as other members of the clan appeared from their tasks. Yara took the spot right behind him, followed by Nikolai and Adrenalynne. With five topaz on the chain, the door started to strain, groaning as if it were bending under pressure.

An explosion from the direction of the elevator had Choo-Choo momentarily distracted until he heard someone say that the cavern had been alerted to their presence.

"Pull!" shouted Duro.

The entire team was on the chain while Brazio drilled into the door while getting pelted with bullets. His suit looked like swiss cheese and the gas had to be leaking into it, but he kept working. The runes on the chain flared with light as they fought to hold the metal together under the strain.

"Pull!"

The collective yank snapped something inside the vault door, and the *pop-pop* of gunfire ended, leaving Brazio to stumble back to the group, ripping off his hazmat helmet and throwing a jar of powder into his face, which seemed to counteract the acidic gas. Pockmarks dotted his face where the acid had burned his skin despite the steel protection. The way Brazio heaved with breath suggested that standing inside the gas had been extremely painful.

"Everyone, get ready," said Duro, pulling out his blades.

The collective whisper of steel sliding from sheaths was followed by another explosion from the elevator area.

Duro was standing in front. His head made a quarter turn.

"No mercy. Kill them all. El Clan Eto Vas!"

Choo-Choo found himself shouting with the rest of his clan. "El

Clan Eto Vas!"

Thirty

The explosion near the elevator had Camina ducking even though she knew she should have been expecting it. *Fuck*. As the silvery vault door opened, green smoke drifted into the air and made her eyes water. Duro threw something through the gap that exploded with a flash of light and a concussive boom before he ran through the smoke.

As the others ran ahead, her limbs shook with anticipation. Camina knew that once her blade clashed with another, she'd be fine, but the buildup left her shaken.

"Come on!" said Yara as she ran ahead.

Camina held her breath and squinted as she followed, the lingering acid feeling like being pepper-sprayed. Once she was through, she stepped over four dead bodies. Two of them looked like the explosive had gotten them while the next two had slashes through their necks.

She'd expected the others to be right beyond the door, but sounds of fighting from nearby told her they'd immediately rushed deeper into the complex. Camina followed Yara through a kicked-open door to a room where three men and two women with the blue dagger tattoos on their forearms were waiting.

The fear coursing through her veins turned to energy as she blocked a strike almost a hair too late, but managed to kick the woman attacking her in the pelvis before she could bring her other arm around. The tight space was filled with slicing blades, cries of impact, and the gurgle of death wails.

Less than ten seconds after they'd entered the room, five alliance clan members lay dead on the ground while Camina heaved with breath. Yara grinned at her with blood splattered across her face. Before Camina could say something, Yara rushed through the next door, forcing her to follow.

They found themselves in a large industrial kitchen. Yara went screaming around the stainless steel counter, but stuttered to a stop with her blades raised. Camina joined her to find a group of men and women cowering near the walk-in freezer. One woman with thick black hair and a scar on her cheek started speaking rapidly in a language Camina couldn't understand. The woman gestured them away angrily.

"I don't think they're here of their own accord," said Camina.

The swinging doors led them into a huge cafeteria that looked large enough to hold a hundred people. A melee was already underway on the opposite side. When they rushed in, a small group of alliance clan hit the cafeteria at the same time. Camina locked eyes with a hulking guy who held an axe in one fist as if it were a dagger.

The fear came back as she crossed the cafeteria. The axe-wielding waku kicked a table into her way, which she narrowly jumped. The way he knocked it over suggested he was a topaz. With no offensive stones, she felt outclassed, but tried to remember everything Pandora had drilled into her about using the opal.

"I'm gonna wear your corpse like a cloak," he said, grinning with golden teeth. His axe snapped a table in half as she leapt out of the way.

"Come on, Camina," she muttered to herself.

So far she'd been acting on instinct, but she wasn't going to survive against this beast of a man unless she fought smarter. Camina flooded her amber to sense where he was going to strike next. She caught the twitch of his muscles a moment before he lunged, which allowed her to dodge backwards, avoiding the swinging axe rather than trying to block it.

But even anticipating the blow, it was still hard to avoid as his topaz gave him supernatural speed. She tapped into her opal, coaxing own muscles and adrenaline system into overdrive right as he kicked a table, forcing her to jump over it. She landed as the axe came screaming at her head. Bending backwards avoided decapitation, but then he punched her

in the jaw, spinning her into shelves filled with ceramic bowls and plates.

The entire unit crashed upon her, trapping her. She fought to escape as

the axe guy approached with supreme confidence. The rest of the cafete-

ria was surprisingly empty, as the battles had moved to other rooms.

He lifted his axe as she pulled herself from the wreckage, flinching

when she heard a gunshot. Camina and her opponent looked to the op-

posite side of the room to see Nikolai sighting down his rifle. The first

shot had nicked the hulking waku. Before Nikolai could take a second,

the spinning axe took him in the chest.

Camina darted out, hoping to get away in the distraction, but her

opponent grabbed her by the arm. She slammed curled knuckles into his

throat, which made him red in the face. He threw her through the swing-

ing doors of the kitchen to crash into the hanging pots and pans, spilling

equipment everywhere.

Pain lit up her entire body. Her right arm was fractured, if not bro-

ken, and possibly a few ribs. Camina tried to sit up, but the agony was

immense. She pushed her opal energy into the cracked bone in her left

arm as the hulking waku burst through the door.

She threw cast iron pots, which he blocked with easy swipes. The

opal exuberance she'd briefly enjoyed was gone, the effort of maintaining

it too difficult as her body shuddered with injuries. Camina leapt towards

the opposite door, only to find herself blocked by the speedy waku. He grabbed her by the throat, crushing her windpipe. Spots formed immediately, and she saw the world disappearing behind a curtain of blackness. Kicks and strikes did nothing to dislodge his supernatural strength. She was caught in a human bear trap.

There was nothing she could do.

An attempt to use her opal to equal his strength proved fruitless. He was too strong and she was too exhausted from her injuries. He pulled her close to bark into her face.

"Die, bitch!"

Before she blacked out, Camina jammed her palms against his eyes, pushing everything she had into them. She imagined a white-hot bonfire erupting from her hands. The guy screamed and launched her away. She crashed through a wall, landing in a pantry filled with cooking supplies. Camina could barely breathe as her windpipe had nearly been crushed, but she managed to use her opal to fix the worst of the damage.

Camina managed to climb back into the kitchen to find the hulking waku still screaming with his hands over his blackened eyes. She'd burned them out with her opal, leaving him blind. A cleaver on the wall made a convenient weapon. While he reached out, trying to figure out where she was, Camina stepped to the side and severed his spine at the neck. He collapsed like a marionette with his strings cut, leaving her to lean against the table in exhaustion.

When she confirmed no one else was nearby, Camina knelt by Nikolai's fallen body. Surrounded by a pool of blood, he lay with his eyes wide, the handle of an ax sticking out of his chest.

"Thank you, Instructor Nikolai."

Camina bowed deeply, holding the bend until tears dripped from her eyes. Then she stood and went in search of others to kill.

Thirty-One

The fighting had spread out amid the complex, which went back further than Brazio had expected. It appeared each clan leader had their own apartment section where they lived with a small group of personal guards. Brazio faced a knot of Voyna protecting Olek Koval. They bristled with spears and swords, while Olek, who stood in back, held a huge handgun.

Brazio wiped the blood from his sword Reaver with a rag he'd found, then tossed it over his shoulder.

"I'm sorry, Olek. I respected how you ran your clan, but you never should have allied with Dominion."

"Allied?" Olek laughed, clutching his handgun in both hands. It

looked big enough to take down an elephant. Brazio wasn't looking forward to getting hit with it, even with his steelskin.

"That option left the building the moment Dominion took Lionel's
head off." Olek held up a hand. The pinky looked mangled. "He made
me do this to myself. Can you believe it? Now we bow and scrape and
hope that he'll let us live a little longer. Maybe I'll let you kill me just to
escape him."

The leader of Voyna made no motion to stand down his men.
There were six of them.

"Join me and we can take him. You can merge with the Drops.
When we run the entire Undercity, you'll have a place of honor and
respect as you deserve. Not cowering in your apartment waiting for your
favor to turn."

Olek's laughter sounded hollowed out.

"Brazio. I wish I could believe that you'll win, but you don't stand a
chance against his maetrie mercenaries. You'd best put the blade to your
own throat."

"What about your daughter? Didn't she just get married? Think
about her."

"I am. If you kill me, then she'll still be alive, but if I side with you
and we fail, then she'll lose her life too. I'm sorry, my old friend. There
was a time I wished I could have dueled you, but you long ago surpassed
me, and now I'll have to rely on my cunning rather than skill."

Brazio knew Olek had been trying to distract him, but he'd been running his amber the entire time and knew three waku were sneaking up behind him with sabers. Brazio casually reached into a pouch and tossed a smoke cannister into the room as the three waku attacked.

His sword, Reaver, sliced the first in half at the waist, giving him a straight shot at the other two who'd thought to use the attack to flank him. The woman's right leg was too far forward by two inches, leaving her slightly off-balance. He kicked at her knee, forcing her to stumble backwards while bringing Reaver around to block the third attacker. He switched the blade to his other hand, curling the tip behind him to pierce the woman's throat, then spun back to catch the final attacker in the stomach.

The cannon-like blast of a handgun nearly took his head off. Brazio leapt with Lightness, running across the ceiling of the smoke-filled room. He landed behind Olek and gently pushed Reaver through his heart from behind. The other six waku fell like wheat to a scythe.

"I will give your daughter my condolences," said Brazio, touching the fallen man's lifeless shoulder.

He wished they'd gotten detailed schematics of the interior because after he left Olek's apartment, he got turned around in the hallways. Brazio moved towards the sounds of fighting, but whenever he reached them, he found the battles over or moved on.

"Brazio."

The name was spoken from a direction he hadn't sensed anyone approaching. Brazio turned to find a familiar—yet unfamiliar—face staring back from across the room.

It was Gregor Anderson, head of the Crows, but he looked much different. The outline of his shoulders was jagged with metal and his face was darkened by shadows. The only bright colors ceom from the bracers on his wrists. Gregor held a maul the size of a trash can. He shouldn't have been able to carry a weapon that heavy, but something had been done to him, making him different. Shadowy smoke lifted from his arms.

"You don't look so well, Gregor."

"I've never felt better," said Gregor, his voice vibrating with strange energy. "Now I get to finish what Titus should have done for me. You can join your brother in the earth."

In years past, anger would have flooded through him and he would have leapt to battle, but the wisdom of age told him he was being baited. While Brazio didn't fear this new version of Gregor, he wasn't about to rush in without understanding the dangers.

"Only a coward strikes a friend in the back."

Gregor grinned, which turned his face into a horrifying mask. "Do not invite the viper into your home and be surprised when it bites you." He spat on the ground. "You and your brother thought your honor protected you. You believed it made you better, but it was a weakness that I exploited. It was your downfall."

"Without honor, it's a race to the bottom where no one wins. Look at you now, Gregor. You're not even human anymore. I don't know what that cursed city elf did to you, but I don't think you can live like that."

"He gave me a chance to fight. To squeeze the life from your arrogant eyes."

During their conversation, Gregor had been moving closer. He was within fifteen feet. Brazio was studying his muscles for the twitch of movement and then he could counterattack.

When the moment came, Brazio sped forward on a cocktail of speed and Lightness. Reaver sung through the air. The man's head should have been taken clean off, but when Brazio landed, he found Gregor had avoided the strike and was bringing the enormous war maul around for a crushing blow.

Brazio switched to steelskin before impact. He was thrown through the wall, snapping interior structural pieces. Before he could regain his feet, Gregor had somehow followed him through and had grabbed him by the neck, smashing him through the rest of the wall with his head. Brazio felt like a human battering ram demolishing more of the wall. It took all his energy to maintain the steelskin.

"Why won't you die, you stupid waku!"

The ceiling collapsed upon them both when the final struts were removed. Brazio used the distraction to burst away and let his steelskin drop. The pile of debris exploded outward as Gregor climbed from the wreckage.

The strength and speed of the Crow leader surprised Brazio. He examined him with the amber, sensing raging energies contained within him. It was like peeking under the hood of a sedan to find a nuclear reactor.

"You know you're not going to survive whatever Dominion did to you," said Brazio, backing up. "Your body wasn't meant to hold that kind of power. It's maetrie work. That kind of elder fae energy is death to humans."

Gregor smirked. "It's not your concern, Brazio. You'll be dead long before it matters and even if you manage to kill me, there's no way you can stop Thule. He's anticipated you at every turn. He knew you would try to kill him. That's why he gave this gift to me."

The swing of the maul put a crater-sized hole in the stone as Brazio leapt away barely ahead of the weapon.

"You were seeking honor when you should have been looking to maximize your power. That's the secret of Dominion's ascent. You were searching for partners for your dead clan when fear should have been your tool. You can only convince some people to love you, but you can always make everyone *fear* you."

Brazio tried to anticipate the attack, swinging Reaver at the neck of the war maul, but the blow came faster than expected, sending him spinning into the furniture of the living space. Brazio released his steel-skin and climbed to his feet unsteadily. Gregor's eyes burned black and tendrils of corruption ran down his arms. The attachment was killing him quickly.

The next few moments seemed to freeze in time. Brazio leapt with Lightness, preparing an angled attack from above, when Gregor swung the maul upward. The flat head slammed into Brazio's chest, knocking the air from his lungs as he bounced off the ceiling and collapsed onto the ground. Before he could leap to his feet, Gregor had a foot on his chest, and no amount of struggling, not even using his full topaz, could dislodge the Crow leader.

"Give your brother my regards," said Gregor, lifting his maul while smoke-like energy wafted from his arms.

Brazio reached for Reaver, but he'd dropped it when he landed. He couldn't breathe.

As the maul reached the zenith, Brazio saw there was nothing he could do to stop it. He hoped the others were more successful—maybe he'd pushed Gregor hard enough that one of the others could defeat him.

A figure blurred into the room behind Gregor, grabbing his arm before the maul could be swung down. Choo-Choo's slick, bald head was visible from above Gregor's shoulder. Brazio resumed his fight, hoping to keep the Crow leader off-balance. But Gregor was too strong for Choo-Choo and he slowly pulled the maul away from his grip.

"Grab the metal!" Brazio coughed out.

Choo-Choo's forehead scrunched, but he switched one hand to the jagged metal pieces attached to Gregor's shoulder, digging his fingers beneath the flat pieces, which squelched and spat black smoke. Gregor screamed in agony.

Brazio grabbed Gregor's foot to twist it off his chest while they fought for control of the maul. Choo-Choo had his fingers beneath the black metal and yanked hard, pulling a section from Gregor's flesh. It let off an awful hiss, and black smoke leaked out around it.

The full attention of the Crow leader was focused on Choo-Choo, which gave Brazio the chance to lunge for Reaver. Before Gregor could stop him, Brazio shoved the blade through his groin, spilling blood onto the floor in a splash. Gregor fell over, the maul landing on his head as Choo-Choo released it.

As Gregor died, the black smoke leaked from his wounds and fled towards the hallway like a living thing.

There was a moment of indecision in Choo-Choo's eyes and then he held his hand out. Brazio took it, letting the younger waku pull him to standing.

"Thank you."

Pain reflected in Choo-Choo's eyes, but he said, "El Clan Eto Vas."

"El Clan Eto Vas."

Choo-Choo removed the enormous war maul from Gregor's grip and hefted it a few times for balance.

"Let's go finish this."

Brazio grinned and motioned for Choo-Choo to lead on.

Thirty-Two

Bullets pinged against the cliff, or chewed through the walls behind the elevator where Tick crouched with Xylos, who aimed a rifle he'd taken from the fallen alliance. A loud pop was followed by Xylos' laughter as he leaned behind the barrier again.

"Got 'em!"

The floor beneath the cliff looked like an anthill upended. Dozens of people—mostly soldados but some waku—were trying to reach the vertical wall. A group of automatic-wielding Voyna were spraying bullets across the upper section, trying to pin them down, but the angle and height gave Tick and Xylos the advantage.

"It's like shooting fish in a very large barrel," said Xylos, grinning as he leaned around the corner to squeeze off another round.

"I don't think that's how it works," said Tick, grimacing as the stone kept exploding from impact, sending shards into the top of his head.

When he'd been told he would be guarding the elevator, he thought he'd gotten lucky. Inside the complex, he'd be forced to fight one-on-one with other waku. He was the worst fighter of the team, losing all their training matches except when Brazio allowed him to use his tiger's eye. But now he wondered if he'd gotten the short end of the staff.

"There's a group running for the wall under a piece of sheet metal," said Xylos, aiming down his sights. "Ready another charge."

Tick looked into the bag. "There's only two left."

"Don't be shy."

Tick armed the explosive then army crawled to the edge where the men and women had reached the wall. A group was climbing while the others fired weapons up the face. Tick released the brick over the edge, putting his fingers in his ears in expectation.

The explosion rattled the cavern, sending streamers of dust from the ceiling. When he peeked over, he saw a pile of bodies near a piece of mangled sheet metal. Tick rolled onto his back. Even though he'd been in a fight before, it'd happened so fast that it was over before he had time to think about it. But now he was forced to keep throwing himself back into danger, knowing a lucky shot would be his end.

"Do you think they're done back there?" he asked Xylos.

"Not likely. Don't worry about it and keep firing."

Tick grabbed the other weapon and squeezed off a few bullets. He wasn't a great shot, but he held his own with Xylos, who seemed to revel in the chaos below.

After taking down two soldados who'd thought to climb onto the roof of the Eleventh Gonka, Tick leaned back around the wall.

"How can you be so happy?" he asked his friend.

Xylos ducked below the edge as he reloaded the weapon. "You gotta embrace it, or it'll drive you mad. There's time for crying in your room later. If you survive."

The cold analysis shocked Tick, who'd thought Xylos was immune to fear.

"Holy balls," said Xylos. "Those wayhos got three teams on the way."

Three separate groups were running under the cover of a piece of sheet metal.

"We only have one explosive left."

"Then you'd better make it count." Xylos glanced backwards. "You gonna unleash whatever it is you have in that sack?"

As if it'd heard, the sack shifted with coiling movement. Tick sent calming thoughts to the creature.

"I don't want her to get shot."

"Her?"

Tick scrambled back to the bag. "Which group should I drop it on?"

Xylos yelled over his shoulder. "Just pick one!"

The explosive went over the edge like the others. When it triggered, there were cries from the other two climbing teams.

"Ha! Some of them lost their grip," said Xylos.

"They're moving fast," said Tick, daring a look when he fired his weapon.

The soldados on the cavern floor were keeping them pinned down with suppressive fire so they couldn't lean over the edge and take shots at the climbers.

"I think it's time to pull out your ace in the hole," said Xylos. "They're about halfway up already."

"Fuck," said Tick, wishing he was with Kuma and Camina because they'd be able to keep him safe. He crawled to the sack, unloosening the end.

"Come on, girl. Don't be shy."

A pair of red eyes above a flickering tongue stuck out of the opening. The brown and gold patterns on the head gave Koro a regal look, while the spots along her belly made her approachable. Tick reached out and stroked the snake's head as she maneuvered out of the sack.

"What in the shadows is that?" asked Xylos, recoiling.

"Her name is Koro. Short for Koroleva. When I was relocating the snakes from the Night Wall, I thought she'd make a good pet."

"Oh, baka, get it away from me," said Xylos. "I hate snakes."

Tick whistled softly and coaxed Koro to leave the sack. When she was halfway out, Koro unfolded her leathery wings, which looked gossamer-like when they were stretched wide as the light filtered through the membrane.

"I hate to do this to you, but if I don't, they'll kill us both. I hope you're small enough they can't hit you," said Tick.

The flying snake stared back with crimson eyes, flicking her tongue. He sensed apprehension from Koro.

Tick reached out to the snake with the tiger's eye and gently impressed upon her the importance of flying over the edge. He sent pictures of the men climbing and then images of himself being stabbed when they reached the top. Koro darted over the cliff, and moments later, screams erupted, followed by the heavy crunch of impact.

"Kill the snake! Kill that fucking snake!" came the cries from below.

Tick used the distraction from Koro to lean over the edge and fire at the climbers. He picked off one that was only twenty feet from making it to the top, but there were a dozen more spread out along the wall. Koro flew around the climbers, biting some and avoiding getting shot, mostly because they weren't firing when she was near the others because they could easily hit their clan mates. The snake wanted to escape rather than fight, but Tick kept the compulsion on her.

"I'm sorry, Koro," he whispered as he leaned over for another shot. "Got another, Xylos!"

Tick kept firing. One by one, with the snake's help, he cleared the wall, then leaned back around the elevator and sent for Koro to return. He leaned towards Xylos, who was lying in a prone firing position with the rifle in his hands.

"Hey, we got 'em. You can pull back now. It'll give 'em something to think about for the next attempt."

When Xylos didn't move, a pit formed in Tick's stomach. Then he saw the thick crimson liquid running down his friend's neck. A bullet had taken him in the throat and he'd died choking on his own blood. Tick had never heard his struggles in the chaos.

The flying snake made it back to the top and gently landed in his lap. Tick stroked Koro's neck as he thought about Xylos' ever-present laughter. He'd never hear it again.

Tick checked back over the edge to find they were readying for another assault on the cliff. Even with Koro's help, he wasn't sure how he was going to fend them off this time. He checked back to the main door, hoping the rest of his clan would appear soon. Otherwise, they were going to be trapped.

Thirty-Three

Kuma leaned on the table to catch his breath. The three Antimagus had caught him off guard. Blood ran from a deep slice on his upper arm, so he cut a piece of shirt from the fallen for a wrap.

"How did we get so split up?" he said to himself.

One minute he'd been fighting with Navos and Adrenalynne, and the next he was all alone. When he'd tried to follow the sound of battle, he got turned around and ran into the Antimagus waku. He was lucky they didn't know how to scrap and he'd managed to use his ruby to borrow the topaz from the best warrior.

Kuma wiped the sweat from his hands. He didn't want to lose his grip on the hilts of his blades in the middle of a fight. After sending his amber sensing out, he moved back the way he'd come in hopes of finding Deacon. He'd seen no sign of the Crow, but that didn't mean he wasn't lurking somewhere in the complex.

A faint exhale of breath warned him of a person hiding around the next corner. Kuma threw himself through the opening with Lightness, then kicked off the opposite wall for a double "X" attack, when he realized it was his cousin.

"I almost took your head off," she said, shaking her head.

Wisps of black hair were plastered to her forehead along with specks of crimson.

"It's a fucking mess back here. Where is everyone?"

Yara frowned. "I found Nikolai with an ax in his chest near the cafeteria. Otherwise, every time I try to find someone, I end up in a scrap."

"Let's stick together then."

Yara's jaw pulsed. "I get to kill him."

"Come on, Yara."

"Promise me that. I get to kill Deacon."

The pain in her brown eyes had Kuma relenting. "Okay."

"No," she said emphatically. "Promise. Swear."

"Alright, alright. I swear. Shadows below, what did he do to you?"

Yara looked away. "It doesn't matter. What matters is I'm going to kill him."

He'd never been close with his cousin but for the first time in a long time, he wanted to put his arm around her shoulders. His arm started to twitch that direction and she glared at it as if it were a live wire.

"Don't even think about it."

Kuma held his arms up. Yara grumbled and went ahead of him down the hallway, the opposite direction he heard fighting, but he didn't want to contradict her.

In the next room, they found the bloated corpse of Gregor Anderson. His death had to be recent by the spilled blood, but he looked grossly deformed as if he'd been sitting on the bottom of a lake for a week.

Yara kicked the corroded black metal on his shoulders, waking faint runes on its surface. "What's this?"

"I'd leave it alone."

Yara glared at him.

"Despite our past, Yara, I do care that you stay alive."

"I wouldn't put it past you to let me die just so you could kill Deacon."

"You know that's not true."

"Feels true," she grumbled.

Kuma crouched by the golden bracers. "These don't look so bad."

"I thought you said not to touch."

He gestured to the front of the corpse. "Something bothers me about those. When I use my amber, I swear I hear voices inside the metal. Not so much for the bracers."

"Your funeral."

Kuma removed the bracers, though it took some work since Gregor's flesh had expanded. He shoved them into a pouch. The rattle of an explosion from the front of the complex had them both looking up.

"I hope Tick's doing alright," he said.

"Me too."

When Kuma arched an eyebrow in her direction, she said, "I care."

"Hard to tell. Whenever I turn my back on you, I always imagine that you're debating the pros and cons of putting a knife in it."

"That's not fair."

"But it's true."

She sulked. "Okay, I do think about it. But I wouldn't really do it."

"I hear something near the cafeteria."

Yara followed him that direction. "It's never been easy living in your shadow."

"My shadow?" he asked, genuinely surprised.

"You've always sucked the air out of the room. Even my father thinks more of you than he does of me," said Yara, scowling.

"That's not true. You're one of the best warriors in the Academy. You'd probably be the best if it weren't for your anger issues."

She stomped her foot as she spun around. "I do *not* have anger issues."

Kuma raised an eyebrow.

"Okay, so I do a little bit."

"Yara, you could be as great as your father if you'd stop trying to prove something to everyone and just be yourself." He paused. "That's why you were with Deacon, wasn't it?"

"At first," she said. "But then it wasn't so bad."

"Why do you hate him so much?"

She growled out her answer. "Because he drugged me. He thought I would stay at his side, like some sort of dog, after they wiped out our family. Your father, my uncle. Everyone. I was fucking the traitor! And he thought I would stay with him. Do you know how demeaning that is? I've always had something to prove because of my father, and then with you outshining me at the Academy. Then to have him put that on me? You know people looked at me differently after we had to join the Drops. They wondered if I was a mole, if I was the one."

"I'm sorry, Yara. I didn't know."

"Of course you didn't. You were always in the center of—"

She turned her head, signaling someone was nearby. Kuma followed her into the cafeteria, where more than one battle had occurred. He thought they'd been mistaken until the gray-skinned assassin strolled through the opposite door.

A hiss slipped through Yara's teeth and she moved like she was going to charge him, until Kuma said, "Careful."

"You're right to be worried," said the maetrie assassin with a sneer that could curdle milk at a hundred paces.

"You're Kavano."

"The boy knows his maetrie well. When you and your uncle played hide-and-seek with me in the city, I thought we'd get to meet that day."

The casual arrogance of Kavano was more than just the awkward saunter, or the way he dragged the tip of his sword along the tiles. It wasn't just the slash of his mouth—one part serial killer smile, one part grimace—or his fearsome reputation. He oozed superiority as if he'd never faced an opponent he couldn't destroy. Demean even.

"I'm not interested in killing pups," said Kavano with a smirk. He jerked his head. "Best to leave the complex before I change my mind. If I see you again, I won't be as kind."

Kuma wasn't sure that they shouldn't flee as fast as they could and forget the mission, but Yara stepped forward with her blades wide.

"Yara. We can't take him."

"Anyone's beatable," she said, muscles rippling with intent.

Kavano laughed. The sound was like having a spike slammed into Kuma's chest.

"Truth, girl. Anyone *is* beatable. But even your best isn't good enough. Not even the both of you together. Now get, before I change my mind," he said, jerking his head as if they were a couple of mangey dogs hanging around.

Yara raised her blades wide and let out a war cry, which had Kuma shifting forward to follow her into battle. He used his ruby to borrow her topaz and matched her Lightness-aided leap.

The maetrie assassin never moved. He stared at them passively with the sword leaning against the tiles, staring up at their approach through the curtain of his dark hair. The angle of his shoulders was all wrong, tilted away, making a counterattack difficult. Kuma thought for a split second that they might have caught him off guard and sent out a sapphire Push to keep the assassin from blocking.

Then Kavano moved.

Whenever he'd watched Duro fight, it was like seeing a person blur from one location to another. Kavano moved even faster, making it appear that he'd teleported to the new spot.

Landing where Kavano had been standing, Kuma spun around, looking for the assassin to find him where they'd been moments before. Kuma checked himself to find no wounds, but heard a gurgle from Yara, who had fallen to her knees. Blood ran down her cheek. A crimson line went from a spot beneath her left eye to her shoulder. Kuma clamped his hands over the wound as Yara stared at him with fear in her eyes. They needed an opal waku, or she'd bleed out.

"It should have been her throat that was cut," said Kavano, examining the tip of his sword as if it'd betrayed him. "I guess your little crystal tricks can be interesting."

The last part was said as if he were a food critic describing a gourmet meal he'd just eaten. Kavano held his blade out. A low hum emanated from the weapon, making Kuma's teeth hurt.

"I'm afraid playtime is over, boy. I'll try to make it quick," said Kavano, approaching in a casual saunter.

Kuma kept his hand on Yara's neck while facing the assassin, holding a single knife. The closer Kavano got, the more his teeth hurt from the strange vibration in the sword.

Thirty-Four

The occasional clash of blades rang out in the distance. The many walls between muted the sharpness of the sound, but she could feel the intensity in their impacts. Pandora thought to move in that direction, but every time she'd previously tried to track down battles she'd come upon them too late.

A few minutes before, she'd been fighting with Adrenalynne at her side, but then when they moved after a fleeing Blue Dagger, Pandora found herself alone once more. Had she not spent the near entirety of her childhood in the Eternal City she wouldn't have recognized the directional confusion of the maetrie realm, but why was it affecting the Undercity? It was clear that her grandfather had introduced it as another layer of protection and it was working quite well, splitting up their attacks, which might have worked better if they weren't better warriors than the alliance clans. But the bigger question was how.

Pandora considered the door to her left, which she thought led back to the cafeteria, where she was most likely to find her clanmates, but that's not how travel in the Eternal City worked. The realm was immense, almost infinite from a theoretical point of view, which made normal travel obsolete. As a realm of high magic, one only had to fix the location in one's mind to reach the destination.

The image of her grandfather rose like a vision in her thoughts. Traveling towards specific people didn't work in the Eternal City, but she hoped that it would be enough to bring her to the location he typically enjoyed spending time.

Pandora went down the hallway, ignoring the sounds of battle to her left through a set of double doors. Two turns later, she found herself in a conference boardroom with ten chairs around a gray marble table. Opposite where she was standing was an enormous painting of an olden forest that seemed idyllic at first glance, but her attention was immediately drawn to the single figure at the end of the table.

"Grandfather."

"Pandora," he said. "You've grown. The quickness of human growth always surprises me no matter how many times I witness it."

Dominion Thule had always been the most human looking maetrie that she'd ever known. While some of the race turned themselves ghoulish during the long passage of time, delighting in the horrific nature of their new visages, others like her grandfather enjoyed staying under the radar with a benign appearance—at least for the maetrie. He wore a pin-striped suit and a black tie with a faint grid of golden lines. At first glance he was normal enough, but the longer one stared at him, the more unease grew. Pandora had never enjoyed her interactions with him even as she shared his blood.

"It was a valiant attempt," he said, drumming his fingers on the thick marble. "I really admire the way you threw yourselves into the trap with glee."

"Trap," she said in a growl. "We've slaughtered the leaders of your clans and taken the lives of its best warriors. Once you're out of the picture, we'll have the entire Undercity under our control."

Dominion smirked. "*Once you're out of the picture?* You can't even say it, granddaughter. You're here to kill me. Or do you not have the nerve? It's that human weakness. I told your mother you were too human to be worth much. But true to your kind, she refused to see the truth, letting love blind her to the fact that you would always be a disappointment."

"Love is not weakness."

"I killed my father when I was your age. In maetrie terms. If I hadn't, he would have killed me in turn. That's the superiority of the maetrie. We are competition incarnate. Humans call it survival of the fittest. It's one of the few things they got right."

Pandora lurched forward with murder on her mind. Her grandfather held up a hand. The gesture was a throwaway. Like the dismissal of a servant, but her limbs froze solid as if she were encased in ice. She strained against the magic fruitlessly.

"Thank you, granddaughter, for the chance to practice. It's been so long since I've used my eldritch charms."

"I hate you."

Dominion chuckled. "Finally, that maetrie heart coming through. You know that this raid has been a failure, right? While I wasn't sure exactly how you would make the attempt, I knew it was coming. The best part is that you've done for me what I couldn't yet do myself. The *alliance* part of this business was becoming a bore and interfering with my work. By eliminating the petty leaders of its clans, I can consolidate my power absolutely, and with the Drops out of the way, the Undercity will be under my control. Not only have you failed, but your failure has made me stronger. If you were a better student of maetrie warfare you might understand this concept."

"Vygragot."

The maetrie word felt awkward on her tongue, only because she hadn't spoken the language in years.

"I believe the humans call it heads I win, tails you lose. It's not exact, but close enough."

"No one will let a maetrie have control of the Undercity, or the faez crystal trade," said Pandora, fighting against the compulsion that had stilled her limbs.

"That's where you're wrong, granddaughter. You see, other attempts by the maetrie courts to take control of human endeavors have failed spectacularly because they always approached the humans on maetrie terms. That's why I've spent the last forty years in these lands so I could better understand your kind. Eventually I found a human that closely matched the maetrie heart, but unfortunately, he stuck his neck out too far and had it chopped off. It sorely set back my plans, but then when the faez crystals were discovered, I knew a new opportunity had revealed itself."

"Maetrie culture is flawed," said Pandora. "No one wins if everyone is always fighting, which is why the human ability to love and care for each other is more important."

"Yet here we are," said Dominion, spreading out his hands palms up. "Do not underestimate the ability of humans to succumb to their base desires given the right incentives. Put ample flaws in the system, make people's intentions opaque enough, while making vast rewards available to the winners, and then watch them fall all over themselves to cut each other's throats."

"You're not stopping at the Undercity," she said.

"Why would I desire to control this playground of petty gangsters and fungal delights? The only reason I bother is because the faez crystals will fuel my empire's growth. With the Halls weakened from the invasion, the window of my opportunity widens."

Dominion reached under the table and a soft chime sounded from nearby. His sour expression was tempered with superiority, making her want to spit on him. It was hard to believe they were related. Two men with the tattoos of Blue Daggers entered from the opposite door with two sets of runed manacles. They clamped them around her wrists and ankles. She felt the energies contained within the metal holding her limbs at bay, but she sent out a tug of sapphire only to see it barely move the chair to her right. The manacles were dampening her stones.

"What are you going to do with me?" she asked.

Her grandfather approached. He put a finger under her chin, lifting it slightly.

"Doing what I should have done a long time ago. I'll be sending you to the Eternal City, where you will have one final chance to prove yourself." He arched an eyebrow. "If you cannot, then I will have rid myself of a troublesome granddaughter. Be warned I have little patience for defiance."

He gestured to the two waku and they grabbed her arms, dragging her towards the opposite door.

"Be grateful you're not like the rest of your clanmates. Kavano should be soon finished with them and then I can get back to taking control of the Undercity."

In the wake of her grandfather's leaving, she felt a great pit open inside. The world crashed in upon her, leaving her too stunned to fight the men leading her away.

Twenty-three tiles.

Seventeen links.

Zero chance of escaping.

Thirty-Five

The truth that Duro had learned many years ago when he was first a soldado, and then reinforced when he became a waku—a wielder of stones—was that the shortest path between two points was not always a straight line. It only took watching water flow through channels in the stone to see how nature defined its boundaries.

Scrapping, the art of the warrior, was much the same. Punches should be thrown at the point of maximum impact from the center of the body. Two points. One line. The arc of weapons and bodies during a fight created the barriers that required adjustments. Curved spaces and angled attacks, but within these parameters the truth remained.

When Duro's eyes fell upon the angled shoulders of the maetrie assassin as he entered the cafeteria, doubts assaulted his theory. Strange energies permeated the one named Kavano. Duro felt like a Renaissance painter encountering cubism for the first time. Nothing made sense about the assassin, let alone the weapon in his fist.

Duro paused at the kneeling Yara, gently moving Kuma's hand away from her neck before sending healing energies into the wound. It would need more repair, but it was all he dared expend given the challenge that lay before him.

"Get the others and get out of here. Forget the rest."

Kuma opened his mouth, but Duro put a hand on his shoulder gently. "If you don't leave now, no one will survive."

The grave news seemed to stun the young waku, but he nodded rapidly, adding a quick bow before helping Yara to her feet and leading her from the room. Kavano had been watching with faint amusement, like a cat who had broken the legs of its prey and was deciding when it was appropriate to make the final kill.

"Tired of running?" asked the maetrie assassin.

The maetrie's aura warped the edges of Duro's thoughts, so he tapped into his opal to counter the effects.

"It wasn't the time. There was no benefit in fighting you before. Now, there is much to gain." Duro paused then offered a ceremonial bow. "May the shadows keep you safe."

Kavano let the tip of his tongue rest on the bottom of his teeth.

"And the light blind your enemies."

Duro approached the assassin at an angle with his blades held at his side. Kavano matched his direction, and the two were like countervailing winds preparing to form into a hurricane. The amber gave him what Duro liked to think of as truth sight. In a typical opponent, he could see every intention lurking within their muscles, their will to fight, and the limits of the capacity. The maetrie assassin was like a black box filled with nuclear materials. The container glowed perilously, but Duro couldn't tell how the dangers would unfold. The black sword in Kavano's grip was another matter entirely. The slim light-defying metal hummed with fell purpose, a vibration that made his teeth hurt, and concerned him as much or possibly more than the person holding it.

"Blightmane," said Kavano with a smirk. "Or Grivashka in my tongue."

As the words left his lips, Duro leapt in an attack. The maetrie assassin had been on his back foot, a position that should have made him a quarter of a second too slow. Duro's blades sung towards Kavano's throat, but found empty air instead. The assassin chuckled from a dozen feet away. The absolute misjudgment had Duro questioning his chances in a fight for the first time.

"I'd hoped this would be more interesting," said Kavano, swiping through the air lazily.

Duro pushed away his doubts. Water flowed from point to point without thought or concern, and so should he. The opal pinned to his chest gushed with useful energy, making his limbs loose and spry.

This time, Kavano attacked first.

It started with a foot stomp. A curious vibration that made the assassin's whole body hum, and then he leapt with the force of a category five tornado touching down in the soft earth.

Three strikes.

Kavano's blade moved in a blur. It wasn't until after the pass was over that Duro's mind caught up to the exchange. Blood ran down either arm where the assassin had touched him twice. The third, he'd managed to block, keeping his throat intact.

"You move fast. For a human," said Kavano.

The throwaway comment clearly meant to cause insult, but Duro let it pass through him untouched.

"Where did you get that blade?" asked Duro, hoping to distract his opponent while he considered a new strategy.

"I took it from its previous master."

"Afraid someone will try to take it from you?"

Kavano let his limbs relax into an awkward stance. "No." His eyebrows rose slightly. "Of the eleven wielders, only one would concern me and he long ago lost the will to fight."

The two warriors leapt at the same moment. Kavano was faster, but Duro wanted to overcome him with power. Anticipating the angle of the sword, he brought his full topaz force against the blade, hoping to knock the weapon from his grip. The impact was like two meteors crashing into each other in midair. The explosion spun Duro away to crash into a table, splitting it in half and sending the chairs spiraling away.

As he climbed back to his feet, he found one of his blades sheared at the base. The assassin stood across from him, the black blade not even scratched.

"You have me at a disadvantage," said Duro, tossing away the broken hilt.

Kavano's eyes shot to the fallen form of Nikolai near the entrance. He gestured towards the body.

"Please. I would not want you to say this fight was unfair."

Duro was sure the assassin was mocking him, but he wasn't going to pass up a moment of generosity, especially when he wasn't quite sure how he might beat him. But Duro had always trusted his ability to find a way in even the most difficult situations.

The new weapon wasn't exactly the same as his original. Nikolai preferred a straighter blade and used them like short swords rather than the angled attacks the curved ones suggested. After hefting it a few times to get a feel for the balance, Duro approached the maetrie assassin, giving him a short bow for allowing him to rearm himself.

"Thank—"

Halfway through what he was going to say, Duro propelled himself forward, staying low to the ground. He made himself into a living blender, each attack coming a fraction of a second after the previous. He knew for a fact he'd never moved faster.

But it wasn't enough.

The assassin moved with speed, distance almost having no meaning. When the pass was over, a searing pain invaded Duro's arm—the betrayal of weak flesh. His left grip was wet with slick blood, the end of his pinky severed. He quickly quenched the bleeding and wiped the sticky liquid on his pants to have a clean grip. Missing a digit would make his attacks slightly less effective, but he was not dissuaded.

After he'd healed himself, Kavano surged forward, his blade singing through the air forcing Duro to make numerous blocks. Sensing a counterattack opportunity, Duro switched his weight as he blocked, but before he could swing, Kavano kicked him in the chest, sending him across the cafeteria. He slid to a stop beneath a pile of tables, knocking them off and climbing back to his feet to find the assassin staring at him with disappointment.

"Is there something wrong?" he asked the maetrie.

"I'm afraid our fight has come too soon. Maybe in a few decades you might have learned enough to give me a challenge, but Dominion's plans require your death today. My apologies. I would have preferred a different meaning to our encounter."

Duro sensed the change in the maetrie before he figured out what he'd noticed. The corner of Kavano's lip twitched with perverse excitement. When Brazio entered the room with his blade, Reaver, balanced on his shoulder, Duro calculated an increase in his odds of survival.

"I'm sorry I'm late," said Brazio, nodding to Duro.

Duro returned the gesture to his friend.

"This day has grown more interesting," said Kavano, backing out of the middle so as not to have one of them at his back.

"I would hate to deprive you," said Brazio as he settled into a fighting stance with his feet wide and his body at an angle. The posture was more defensive than offensive, and Duro understood his role at a glance. He shifted his weight forward and his friend creased a grin in response. They were of like mind when it came to fighting.

"May the shadows keep you safe," said Brazio to the assassin.

"And the light blind your enemies," responded Kavano.

Duro leapt like a spear of light, his blades pointed at the assassin's heart at the same time that Brazio moved low to force him to block. Movements turned to a blur and when the pass was finished, Kavano looked down to his left arm where a cut the size of a pinhead beaded black blood. The assassin smiled, seeming to relish the minor injury, and he paused, bending deeply at the waist, before returning to a ready stance.

"Now we can truly begin."

Thirty-Six

The wound burned like bright fire, but not as hotly as the ache in Yara's chest. She stumbled alongside her cousin as weakness had invaded her limbs and she felt her knees close to collapse. He was leading her back to the front as the sounds of blades rang out in the cafeteria behind them.

"I can walk," she said, trying to push him away.

"You can barely stand," said Kuma, keeping his arm around her shoulders.

The entirety of her shirt was soaked through with wet, sticky blood. Her blood. The end of the cut near her shoulder leaked still, sending a rivulet between her breasts. Her left eye twitched as the blade had cut near the muscles that controlled it.

"I need to go back," she said, hearing the exhaustion in her own voice. "I have to kill Deacon."

"You lost a lot of blood before Duro healed the wound, and you heard what he said, we have to get out of here. We killed most of the clan leaders. Our mission is as complete as it's going to get. Deacon can wait and I'm not even sure he's here," said Kuma.

Yara felt it hard to disagree. She'd kept expecting him to appear in a doorway with a blade in his hand, but the longer it went without seeing him, the more she was certain he wasn't in the complex.

"You need to rest. The waterfall isn't going to be easy for you. You're like your father after Titus nearly killed him," said Kuma.

The name brought heat to her cheeks. "Where is he?"

"Deacon?"

"No, the mercenary. Titus. Shouldn't we have seen him?"

Kuma slowed his carry, and Yara almost slipped to the floor. "Maybe he's on another errand."

Yara didn't like that neither Deacon nor the maetrie mercenary was around. It felt off. If they'd anticipated their attack, as Kavano had suggested, then the two of them should have been in the complex for the defense. It was almost like Dominion had wanted them to succeed.

"I have to kill Deacon," she said, as much to herself as her cousin.

"I understand."

The agreement should have pleased her but it only made her mad. She continued as if he'd denied her.

"If I don't, it'll always be hanging over my head. What he did to me. I've got nothing left."

"You have family."

Yara squeezed her eyes shut, not knowing why she was telling Kuma these things. "Sometimes that's not enough for me. Whenever I close my eyes, all I see is red. It's like he cut my heart wide open and I haven't stopped bleeding."

"Hold," said Kuma suddenly, leaning her against the wall as he pulled out his blades.

Yara reached for her own, but found them absent. She'd lost them in the fight with the maetrie assassin. It made her feel even weaker than she already did to be weaponless.

When Choo-Choo and Camina appeared around the corner, both of them looking like they'd been through a blender, she allowed herself to relax, even though there would have been nothing she could have done. Choo-Choo, who limped heavily and could barely put weight on his left leg, was half carrying Camina, who had dried blood covering her face.

"I think she's concussed," said Choo-Choo, then he squinted at Yara. "You look worse."

"We fought the maetrie assassin," said Yara.

Choo-Choo's eyes opened wide. "How...?"

"Duro came and sent us away. He said to leave. We've done everything we could do." Kuma nodded towards her. "Can you heal her?"

Camina broke free from Choo-Choo, stumbling towards Yara. "You look like shit, Yara."

"So do you," she said, hearing the smile in her own voice.

The warmth of magical energy stopped the remaining blood loss.

"Your shirt's ruined," said Camina as she helped Yara back to her feet.

"So is your face."

"Come on, you two. Let's get to the front," said Kuma, who was the least injured, which aggravated Yara. Why was he always the one to come out of these battles with a cloak of splendid shadows?

The acidic gasses at the vault door were no longer present, so they passed through. As they neared the elevator, the sound of gunfire grew louder. They found Tick hiding behind the wall, occasionally leaning out to fire down the cliff. The motionless body of Xylos lay near him.

"Oh, thank the fucking shadows. They're almost up the wall and I'm about out of bullets. Please say we're leaving," said Tick.

Choo-Choo surged towards the cliff with the automatic weapon he'd taken from the fallen alliance clan member at the vault door. He leaned over the edge and sprayed bullets down the cliff face, before slipping back as return fire peppered the ceiling where he'd just been standing.

"That should give us another minute," said Choo-Choo.

"Where's Pan?" asked Kuma.

No one answered.

"I haven't seen her since the beginning of the fighting," said Choo-Choo.

"She was heading into the back, last I saw," said Camina.

"What about Navos?" asked Choo-Choo.

No one answered. Choo-Choo started heading back into the complex.

"I'm going back for him."

Kuma grabbed his arm. "Let me. You can barely stand yourself and they're going to need help after the waterfall."

Choo-Choo tried pushing past Kuma, but he held him back.

"He's right," said Yara from her spot against the wall. "As much as I hate to admit it, Kuma's got the best chance to find them and get back before they make it back up the cliff. You can barely walk. It'd also be a great chance to get rid of my annoying cousin."

She winked at Kuma, who returned the gesture. Choo-Choo relaxed, checking back to the others.

"Go," said Kuma. "We don't have time to argue."

"Before we do," said Tick, closing his eyes momentarily. When he opened them, he sighed. "I had to send her away. Hopefully she'll make it safely."

Yara had no idea what he was talking about, but she didn't care as he joined her and Camina as they headed towards the waterfall, which was on the eastern side of the high area. As the three of them headed through a steel door, she saw Kuma and Choo-Choo speaking quietly but was too tired to use her amber to listen in.

In the next room they found a set of double doors. The sound of rushing water could be heard through the barrier. When they pushed through, they were assaulted by noise and mist. A semicircular ledge was half covered by falling water that came from a river at least thirty feet higher than their location. The hole went deep below them, out of sight from their viewing spot.

"Duro wants us to jump into that?" asked Tick. "I think I'll take my chances with the army coming up the cliff."

The power of the waterfall was daunting. None of the others looked ready to leap.

"I'll go first," said Yara, stepping to the edge. She might not have been able to kill Deacon, but at least she could show her fellow clan members she wasn't afraid, or a traitor. The punishing impact of the waterfall left her stomach twisted and her hands trembling, so she squeezed them into fists to hide her fear.

Camina shook her head. "Fuck. If you're going to be stupid, then I will too."

Choo-Choo hooked his arm around Tick's and led him to the edge. The smallish waku put up a fight briefly as show and then relented.

Yara held out her hands. "We'll jump together. Take a big breath. When you hit the water, kick towards the surface, then as the river takes you into the canyon, keep your feet forward. Hopefully we can stay together."

"Twelve," said Tick.

The four of them spoke together. "Big breath and take a dive. Hope you survive."

Yara looked at their faces. She knew despite their expressions that they were as terrified as she was.

"One. Two. Three."

They jumped.

Thirty-Seven

Before Kuma could enter the complex to find Pandora and Navos, Choo-Choo grabbed his arm. The bald waku's head was covered in a sheen of sweat that glowed in the dim light. Gunfire echoed from the room behind.

"Hey," said Choo-Choo, his forehead hunched and a thousand thoughts crossing his eyes. "Good luck. Maybe you're not as bad as I thought." He grinned ferally. "Tiny Bear."

Kuma patted him on the shoulder. "You too. Take care of them. I hope to see you soon."

"Get them back," said Choo-Choo with fear in his eyes as he turned and limped through the door to where the powerful waterfall was pummeling the earth.

Kuma slipped around the elevator area, briefly checking over the cliff to see two teams halfway up the wall. He didn't have much time to find them and get out without having to fight. The halls seemed more dangerous heading back through even though he was sure that they'd killed most of the inhabitants of the complex. The only one he didn't know if they'd gotten was Pandora's grandfather, Dominion Thule. Even after all this time, it was hard to believe that she was his kin. Whatever they'd done to her had to have been awful.

The sounds of battle in the cafeteria had Kuma slow past the open door. He wasn't sure what he was seeing at first. Three blurs moved through the space while the clash of steel echoed. When part of a wall collapsed, Kuma spotted his uncle Brazio pulling his blade from the wreckage and rejoining Duro against the maetrie assassin.

If there'd ever been any doubt that Kuma had more to learn, it was dispelled by the few seconds of battle that he witnessed. The two waku and the assassin were operating at a level far beyond what he'd thought possible.

Kuma wished he could stay and watch, but he had friends to rescue. Using his amber, he surveyed the surrounding area, hoping to pick up Pandora's or Navos' speech, or some other sign of their existence. He found it difficult to pick out directions, even when he could identify sound. It was as if something was interfering with his sense of location.

"I just need to find Pandora," he whispered to himself.

With the image of her face in his mind, Kuma jogged through the hallways, letting himself be tugged forward by an invisible string. He wasn't sure why, but he thought he might be moving towards her and hoped that Navos was there too. When he heard her voice through a set of double doors, his heart soared and he pushed through without regard to what he might find on the other side, a choice he instantly regretted as he found a large group of alliance clan warriors dragging their captives towards an opposite door.

"I told you if you touch me like that again, I'll rip your teeth out and cut your dick off with them," said Pandora.

She was at the back of the group while Navos and Adrenalynne, looking severely beaten up, were being half carried since they were barely conscious.

"Another gift for the boss," said a tall waku with the colorful tattoos of Yami no Kishi as he unsheathed a blade. Two others joined him with short metal spears. "Get them out of here."

Three against one wasn't good odds, especially with little time to get back to the waterfall. Kuma knew he had to take chances if he was going to rescue his friends and escape. Navos and Adrenalynne disappeared through the door, while Pandora fought the two holding her like a wild cougar.

The key to fighting against multiple enemies, Kuma reminded himself, was to use their movements against each other. He never wanted to get trapped by all three. Even the fastest waku would have difficulty blocking all the attacks. Kuma leapt to the left when the three reached him, using his blades against the tall waku with the sword and forcing him to back into his companions.

The quick strike clued Kuma that his opponent had a topaz, so he tapped into the ruby to borrow speed and strength from him. The two spear waku danced around the tall one, but Kuma kept shifting and kicking out at his main target, keeping them off-balance. The battle was a stalemate, but if he made a single mistake they'd make him pay.

"Nawi," said the tall waku as he backed away, using his sword defensively. "Help us with this fool."

One of the people holding Pandora broke away, removing twin short swords from her sheaths. She twirled them expertly before leaping into the fray. The four combatants made it impossible to fight only one, so he was forced backwards dodging two sets of weapons. Only with the combined might of his stones—owned and borrowed—was he able to keep up, but it was only a matter of time before they'd break through his defenses.

Thirty-Eight

The moment Pandora saw Kuma enter the room, she knew she had to escape her bonds somehow to give him a chance. There were too many waku in this group, which had been held back from joining the defense of the clan leaders. She saw how her grandfather had served them up, which would only strengthen his hold on the alliance. They would see him as the final protector of the clan and rally to his side, much as they had with the Drops. They'd been fools to make the attack.

Three waku headed towards Kuma, who stood with his curved blades wide, ready to scrap. When the woman holding her arm tried to break away to join them, Pandora kicked her in the leg and started wrestling away from the other guard, forcing them to hold her down. The woman kept punching Pandora in the chest while she used her legs to strike their knees and groin areas.

"Stop fighting or I'll stick you like a pig," said the woman.

Sensing a line, Pandora stilled for a moment, readying herself to leap into action. The woman was called to the fight with Kuma.

"If you fucking move, I'll cut your throat, to the shadows what *he* wants to do with you."

There was no question the *he* she meant was her grandfather, but it made it clear they didn't know she was his granddaughter. As the fourth guard moved away, Pandora hunched into a ball, as if she'd been cowed by the guard's comment. Her sapphire could barely make a chair tremble, but it still gave her the radar sight. When she sensed her guard paying attention to the fight with Kuma, Pandora sprung upward, breaking his grip and looping the chain around his neck. Before he could get his hands in the way, she fell onto her back, yanking on the chain with all her strength. He fought hard for a short time then slowly went limp as she choked him out. When he was unconscious, she pushed him off and used his blade to cut his throat in case he wasn't dead yet.

Before the others could notice her escape, Pandora charged the attackers surrounding Kuma, throwing herself into their backs, knocking them to the floor. Kuma watched her approach and timed his attack at the height of chaos, using the distraction to spin past the long spear and puncture the chest of the wielder. In the tangle on the ground, Pandora jabbed with her dagger as fast as possible, making it impossible to strike back.

When the two waku she'd knocked down were dead, she found Kuma standing over her with his hand out. Once she was standing, they searched the bodies for a key.

"We have to get out of here," said Kuma. "The others went down the waterfall already."

After finding the key, Kuma released her from the manacles. He started moving towards the entrance, but she held him back.

"The others. We have to get Navos and Adrena."

Kuma's face broke. "There's about to be twenty or so alliance clan entering the complex in about thirty seconds, if they haven't already. We don't have time to catch up and kill their guards."

"We have to," she told him.

Kuma sighed. "We'd better be quick then."

They ran towards the opposite door. On the other side, there were two more exits, but no clear indication as to which way they'd gone. Pandora opened the one on the right while he opened the left. Her room was empty with no ways out.

"Can't be this one."

"Nor this one," said Kuma.

It wasn't clear where the others had gone, but the complex had been acting strangely. Her grandfather had done something to bring the effects of the Eternal City into its borders.

"To the front," said Kuma, frowning.

They made it halfway back before they heard the cheer of the waku that had reached the cliff.

"Fuck. Trapped," he said. "Maybe there's a way around."

She grabbed his hand. "Let me lead."

Pandora imagined a route that would let them escape. She hoped there were secret exits that her grandfather had installed to help him get away in times of trouble.

When they found themselves back in the boardroom with the strange painting on the wall, she worried they might run into her grandfather or Titus.

"What the fuck is that?" he asked.

"Nothing that matters right now."

She led them through the door she'd seen her grandfather enter from, finding a hallway and two doors. The last one seemed to tug at her heart and they found a glistening black stone on the opposite wall. The edges were rough, looking like they'd been hacked out of the earth.

"What's this?"

"A portal. To the Eternal City, I believe. It'd be the way he's coming and going, which meant we never had a chance to kill him." When Kuma turned to leave, she grabbed his hand. "I might be able to get us through since I'm part maetrie and related to Dominion."

"There?" he asked incredulously. "Are you crazy?"

"Better than staying here."

"Won't we run into his guards, or other maetrie on that side?"

"If this goes where I think it does, then we'll be fine. He'd never allow a portal to enter his ancestral home. It probably puts us on the streets."

Kuma swallowed.

"Are you sure? I thought the Eternal City was one of the most dangerous realms."

"It is, but you happen to have someone with you who understands the dangers. I can get us to safety, maybe find allies who despise my grandfather and then return." A thought popped into her head. "Dammit. There's only one problem. Once you're there, you won't be able to eat or drink or you'll never be able to return."

"I don't like the sound of that."

The sounds of guards entering the boardroom in search of them made their time short.

"There are ways of protecting humans, but I don't have them."

Kuma's face wrinkled and he reached into a pouch. "Something like these?"

Her eyes lit up at the sight of the golden bracers. "Yes! Where'd you get them? Put them on. Quickly."

The voices grew closer. As Kuma shoved the bracers around his wrists, she grabbed his hand and pulled him to the obsidian wall. It was cool to the touch, but warmed the longer her palm pressed against it. As the voices reached the door and it began to open, Pandora flooded her mind with thoughts of the Eternal City. She imagined the decadent rot, the ancient buildings long in disrepair, the skeletal skyscrapers that moved whenever you weren't watching, the oily streets and dangers that lurked around every corner. Vertigo rose up from her gut and sent her mind spinning away as the darkness collapsed around them as they went through the portal to the Eternal City.

Thirty-Nine

Duro wasn't sure at what point he knew they couldn't win the fight against the maetrie assassin, but he saw it in Brazio's hunched forehead when there was a brief break due to the return of the alliance clans from below. One of the younger Blue Daggers had aimed their gun at him, but Kavano had broken away, cutting the arms from his body before a shot could be fired.

"Leave these two to me," said the assassin. "Find the others."

The rest of the alliance clan hurried deeper into the complex with expressions of abject terror.

"Right?" he asked Brazio, receiving a disappointed nod.

The back way out of the cafeteria led through an industrial kitchen and then to the hallways leading through the open vault door. Duro cut down three warriors who barely had time to raise their weapons before they were bleeding on the floor. When he hit the rocky field above the cliff, he found Kavano waiting for them at the edge, blocking their escape.

"I thought we were enjoying ourselves. I haven't had a challenge like this in decades, centuries perhaps."

To his right, Brazio was breathing heavily. Black lines on his neck and wrists revealed the breakdown of his body due to the heavy load of five stones, including the protective black diamond. Without it, they would have been dead within the first minute of the fight, but Brazio's ability to withstand the assassin's blows had given them a slim chance.

"We wanted a better venue for our scrap," said Duro, gesturing casually at the cavern.

Kavano was kind enough not to call out the lie, even though it was clear he knew it. The assassin held out his blade in a human *en guard* position with a smirk. The hum from his weapon increased in tenor as if it was anticipating their flesh. Duro caught a glance from Brazio, staring at the cluster of pillars on the left side of the cavern. Its meaning escaped Duro until he remembered the unwinnable fight Pandora had with the traitor Irena.

"Let's begin again," said Kavano.

The first round of the fight had taken every trick and skill Duro had to stay alive. He'd pushed his own stones to the limit, the combination of opal and topaz turning him into a human blur while the amber helped him anticipate the assassin's moves. As Kavano met their blades with Blightmane, Duro knew the assassin had been holding back. He found himself flying through the air from a kick to the stomach, hitting the constructed wall like a meteor. It was a miracle nothing was broken, but it took Duro a moment to stumble from the wreckage while Brazio withstood the assassin's assault. Only the black diamond was keeping him alive, but as Brazio had proved in his duel years ago, the protective stone wasn't a panacea. Eventually the shielding layer of the steelskin would fail or be circumvented by other means.

Duro rallied his flagging energy, flinging himself forward like a rocket. Like many times before, he'd though he'd caught the assassin off guard and slipped a blade past his defenses, but Blightmane blocked his attack at the last second. But Duro did not let up, using Brazio's defensive posture to push the assassin towards the section of stone pillars. It took every ounce of his skill but they managed to maneuver Kavano until his back was against the natural structure.

Though Duro had only known Brazio personally for a few short months, he'd been an admirer for over a decade. The familiarity helped them fight together as a single unit rather than two separate warriors. He could sense Brazio's intention and not just because of the amber. Duro focused on attacking Kavano's hands to keep him off guard until Brazio

could disguise an attack that hit the pillars instead of him. As Reaver
sliced through the rock, chunks broke free, landing on the assassin's back,
sending him to his knees. Duro doubled his attacks, keeping the maetrie
pinned while Brazio rained more hunks of earth upon his back. The
assassin was half covered, and Duro thought they might have a chance
when suddenly Kavano was no longer beneath the stones.

"Not very fair," said Kavano from near the cliff's edge. Blood was
streaming from his forehead and his clothing looked rumpled. He wiped
the cut, closing it instantly, and licked the liquid from his fingertips.

Seeing another opportunity, Duro leapt at Kavano the same time
as Brazio. They attacked the assassin in a fever, not to land a blow, but
to push him over the edge. Kavano countered their blades but their
combined efforts forced him backwards. When the assassin's heels were
sticking over, Brazio slammed Reaver into the rock near his feet, crum-
bling the earth and sending him backwards.

Duro moved to the edge to see the assassin's demise, but the darkness below hid his fall. No sound of impact or cries of pain followed.

"What now?" asked Brazio, examining the edge of his blade for
damage.

Duro nodded towards the rope line that extended below. "That or
we try to head to the waterfall."

"I don't think he'll allow us to make it that far," said Brazio, chuckling.

"I think you're right, my old friend."

Brazio put a hand on his shoulder. "I wish we'd combined our clans long ago. Not just because we might have been able to counter Dominion's moves long before, but because fighting beside you has been an honor I will never forget."

"The same, my friend. The same."

"Shall we?"

The climb down the cliff took less time than Duro would have liked, but destiny meant sometimes the only way out was through. The assassin at least allowed them to reach the bottom before he made his grand return. Kavano stood on the far shore of the lake. The black surface was a mirror between them.

"I appreciate the chance to climb down without interference," said Brazio.

"It was the least I could do for two warriors of your caliber," said Kavano, inclining his head.

"You could always let us pass," said Brazio. "A few more decades, as you suggested, might improve our battle."

"Alas, as much as I would love to allow it, my benefactor was clear about my role in today's events. He paid me an exorbitant sum for your deaths. Had I known how delightful this fight would be, I might have turned down his offer and sought out a battle on my terms, but my word as a mercenary would be meaningless if I did not carry out my assigned task."

"Would you like to be something more than a mercenary?" asked Duro.

"There was a time I sought other meaning for this existence, but in time, I realized that nothing matters but my own survival."

"Clearly that is not the case," said Duro. "Otherwise you would have killed us already."

"It is true, there might be flaws in my internal story but to reexamine them now might put in danger my very actuality," said the assassin. "It is a curse that you would not understand, being short-lived creatures who burn bright, but burn out before you can truly understand the emptiness of eternity."

"That might be true for the maetrie, who live in constant battle without friend and with infinite foes, but do you not see there are better ways? El Clan Eto Vas."

"The Clan is All," said Kavano. "I know your motto."

Duro gestured towards Brazio. "Once we were enemies, but now we are friends. Join us, friend Kavano, and let us help you shake off those bonds that Dominion has laid upon you. You are more than a mercenary. There is purpose in the honing of skill. You could be a great teacher, or if that wasn't for you, even the fellowship of clan might provide that which you lack."

The casual stance of the assassin hardened like molten steel into a fell weapon.

"Do not presume you comprehend my woes," said Kavano with a sneer. "Nor that you can fathom the extent of your situation. Now that the Courts have decided your realm is worth conquering, there is little you will be able to do to stop it. There are countless worlds, broken like glass, because it amused them to do so. Better to be the tip of the spear than the one being pierced by it." He slapped the water with his blade, sending a wave of ripples across the surface. "Be honored that you amused me enough to prolong your existence."

The once mirror-like surface of the lake was broken. The assassin leapt forward, bounding across the ripples as if they were ridges on a sand dune rather than liquid. When Kavano hit the beach, Duro was there with Brazio to oppose him, but their defense seemed laughably weak.

Blocks were swatted out of the way with barely restrained anger. The assassin's boot found their chests every time they gained their feet. He could have killed them half a dozen times, but he kept up his punishment. The first time the blade known as Blightmane sliced through the meat of his upper arm, Duro felt horror as much as surprise. The slice was paired with the images of a shattered realm, fiery wounds smoking from the earth, the crumpled remains of civilization long ago destroyed. The sounds of weeping stunned him as it was the voices of millions. Despair wracked his limbs.

When Duro looked up, the blade was in his chest. It felt like ice against his heart. He glanced over to see Brazio already on his knees, blood spilling from his throat. He reached out and grabbed his fellow warrior's hand as he collapsed and felt his soul slipping to places unseen.

Forty

The word had come an hour before that they would be abandoning the Pajot. Vasilisa was aghast, and told her mother that they couldn't leave because Emilio wasn't back. Her mother barked back in a voice that she hadn't heard since Valeria had died. It was both heartbroken and angry.

"No more than what you can easily carry!" cried her mother from below.

Vasilisa stared at the meager backpack surrounded by the stuffed animals and other trinkets of her life in the Undercity. She wanted to take it all, but had settled on being practical and only taking clothes, except for a small plushie of a mystdrakon that would fit in a side pocket. Buttons stuck to the outside said things like: "Hundred Halls Sux!" or "Mage No More!"

"Hurry up, Vasy! We have to leave!"

She glanced towards the ladder.

"Sorry," she said to the stuffed animals. "Maybe things will settle down after a few months and we can come back."

She knew in her heart this was unlikely, but hope wasn't a thing she wanted to let go of.

In the living room, she found her mother loaded down with a backpack and three small sacks. Her eyes were rimmed with crimson and she was sniffling.

"We have to take Emilio's things too."

"Let me take one, Mami."

Her mother wouldn't let go at first, so she had to pry away the sack with one hand.

"Yes, of course. I wouldn't be able to carry it."

They joined the flow of people headed to the western side of the Pajot. Without her brother and the other top waku to guard them, Vasilisa felt vulnerable. The other Drops members looked equally concerned.

"He'll catch up to us, right?" she asked her mother, receiving a stern, but empty stare as a response.

Was she going to lose a second sibling in her short life? It didn't seem fair. While she'd been too young to really know Valeria, the ache was like a blot on her heart. It was proof that the world wasn't fair and bad stuff could come crashing down at any moment.

Outside the processing building, Daraja was greeting them. She stood tall, her ebony skin glistening in the hot lights that hung from the ceiling. She was wearing a patterned black, gold, and green suit. Like the rest of her clan, Vasilisa had always admired the clan leader even though she seemed quite different on the surface. Though she didn't have the tattoos or the same background as most of them, she was true Drops in the heart.

"How are you, Vasy?" asked Daraja, leaning forward with a kind smile.

"When will Emilio be back?"

The clan leader faltered. Most had forgotten his real name, but eventually her eyes creased.

"They'll meet us at our destination."

"If they'll meet us, then why are we leaving?" asked Vasilisa.

Daraja glanced away. "It's the safest course until we know for sure what happened."

The clan leader caressed her shoulder then moved her along to talk with the other members. Vasilisa didn't like the explanation, but she knew she didn't deserve anything more. The fact that they'd been train- ing for a secret mission hadn't been that hidden. When Emilio hadn't come home from training last night, she'd known that it had begun and she'd barely been able to sleep. A million what-if's had ricocheted through her mind all night.

After gathering in the cavern before the western exit, Vasilisa talked briefly with her classmates, but no one knew anything new and most were hesitant to speak with her because of her brother.

"What will our new home be like?" she asked her mother as the procession started moving out.

She didn't answer at first until Vasilisa asked again. "I don't know, Vasy. Like everything else, it's been a secret. But I trust Daraja to have found us a good place to live."

"I hope it's not outside," said Vasilisa, staring at the comforting rock ceiling. "I don't think I can live with all that sky."

"You're a resilient young woman. I'm sure you'll adjust," said her mother absently.

"He'll come back," said Vasilisa. "I know he will."

"Yes. He will," said her mother, but her heart didn't sound in it. She was already grieving for her son. Was that what it was like to be an adult? To have no hope? Vasilisa didn't want to be that way. She loved her mother, but she was so rigid. Especially when it came to her dead sister Valeria.

The tunnel required a single-file line at times, so Vasilisa trudged ahead of her mother, hauling the sack of Emilio's clothes. It grew heavier as they walked, but she refused to let it slow her. When a gap formed between her and the next person, one of the soldados that had been guarding their passage tried to take the sack out of her hand.

"Only what you can carry. Can't have anything slowing us down."

Vasilisa ripped it right back. "I *can* carry it."

The soldado reached out a second time, but Vasy turned her body in the way and rushed to close the gap.

Shortly after, Vasilisa's thoughts revolved around the idea that she'd forgotten something important at home. She felt like she hadn't properly said goodbye to the place she'd lived her entire life. Even though it was only stone and rock, it was important to honor the protection it'd given them all these years.

"What do you think will happen to it?" she asked her mother when the tunnel opened up wide enough they could walk side by side.

"It?" asked her mother with growing unease.

"The Pajot. Our home," said Vasilisa.

"They'll probably send workers to work the terraces. The drugs we made were valuable. I'm sure they won't let that go to waste."

Vasilisa wasn't sure she agreed, but she wasn't going to disagree with her mother considering the mood.

Two caverns later, shooting started. Screams, followed by a compression of the line as those in front moved backward until they were crammed into the tunnel shoulder to shoulder, brought a rare case of claustrophobia to Vasilisa, who just wanted space to breathe. When she saw her mother had it worse, she talked to her in a quiet voice.

"It's okay, Mami. We'll be okay. Our waku and soldados are the best."

Vasilisa said the words even though she knew in her heart that it wasn't the case. Their best waku had been sent away on a secret mission, and if there was shooting going on, it meant they'd failed. The idea that she was the only sibling left was a yawning chasm at her feet that threatened to pull her into its depths, but she knew she had to be strong for her mother, who stared blankly at the wall like an automaton.

When the line started moving again, a flicker of hope climbed into her chest only to be dashed when she saw the black-clad men and women in runed Kevlar armor and carrying automatic weapons ushering them forward. The bodies of their guards lay on the rocks, their eyes wide in the surprise of death.

It wasn't the first time she'd seen a dead body. The Undercity was a cruel place. But the others had been hours or days after the brutal events and they'd often been covered so no one could see the wounds of their demise. Not only did she know that they'd just been murdered only moments before, but she knew them well. That was Hector and over there was Juliana, her bright red hair dimmed by death.

They were led into a wide cavern, surrounded by the men and women in Kevlar armor. Daraja was kneeling on a short rise that looked over the entire group with one of the city elves standing above her. She knew about the maetrie, but he looked nothing like what she expected. He was broad-shouldered and thick like a bodybuilder rather than the slender city elves of the stories she'd heard. Vasilisa expected him to be smoking a short cigar.

"Greetings, I'm Titus Cabone. As you can guess, I work for your new boss, Dominion Thule."

A grumbling fervor swept through the crowd even as they already knew who had captured them.

"At this moment, your treasured waku, the ones you sent to assassinate the heads of the alliance clans, they're all dead."

The announcement brought a wail from her mother, who dropped to her knees. There were other outbursts, but none as loud as Triana's. Vasilisa tried to console her mother, but she was rocking back and forth, clutching the collar of her shirt and mumbling to herself.

"He can't know that," said Vasilisa quietly. "He's guessing."

She knew it wasn't possible given the timing of when they'd left last night compared to the time it took to traverse the Undercity. But the logic didn't persuade her mother that disaster hadn't occurred.

"My Emilio, my sweet Emilio," she kept muttering.

Titus waited until the worst of the outcries had subsided. "This news is troubling to be sure, but in time you will forget them. More important is that you're alive and that life will continue much as before, though with a few less people around."

The mercenary smirked and Vasilisa wished she could shove a blade in his throat. She had one stuffed in her left boot and she was really good at throwing them, but she had no doubt that the maetrie wouldn't die from a simple knife. They were much harder than that to kill.

Titus grabbed Daraja by the back of her neck and dragged her to her feet.

"Tell them that everything will be fine and you'll be working a *few* more hours than you were before."

Daraja spat on his protective jacket. The mercenary chuckled, removed a knife from a side pocket, and slipped the tip of the blade into the back of Daraja's thigh. Her momentary gasp was quickly bottled up. She stared at him with an inferno on her brow.

"I want you all to know that it doesn't have to be like this," said Titus. "Your new clan leader, Dominion Thule, is not an unkind man. He only wants to consolidate the clans in the Undercity, end the senseless wars and stupid honor duels. From this day forward, you'll find peace in the shadows where before there was only danger."

Titus leaned down to Daraja. "Tell them. Dominion doesn't need you around, but he thought things might be smoother if your people had a voice. He's generous to those who help him with his causes."

Daraja squeezed her eyes shut and shook her head vehemently. Even before Titus lifted the blade, Vasilisa knew what was going to happen. He pressed it against her shoulder, facing down, as he looked across the crowd.

"I give you one last chance."

Daraja lifted her chin and stared at the remaining Drops. Her expression was both defiance and fear.

"El Clan Eto Vas!"

The words barely left her lips when Titus shoved the blade downward. The gasp on Daraja's lips was followed by blood leaking out. Titus pushed her off the blade, and she tumbled forward down the small slope to land at the base of the rocky mound.

"Does anyone else want to follow her?" When no one answered, he said, "Good. Then we'll be turning around and heading back to the Pajot. Grab your things. We'll be moving quickly."

It took a minute to get her mother to her feet. Vasilisa thought about leaving the bag of clothes that had been her brother's but refused to give up hope that he was alive. She hooked her mother's arm and dragged her along while holding two sacks in her good hand. The entire time she trudged forward, an ache burning in her chest, Vasilisa kept one thought in her head.

El Clan Eto Vas. El Clan Eto Vas.

Forty-One

The canyon walls battered Choo-Choo's back as he struggled to stay on the surface of the raging underground river. He'd lost his friends in the torrent of the churning waterfall and then in the scramble for survival in Canter's Folly. He knew the story that had beget the canyon's name: an early explorer to the Undercity had thought to traverse the waters in a boat of his own making only to be found a bloated corpse days later.

Half drowned, even his topaz didn't seem enough against the twists and turns of the river, which habitually smashed him into the walls. He imagined even a battle against Duro wouldn't be as painful.

Choo-Choo managed to get his jaw above the surface in time to see the river fall away, tumbling his battered body into the air before dunking him deep below. He struggled to find the right direction, and the air in his lungs burned like fire, as he hadn't gotten a good breath before he'd been submerged.

Eventually he righted himself and kicked off the bottom, swimming up to air and a calmer body of water that had spread out in a small lake. Choo-Choo paddled to the shore, flopping onto the pebbles and jagged rocks, but not caring about the pain pressing into his flesh.

A round of coughing spat water from his lungs and left him shivering even though the cavern was warm. He knew it was foolish to lie prone in a foreign part of the Undercity. For all he knew, dangerous beasties were sneaking upon him in his convalescence. With a half-hearted effort, he sent out his amber hoping nothing would require his attention. He sensed footfalls approaching his location, and climbed to his knees while searching for his missing blades.

A bedraggled Yara appeared out of the gloom. Her face was a mess of blood, the half-healed wound beneath her eye jagged from the soaking of her flesh. She approached with a limp motioning quietly for him to follow, making the sign for movement without noise.

Following was painful as his already injured knee had been wrenched further during the battle to stay afloat. He managed to pass through the cavern until reaching a hollow in the back where the diminutive Tick was sitting cross-legged with his eyes closed and head leaning on the stone. A cry almost escaped Choo-Choo's lips when he saw the snake sitting in his lap until he realized Tick was stroking the creature's back, reminding him of the tiger's eye.

Yara tugged him below the edge of the hollow as the sound of a scouting party entered the cavern. Using his amber, he could hear their discussion as if he were right beside them.

"I thought I heard coughing," said a voice.

"If any of 'em survived, they'd surface here," said another.

Splashing was followed by the kicking of rocks. "If someone came out, it was right here."

Choo-Choo dared to peek over the edge to see a group of eight warriors, some carrying automatic weapons. The rest could be presumed as waku. If he wasn't injured and disarmed, he would have argued for a fight, but besides Tick's snake, he didn't see a single weapon amongst them.

"I can't imagine any of them survived. The one we pulled out a while ago was unconscious. Not sure if she'll survive," said the second voice.

Camina. It had to be her. He doubted Kuma had made it back with Pandora in time. If they made it out, they'd be coming along in a few minutes at the earliest, though he'd lost track of time in the struggle.

"Fine with me. I don't think they'll bend the knee, but I'm not about to disagree with the new boss, especially with his gray-skinned friends."

"The one with the sword bothers me. I think he'd eat me for lunch if Dom let him."

"I like him more than the big one. I've heard stories about what they've done in other realms. Real bloody stuff. Almost feel sorry for the poor souls at the Pajot."

"What?" asked the other.

"Yeah, they headed out around the time word came down to be alert for an attack. Heard one of them mention the Pajot. Would make sense to hit them back at the same time. The new boss is creepy as fuck, but he sure knows how to run a clan."

Their words faded away as they headed back up the tunnel. Choo-Choo fell back against the stones, tears welling in his eyes.

Yara put hand on his shoulder. "I'm sure they're okay. Daraja probably got them out first."

He wished he could believe her. If Dominion knew about the attack, then he probably knew about the plan to leave the Undercity.

"What do we do now?" asked Tick as he stroked the head of the snake purring in his lap.

"Maybe some of the others escaped," said Yara. "We can hide out and try to find them."

"I was kinda hoping you'd say we'd be going to the city and find a new gang to run with," said Tick.

"No," said Choo-Choo, shaking his head. "You can go, but my family is going to be at the Pajot."

"They might not be there," said Tick.

"No. Those guys were right. Dominion Thule is too smart. He outmaneuvered all the clan leaders, which includes Daraja. As much as I'd like to believe they got away, without Duro or Brazio to defend them, that mercenary probably stopped them from leaving. They'll need them for harvesting drugs."

"Not drugs," said Yara absently. "Dominion didn't come here for drugs. He came here for the stones, and now he doesn't have any competition. He can mine to his heart's content, if he has one."

"Shadows below," muttered Choo-Choo, understanding completely. "I definitely can't leave the Undercity. And maybe if they're spread out trying to mine, it'll give us an opportunity."

"To what?" asked Yara.

"You still want revenge on Deacon?"

She scowled. "With all my fucking heart."

"Good, because I can't do this alone."

"Do what?" asked Tick.

Choo-Choo frowned. The path forward wasn't going to be easy. In fact, it was highly likely that it would get them killed, but he couldn't leave his family in the clutches of that murderer Titus Cabone, or his best friend Navos captured by the alliance. His family was too important to sneak away and act like nothing had happened.

"Be the resistance."

§ § §

Continue Kuma and Pandora's adventure in Book Four of The Crystal
Halls series

CHAINS

OF

OBSIDIAN

OTHER BOOKS BY THOMAS K. CARPENTER

The Hundred Halls Universe

SEASON ONE
THE HUNDRED HALLS
Trials of Magic
Web of Lies
Alchemy of Souls
Gathering of Shadows
City of Sorcery

THE RELUCTANT ASSASSIN
The Reluctant Assassin
The Sorcerous Spy
The Veiled Diplomat
Agent Unraveled
The Webs That Bind

GAMEMAKERS ONLINE
The Warped Forest
Gladiators of Warsong
Citadel of Broken Dreams
Enter the Daemonpits
Plane of Twilight

ANIMALIANS HALL
Wild Magic
Bane of the Hunter
Mark of the Phoenix
Arcane Mutations
Untamed Destiny

STONE SINGERS HALL
Song of Siren and Blood
House of Snake and Tome
Storm of Dragon and Stone
Sonata of Shadow and Thorn
Well of Demon and Bone

THE ORDER OF MERLIN
The Order of Merlin
Infernal Alliances
Tower of Horn and Blood

ABOUT THE AUTHOR

Thomas K. Carpenter resides in Colorado with his wife Rachel. When he's not busy writing his next book, he's hiking, skiing, and getting beat by his wife at cards. He keeps a regular blog at www.thomaskcarpenter.com and you can follow him on twitter @thomaskcarpente. If you want to learn when his next novel will be hitting the shelves and get free stories and occasional other goodies, please sign up for his mailing list by going to: http://tinyurl.com/thomaskcarpenter. Your email address will never be shared and you can unsubscribe at any time.

Milton Keynes UK
Ingram Content Group UK Ltd.
UKHW040153111023
430351UK00011B/128/J

9 781087 976716